HALSEY FAMILY TREE

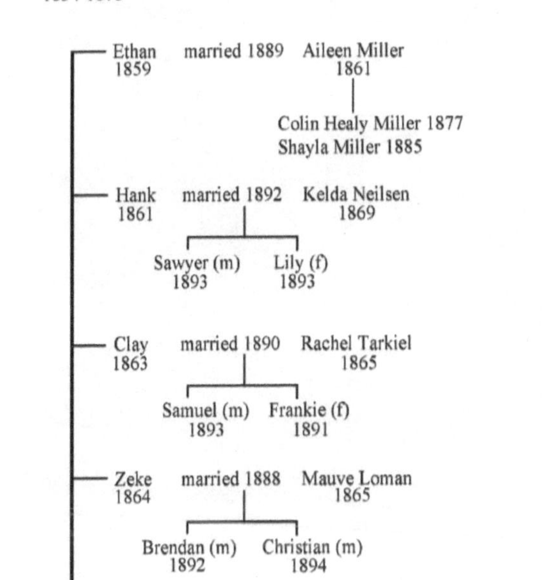

Halsey Homecoming Series

Laying Claim
Staking Claim
Claiming a Heart

STAKING CLAIM

Halsey Homecoming Series

by
Paty Jager

Windtree Press
Hillsboro, OR

STAKING CLAIM
Book Two of Halsey Homecoming

Contact Information: info@windtreepress.com

Windtree Press
Beaverton, Oregon

Visit us at http://windtreepress.com

Cover Art by Covers by Karen

Published in the United States of America
ISBN 9781940064468

This story is dedicated to Paty's Posse.

A group of fans that are dear to my heart.

Chapter One

Liverpool, England
1899

Colin Healy strode down the cobblestone street toward the Liverpool docks. Thoughts of home and his family made his pace quicken. He'd booked passage on the clipper ship, *Americana,* bound for New York today. The letter he'd received from his sister, Shayla, asking him to return for her fifteenth birthday and her graduation from grammar school had clenched his up-till-then indecision about going home or staying on longer at Meath Hall. The estate he'd inherited through his father's family had become as important to him as the family he had left in Sumpter, Oregon. While he enjoyed running the estate, he was tired of being called Sir Colin Healy and having advances made upon him by all the young women hoping to elevate their status by marrying a baronet.

The thought of Miss Gwendolyn Marsh the last time he'd attended dinner at her family's estate made his stomach churn. He had nothing against women, just couldn't cotton to pushy women. He didn't like talking about himself and he didn't like women who asked one hundred questions, all of which made him uncomfortable.

The only people in England who knew how he and his mother had landed in America were his father's cousin, Orin and his son, Denis. Orin had found them in America when Colin's life was threatened by greedy British relatives. After Ethan Halsey married Colin's mother, he took the family to England to arrange for Orin and Denis to run the estate for Colin until he was old enough to take over. Four years ago, Colin had returned to become the baronet of Meath Hall.

He'd been too busy to miss his family and the Halsey family members as he learned his new position and occupation. But he and Shayla had always been close. They'd lived through her father's tirades and thrived in the Halsey family. Thinking of Shayla, he couldn't stop the smile creeping across his lips. He'd answered her plea with a letter stating he wasn't sure he could get away, when he'd already decided to go. He'd surprise the scamp and the rest of the family.

Commotion down a street to his left caught Colin's attention. A young woman, dressed too nice to be walking the side streets alone, had three men taunting her.

Colin gripped the handle of his canvas Gladstone and shifted his direction, striding down the street toward the woman and men.

One of the men, a little younger than the woman, snatched a fake flower from the woman's hat. "Where'd ye get sooch a fancy 'at, Livie?" If the ratty, dirty clothes hadn't suggested the men were from the lower class of city dwellers, the thick Liverpudlian accent gave him away. The gentry and businessmen were easier to understand.

"Get yer 'ands off me. Ah've an appointment to keep." The young woman swat small, white-gloved hands at the men's grubby fingers pecking away at her hat. "Stop!"

"I believe the lady asked you to stop." Colin halted ten feet from the ruckus, set his bag down, and settled his feet in a solid stance to show he meant business.

"We's just 'aving some foon," said the tall and rangiest of the three.

"I could tell from the end of the street she doesn't welcome your *fun*."

He allowed his gaze to wander from the men to the woman. He was dumbstruck by the clarity of her wide, green eyes.

She ducked her head and hurried by him, leaving a hint of roses in the air.

Colin stood in the narrow street like a wall, glaring at the men and daring them to go after her. One by one they slinked away, and he was left standing there wondering at the woman's high fashion, and yet, the man had called her by the name of Livie and acted as if he knew her. The woman was a walking contradiction. The little he'd heard her talk didn't completely fit the breeding her clothes shouted. But then again, he didn't dress and talk like a British baronet. He shouted American from his wool trousers and suit jacket, to his boots and Stetson.

He shook his head, picked up his bag, and headed to the dock. Captain Whiteside had explained the need to have all passengers on the ship before they started loading the cargo. It was how he regulated the ballast.

On his way to the Winterburn Dock where the *Americana* was loading, his gaze swept up and down the streets, looking for the colorful flowered hat and long, bright blue coat the woman wore. No matter how hard he tried to see her in the growing crowd, she had vanished.

Colin strode up the gangplank and shook hands with Captain Whiteside.

"Sir Colin Healy, happy to have you aboard, my good man." The captain released his hand and tooted a whistle. The cabin boy ran up to the captain's side.

"Please, Captain, you can drop the sir, I'm not traveling as the baronet of Meath Hall. I'm Colin Healy heading home." While he was the heir to the estate, he felt like a fraud when people announced him as Sir Colin Healy. He wasn't British gentry, he was American through and through. No matter how many years he spent here, in England, at the estate, he'd never forget the life in Sumpter that had formed him into this man.

"Sure, I understand. Jack, take Sir…I mean Mr. Healy's bag to first cabin ten."

The boy extended his hand and waited for Colin to hand it over.

"You're welcome to follow young Jack to your room or remain deck side," the captain added.

"I think I'll follow along and get a bearing of my room then return and watch the loading of the cargo." Colin motioned for the boy to lead the way and followed Jack's bouncing gait across the deck to a set of covered stairs at the mid-point of the ship.

"Watch yer step, someone as tall as ye might 'ave a bit of a bump on the 'ead," said Jack, scrambling down the stairs with the bag.

The staircase was shiny mahogany and wide enough for two people to pass without touching.

"This way, sir," Jack called at the bottom of the stairs and headed toward the front of the ship. "This is youz cabin." He stopped at a white door with a dark blue number ten painted in the middle about chest high.

"Thank you." Colin slipped a penny from his pocket and handed it to the boy. "I would like a bucket of warm water brought to my cabin every night at ten."

The boy's face lit up at the copper coin. "Yes, sir!" He grasped the coin, shoved it into his pocket, and scampered off.

Colin opened the door and was surprised to see a bed his feet wouldn't hang over the end and a small writing desk beside the built-in cupboard for his belongings. This room with the long rectangular port hole would be a splendid place to go over the papers he'd brought with him about a possible investment.

Within minutes, he stowed his clothes in the cupboard, set his personal items on the small desk along with the papers he would read through, and exited the cabin, pulling the door shut.

Back up on deck, Colin stood at the ship's railing watching the dock workers load the cargo destined for New York. A glimpse of bright blue in the periphery of his vision, turned his attention to a small entourage headed to the ship's gang plank.

There was no mistaking the long, bright blue coat and large, overly-flowered hat.

Where were the people now following her when he came to her aid earlier?

A servant girl followed the young woman. She carried what looked like a hat box and two men followed her carrying two large trunks on their shoulders. While the woman's stride was self-assured, her head pivoted back and forth, her gaze taking in everything.

Why would someone clearly of gentry, use a sailing ship to travel when not one hundred feet away the *Campania,* a steamship in the Cunard line, was getting ready to set sail for America as well?

Before he registered his own movements, Colin discovered himself standing beside Captain Whiteside at the gangplank. The jovial captain enjoyed welcoming the passengers.

One of the reasons Colin picked going home by sailing ship rather than the faster steamship was to have fewer passengers to deal with, or in his case, hide from. He wasn't a socializer like his sister, Shayla. He tended to have his mother's trait of enjoying themselves just fine when alone or with family. Taking the slower sailing vessel gave him the option of never setting foot in a proper dining room or having to sit through conversations with strangers.

"Welcome!" boomed Captain Whiteside as the young woman stepped from the gangplank onto the vessel.

"Thank you, Captain." She touched a gloved hand to her hat, then touched her earlobe showing beneath upswept copper-colored hair.

Colin didn't want to think he was partial to red hair due to his mother's fiery locks. This woman's upswept hair was a more subtle hue. He found the shiny copper color mesmerizing.

"Your name?" Captain Whiteside inquired, holding a script with names and cabin numbers.

"Miss Olivia Leatherby." The woman's green gaze drifted from the captain to Colin. Her eyes widened, showing she recognized him from earlier. She made no move to thank or acknowledge him, and her gaze quickly returned to the captain.

Why didn't she at least acknowledge my presence? Colin continued to study the young woman. The more he saw, the more he was intrigued. She was a good head shorter than he, but her curves and the way she set her feet to take the sway of the ship proved she wouldn't float away in a good breeze.

"Miss Leatherby, you will be staying in first cabin twelve." Captain Whiteside tooted on his whistle and the cabin boy hurried forward. "Jack, take Miss Olivia Leatherby to first cabin twelve."

"Aye, Captain." The young boy waved his hand for the woman and her belongings to follow.

Cabin twelve. That was two cabins down from Colin. Being practically neighbors, bumping into one another would be unavoidable.

He'd moved back to his spot at the railing when his gaze landed on another passenger whose fashionable attire and haughty manner didn't fit with the usual sailing passenger. He'd come across a few men like this one since his return to England and taking charge of his estate. Why would a man of this class take a clipper rather than a steamship? He was the type who would think the accommodations on a clipper ship beneath him.

The wind didn't carry the man's name to him by the railing as Captain Whiteside greeted the stranger. It didn't matter. He could always ask the cabin boy or the captain the gentleman's name.

He turned his attention to the smoke puffing out of the *Compania*. A dark gray cloud puffed out adding more somber gray to the day. Passengers lined the deck of the steamship, waving at the people on the docks.

He could have been on that ship, surrounded by all the people and traveling in luxury, but he preferred the slower pace of the sailing vessel. He'd used his newly acquired connections in the shipping world to obtain a first cabin on the *Americana*. While he didn't need the luxuries one had while on a steam ship, he did prefer traveling on a sailing ship in first class. The rooms were slightly larger, giving enough room to not feel as if he slept in a coffin, and the food, while not being served as elegantly, was filling and tasty.

The quiet, solitude, and time would allow him to go over the ideas his cousin Denis had handed him as he left Meath Hall. Even though he was excited to return to his family in Sumpter, he had become accustomed to riding about the thousand-acre estate talking to the tenants and discussing the best ways for them to grow better crops and livestock. Growing up, all he knew was mining, but living here, overseeing the land, he felt a kinship to both the people and the land.

"I guess you can take the boy out of the country but you can't take the country out of the boy." He grinned and headed to the first-class section of the ship. There would be a few more hours of spring sunlight streaming through his port hole. He'd best take advantage of the light to read the ideas Denis submitted.

He entered the covered stairwell and stopped. Angry words flowed up the opening.

"I heard you were late." The steely deep tone sounded like a threat.

"Ah had to say good-bye…"

He knew that soft wispy voice. Colin hurried down the stairs.

Chapter Two

Livie wouldn't have been late to meet Wilfred's henchmen and her new lady's maid if the three rampers hadn't stopped her in the street. They were friends of her brother, Ellis, and wanted to know why she was all dressed up when he was rotting in Gaol. She tried to slap their hands away as they picked at the hat that Wilfred bought her. Luckily, Abigail had another hat in the box. They'd changed her plucked hat before heading for the ship.

Wilfred grabbed her upper arms, squeezing. "There's no one you needed to say good-bye to. We have a deal and—" His deep angry voice cut off when his gaze travelled over her shoulder.

"The lady might have a chance to converse with you if you weren't hurting her arms."

Livie twisted her neck and peered over her shoulder at the same man who'd saved her from Ellis' friends. Her jaw clenched, hoping he didn't say they'd met before. If Wilfred knew of her altercation earlier, he'd become even angrier. She was on this ship to seduce Sir Colin Healy and learn information to help Wilfred get his family's estate back. If she helped him, he'd help her brother. She'd rejected Wilfred's offer the first time she heard it. She may have grown up in the rookery but she wasn't a liar and she didn't believe in thieving. But after visiting Ellis and seeing the conditions at the prison and then her mother begging her to get her son out, Livie'd conceded. Even knowing Wilfred's awful temper.

"I didn't realize. Olivia, was I hurting you?" Wilfred asked in such a syrupy tone, she thought she'd gag.

"Y-yes, a little." She hated the fact she was scared of this man. A coward who used others to benefit himself.

"Let the woman go." The other man said in as snarly a tone as she'd ever heard.

To her surprise, Wilfred drew his hands back as if her arms had just caught on fire.

The man stared at Wilfred. "I know you have antiquated laws here in England, but where I come from a man who treats a woman that rough isn't a man."

"What right do you have saying I'm not a man?" Wilfred's blotchy red face showed he was working into a rage.

"Ah'm sure he didn't mean it, luv" Livie blurted out trying to coddle Wilfred's rage even though she agreed with the stranger.

"Allow me to escort you to your room." The man cupped her elbow with his hand and turned her down the hall toward her room.

"Ah was going to the deck to watch the ship pull out of the harbor." Feeling safe with the man, she leaned close and said softly. "The small cabin with me lady's maid moving about putting things away made me long for the openness of the deck."

He grinned. "I understand. Let me escort you up top."

The gentleman walked right past the rooms and up a smaller stairway at the end of the hall. They stepped out of the covered stairwell and stood at the front of the ship.

Livie walked forward, grasping the railing, and inhaling the ocean's scent. She'd lived her whole life in Liverpool but never caught a whiff so refreshing. Where she lived the fresh scent of the sea rarely made it beyond the stench of too many bodies and too much squalor.

"I'm Colin Healy."

The minute their hands touched, it struck her. *Colin Healy.* This was Sir Colin Healy, Baronet of Meath Hall. The very same person she was to befriend and discover secrets. This man was her only hope of getting Ellis out of Gaol.

"Pleased to meet you. Ah'm L-Olivia Leatherby." She almost slipped and told him the name she went by from birth, but Wilfred said it was too lower-class to use while pretending to be the daughter of a baron.

This couldn't have worked out better if she'd planned it. Gazing into his dark blue eyes even more tension slipped from her body. His coming to her rescue twice suggested he'd be easy to draw out the information she needed. He obviously was a person who liked to help others, and therefore, she believed he would be personable and social. Not to mention he was the handsomest and best smelling man she'd ever encountered. Even Wilfred with all his money and airs, looked and smelled like someone from the rookery of Liverpool.

He released her hand and stood peering out at the ocean. "It seems you were in need of my help twice today."

The image of Wilfred's angry face flashed before her. She touched Sir Colin Healy's arm. "Please, don't tell Wilfred about the first time, luv." The second the words spilled out she wished they hadn't. One, because it showed she feared the man, and two, she'd called him by his first name, which someone of good breeding would never do when speaking to a relative stranger.

He faced her. "Why? How do you know that man?"

She sighed heavily and worked to come up with a good story. "He's Lord Wilfred Canfield. He has mistakenly decided ah should marry him." She peered out from under her lashes at the baronet. "You saw his anger. Ah told him ah wouldn't be a wife to anyone who couldn't control his temper. Ah came on this trip to visit me cousin in New York and put distance between oos." She gazed into Sir

Colin Healy's eyes and saw what she'd hoped for—sympathy. "Boot he thinks he can persuade me by the time we reach New York." She glanced around them and leaned forward. "Honestly, his following me has only made me fearful for me safety."

The man's sympathetic eyes narrowed. "You let me know if he lays a hand on you. No man has the right to hurt a woman."

The rage in his words made her wonder what had given him such an adamant conviction.

"Thank you. That makes me feel better about this trip. Once ah get to me cousin's, her husband will see to it that Wilfred is sent away."

The main sail snapped open, and the ship lurched forward.

Livie fell toward Sir Healy. He caught her against his wide, hard chest. His arms circled her body, holding her steady.

She wondered at the strength in his arms, yet they cradled her gently against him. He was a contradiction and unlike any man she'd ever met in her life. Most of the men she knew in the rookery would have had their hands roaming all over her body by now. Or backhanded her for falling into them. She could still feel the sting of her father's hand the day before he went missing. She'd never told a soul, but she believed her mother killed him and left him somewhere to rot. Her mother had put up with her husband beating on her, but when he raised his hand to her daughter, she'd broke.

The snap of the sail just above them slapped sense into her. Livie pushed at the chest she'd tucked her head against for a brief moment of tranquility. The arms holding her released, and she took a step, then another, away from the man studying her.

Chapter Three

Colin stared into green eyes bursting with copper around the pupil. This woman had his mind bouncing in all directions. Her speech patterns were nothing like Miss Gwendolyn Marsh. He'd have thought being of the same class, Olivia's speech would be as formal. And the matter of the r on the end of words sounding like uh, spoke more of the common work folk he'd visited. Uncle Orin had taught him how to speak to the entitled and her calling Lord Canfield by his given name…Yes, there were many contradictory things about this woman.

She turned her attention to the ocean as the boat pulled away from the dock. It gave him time to think and study her. She tugged on the pearl dangling from her ear. The way she worried the clasp between her fingers, he'd venture to guess she didn't normally wear the jewelry.

When she'd fallen against him, her soft curves had brought out the first urges he'd had since Denis talked him into drinking one night, and they'd ended up in bed with daughters of one of the tenant farmers. He didn't like to think about that night and how he'd almost ruined his relationship with that tenant.

"Why are you scowling?"

The soft voice drew him from his reveries. Miss Leatherby had a hip resting on the railing. Another action he'd never see a woman of title do. Ladies always carried themselves with a stiffness that made Colin wonder if they had stays in their drawers.

"I was thinking about a time when I should have remained in control." He had to keep that incident in the forefront of his mind and keep this woman at arm's length, but be there if she needed help. He'd spent too many frustrated times wishing he was big enough to defend his mother against Mr. Miller, her second husband and Shayla's father. He'd witnessed the man nearly beat his mother to death the same day that Shayla came into the world and Mr. Miller ended up dead. Many nights he'd dreamed he was the one to end the man's life. So much so, he wasn't sure he hadn't done it, until Ethan Halsey came into their lives and discovered it had been a man wanting to become his mother's third husband. Colin shook the past out of his head. He had to think about now and the future.

Miss Leatherby watched him with a hint of sadness. He couldn't allow himself to get tangled up with a woman. Not now, not when he was confused about his future. Before he asked her what troubled her, he had to get away.

"Excuse me, I need to take care of business before dinner." He turned to the stairwell.

"Will you be sitting with me at dinner?" Her voice wobbled.

He pivoted and she flashed him a weak smile.

"If you are beside me, Ah'm hoping Lord Canfield won't feel free to sit by me."

Against his better judgment, he nodded. "I'll be there."

Colin had planned on asking young Jack to bring his meals to him. Now, he had to keep his word and sit with Miss Leatherby. As much as the seating arrangement and having to dress for dinner irritated him, he slipped his arms into his suit jacket and made sure his vest was wrinkle free. He didn't want to become attached to the woman but found all her contradictions fascinating. His plan was to get her talking about herself, all women liked to talk about themselves and their families. That would help him understand her and perhaps find answers to his questions.

The large bell on deck bonged three times, indicating the evening meal was ready.

He opened his door and stepped into the hall. The click of doors along the hallway brought other passengers out of their rooms. He nodded to the men and bowed to the women. Two doors down Miss Leatherby stepped from her room. Two men who had exited the room between he and Miss Leatherby approached her.

Colin witnessed the widening of her eyes and her hesitation moments before her body started to move back into the room.

"Miss Leatherby," Colin strode past the two men and extended his arm.

A smile spread across her lips and lit up her eyes. "Sir Healy, how thoughtful of you to escort me to dinner." She smiled at the two men and slipped her hand through his arm.

He kept walking toward the smaller, less formal stairway. He wanted more privacy than the larger full staircase. "Please, I prefer to be called Mr. Healy, or when alone, Colin."

She gasped, parting her petite bow-shaped lips. "But you are titled and should be shown respect."

He shook his head. "It's a title I acquired through inheritance. It doesn't make a difference in how I do business or live my life. I'm Colin Healy, plain and simple."

Confusion dulled her eyes and dropped the corners of her lips. "You don't want to be a baronet or own land?"

"Who doesn't wish to own land? I enjoy the land. The challenges of bringing in a good crop and working with the tenants. It's the formality that comes with the land I dislike."

He held the door of the dining hall while Miss Leatherby entered. Orin had tried to explain to him how the titled felt their position placed them above everyone else and how few worked beside their tenants or even knew the first thing about the crops that were being raised on their lands.

Even the Halseys, who now would be considered barons of the Sumpter area, got in and worked side by side with anyone who needed help. He'd learned connections with people were more important than all the money in the world. That's why he visited and helped the tenants, and why he made Orin and Denis promise to check in with everyone on a weekly basis while he was gone.

"Miss Leatherby and Mr. Healy, come, sit at my table," Captain Whiteside greeted them as they came through the door and escorted them to the table at the head of the room.

Colin held Miss Leatherby's chair as she sat. He glanced around the table, returning Canfield's glare before taking a seat beside Olivia.

He registered the moment, Miss Leatherby spotted Canfield. She stiffened and clenched her hands together in her lap.

Leaning toward her, Colin murmured. "Don't look at him. Focus on the conversations with me or the captain."

She nodded and lowered her gaze to the bowl of soup sitting in front of her.

Livie couldn't believe her bad luck. Wilfred sat almost directly across from her at the captain's table. Not only did she have to remember her short course in table etiquette, she had to ignore the angry glare from Wilfred. Which she didn't understand. He wanted her to be friendly with Sir Healy, so why was he mad that they arrived together?

She hadn't had a chance to tell him the story she'd made up. When she'd returned to her cabin, Abigail insisted she lie down and then woke her an hour before dinner and started dressing her. It was a good thing she wasn't really a Lady. She'd never be able to get used to having someone dress her. It took all her control to stand still and allow the woman to do her job.

After dinner, she'd have to find a way to tell him what she told Sir Healy. In the meantime, she'd enjoy food she'd never have the chance to eat again. She dipped her spoon into the bowl of brown, thick broth and chunks of meat. The soup was a bit fishy and the meat chewy.

The captain took his seat at the head of the table to her left. "Do you like turtle soup, Miss Leatherby?"

"Ah don't know. Ah don't believe ah've ever had any." She glanced at the captain. Merriment danced in his eyes.

"You're eating it at the moment." He smiled and slurped a spoonful.

She stared down into her bowl. Should I have known it was turtle soup? Is it something that is served often to the gentry?

"Don't worry. I was taken back the first time I was told I was eating turtle soup." Sir Healy's calm, quiet voice broke into her self-recrimination.

She glanced up into his eyes. There wasn't mirth or superiority shining in the color of a clear summer day. Maybe she hadn't buggered her job.

"You don't have to eat the soup, there will be

several courses." Sir Healy's voice reminded her she'd stopped eating.

"It's delicious." She dipped the spoon and continued to eat.

The clatter of utensils against dishes and the murmuring of other conversations muffled around her, letting her be quiet and sink into her own thoughts. After dinner she should suggest taking a walk on the deck to Sir Healy. Then she'd get him to talk about his estate and his childhood. Wilfred wanted to know more about the family and where the deed to the estate was hidden. He'd sent people into Meath Hall as servants and no one could find the papers Wilfred wanted to disprove the inheritance.

Sir Healy nudged her arm, spilling the soup in her spoon back into the bowl. She peered at him.

"Captain Whiteside asked you a question." Sir Healy's gaze moved from her to the captain.

"Oh, ah'm sorry. Ah was lost in thought." Her cheeks burned with embarrassment. She'd been so deep in her thoughts, she'd ignored those around her. A quick peek at Wilfred only heightened her unease.

"The letter from your father said you were traveling to visit a sister in New York. What is her husband's name? I know quite a few businessmen in the area." The captain leaned back in his chair having finished his soup.

What name did Wilfred tell her? Did it matter? They were made up anyway. She wanted to glance at Wilfred, get some guidance but that would signal there was more to their acquaintance than she wanted Sir Healy to know. *Bugger!*

"Raymond Smith is Constance's husband's name." Mentally, she fixed the names in her mind. Hopefully, they wouldn't leave her like the ones Wilfred had already given her.

"Smith, that's a pretty common name. Can't say that I remember any businessmen by that name." The captain smiled. "What does he do?"

She hated to act mindless like she'd witnessed Wilfred's sister and her friends do when confronted with a conversation they didn't want to join, but she didn't want to talk about her made up family.

"Ah don't know. Men talk about business when we ladies aren't around." She glanced at Sir Healy. He didn't look convinced. In fact, he appeared puzzled. Surely, he'd been around enough gentry to know the women paid little attention to what the men did as long as they had fine dresses and jewelry.

Wilfred asked the captain a question, drawing his attention from her. Relief washed over her, even though she knew he didn't do it to save her, only his mission.

Chapter Four

Colin was even more curious about Miss Leatherby. She told him she was sailing to her cousin and now the captain said her sister and she didn't correct him. He finished the meal, staying alert to anything Miss Leatherby was asked or replied. She dodged most of the questions and stood as soon as the meal ended.

"Would you walk with me?" she whispered, when he stood to hold her chair.

Etiquette should have had him bow out, but his curiosity about the woman had him offering his arm. They stepped out on the moonlit deck. A brisk breeze ruffled his hair and tugged at her light shawl.

"I suggest we go to our rooms and get warmer coats if you still wish to walk." He headed straight for the middle stairwell without waiting for a response. At her door, he straightened his arm. "Do you still want to walk?"

She kept her gaze on the door. Wisps of copper hair fluttered across her cheek. "Yes, ah'm not ready to retire for the night." Her gaze collided with his. "Ah'd like to get to know you better."

He stared into her eyes. What was going on behind those green and rust orbs? "I'll return in five minutes." Pivoting on his heels, he headed for his room, entered, and shut the door.

He stood in the dark, the back of his head against the door. Miss Leatherby had struck him as an innocent young woman embarking on a new adventure when he first met her. Now, he wasn't so sure. She didn't meet his gaze honestly and all the contradictions he noticed in her speech, her actions, her words… But damn, he wanted to discover why she was so contradictory.

Without lighting the kerosene lamp, he fumbled in the dark, digging his wool jacket out of his bag along with the knit cap Aunt Kelda and Uncle Hank sent him at Christmas. His aunt knit the caps for the loggers to buy and wear while working in the woods. The warm wool worked well in the cold, wet weather in Lancashire. Once he was bundled for the cold wind, he left his room and knocked on Miss Leatherby's door.

She stepped out wearing the vibrant blue coat she'd worn when he first saw her. She'd wrapped the wool shawl from earlier over her head and about her neck. That she took comfort over fashion nudged up his admiration for her.

"Good to see you know to dress warm." He

offered his arm, and she slipped her hand through, linking their elbows.

"Ah don't intend to spend the whole trip in my cabin ill." She held her skirt as they walked up the stairs at the front of the ship.

Once on deck, she followed beside him at a leisurely pace. He nodded to other couples out getting fresh air after their meal. The lanterns hanging from the sides of the structures in the middle of the ship lit the deck halfway to the railing. It was in this shadowed area that Colin stopped and faced Miss Leatherby.

"I don't think you're a daughter of a baron, and I don't think you're meeting a sister or a cousin in New York." He'd expected her to slap him for being so straight forward with his assumption.

She sighed heavily and stared out at the darkness with ribbons of moonlight floating on the ocean's surface.

"Wot gave me away?" she finally asked, so quietly he had to move closer to catch the words.

"I've lived here long enough to know ladies your age and of the gentry speak more refined. You told me you were visiting a cousin, only the captain said the letter from your father said you were visiting your sister. The soup, the way you watched everyone to make sure you were doing things correctly at dinner." He turned her face to him. "The way you avoided eye contact with Canfield."

She flinched, squeezed her eyes shut, then opened them. Sorrow drooped her eyes and her shoulders. "Ah should have known ah couldn't do this."

"Do what?" He hadn't expected her to cave so easily. The second the thought popped into his head, he became guarded.

"Ah'm not gentry. Ah worked for an elderly Doochess. A week afore she died, she sent the letter to the captain and obtained me passage. She had her seamstress make clothes for me and gave me enough money to start a business in America. She'd heard stories of people like me going to America and having a good life. That's what she wanted for me. To be independent."

"Why didn't you just tell me and the captain that?" Colin wished he'd stopped in the light of a lantern so he could read her face and see if this was the truth. He wanted it to be. It made more sense than the other lies she told.

"If the people in the dining room knew ah wasn't gentry, they wouldn't allow me to eat with them or even be in the first cabins."

"No, I don't believe that. If you paid for a first cabin you would get it no matter your class."

"How long have you lived in England?" There was a tinge of humor in her question.

"Four years. Why?"

"Ah've been here a lifetime, and ah still don't understand why a pompous arse of a man or woman who has never worked a day in their life can tell others how to live and wot jobs they can and can't do. That is England. Ah want to go where ah can work at wotever ah want and not be told ah can't do something because ah grew oop in the rookery."

The resentful tone explained a lot about the woman.

This last statement from Miss Leatherby showed him her true person. She was a fighter looking for a better life. He could understand that. His mother had struggled and fought to give him and Shayla a shot at a life she'd had and lost. But now she was happy and content as Ethan's wife.

There was one thing that still bothered him. "I understand your desire to go somewhere where you can start new. But how does Canfield fit into this? He knows you and he's gentry."

The mention of the man changed her composure. She shot glances up and down the vacant deck and moved closer to him. "He knows about me past. His mam was friends with the doochess. When you saw oos together, he was against me pretending to be something ah'm not. Ah asked him not to expose me and he…he said he'd think of something ah could do to repay his silence."

Colin felt her body shake. Anger burned hot in his gut. He understood the man's meaning. "You don't have to do anything to repay him. I guarantee, if anyone gives you trouble about not being gentry, I'll stick up for you. And I don't need any favors for doing it."

"Ah don't want you getting into trouble. Ah'm not worth it."

He couldn't restrain himself any longer. Colin wrapped his arms around Olivia and held tight. He was leery and distrustful of men. More than one had hurt his mother and his family before Ethan showed him not all men had mean streaks.

But women—he'd been taking care of his mother and Shayla since he could remember. He championed them. So many men felt women were nothing but legal slaves. With four strong aunts and a mother whose strength got them through tough times, he knew they were strong, they just had to find that inner strength.

Olivia was just starting to find it.

"Everyone is worth standing up for." He rocked her back and forth, enjoying the feel of her body cuddled against his. Even through the wool coat, he could feel her curves. He kept his hands at her back, not straying lower or to the front. After what she'd just said about Canfield, he didn't want her to think he'd take advantage of her. While his mind stayed rational, his body was heating.

He eased her away from him. "One more question."

She nodded.

"Is your name really Olivia Leatherby?"

"Livie Leatherby. The doochess thought Olivia sounded more like gentry than Livie."

Colin released her completely. "Which do you want me to call you?"

"It's best if you use Miss Leatherby in public. Like this, when it's just the two of oos, Livie would be fine. Ah'll respond better than to a name ah've barely had."

"Livie, I think it's time to retire to our cabins. There's no one else on the decks, and I wouldn't want to start rumors that would sully your reputation." Colin offered his arm.

She slipped her hand through the crook of his arm, they sauntered into the lantern light, and straight for the larger stairwell in the center of the ship.

"It feels better having someone know the truth," she said quietly when they stood in the hallway in front of her cabin door.

"Lies have a way of eating a person up. I won't say a word, but I don't think you'll be treated any different if the truth comes out. Good night." Colin tipped his head to Livie waiting for her to enter her cabin.

She slipped into her room, but flashed him a shy smile before closing the door.

Colin returned the smile and strode down the hall to his cabin. Once inside he slowly undressed, thinking about the interesting woman. It took strength of character to travel alone to a new country with visions of starting over. Not only did he admire her strength, but her beauty. This may be the first trip he took on a ship that he didn't hide out in his cabin. He wanted to get to know Livie better and perhaps help her plan out her life once she arrived in America.

Chapter Five

Livie leaned her back against the door and counted to forty waiting for Colin to enter his cabin. She opened her door, peeked up and down the hall, and hurried beyond the wide staircase to the last cabin door before the lavvy. She scanned the hallway, then knocked quietly. Movement and rustling sounded from inside the room.

The door opened.

One side of Wilfred's face appeared moments before his arm snaked out and pulled her into the room.

Whiskey, pungent male, and burned kerosene assaulted her nose. Livie spun out of his grasp. "Why did you haul me in like a fish on a line?"

"Couldn't have the mark seeing you trot into my room after a stroll on the deck with him."

She'd witnessed Wilfred drunk and disheveled

before. At least twice a week, he'd wobble home mid-day after a night of carousing. And it was at those times she had to keep her distance. The small cabin put her within arm's reach of the man no matter where she stood.

"Ah'll come back and talk when you're not *kaylied*." She spun on her heel. Before she could grasp the latch, an arm came around her middle, and her back slammed against Wilfred's chest.

"Why'd you come here?" His foul, whiskey-laced breath heated the back of her head.

"To tell you, Sir Healy knows ah'm not gentry. He figured it out, so ah told him a doochess ah worked for paid me way and sent me to America to start a new life. He thinks you knew me because your mam and the doochess were friends. And you have threatened to tell everyone me true status if Ah don't…" She swallowed. By saying the words she so flippantly told Sir Healy, she could put ideas in Wilfred's head. Ideas she didn't want to fend off.

"Ahh, that's good. You won't have to keep up appearances while with him. And you've made yourself a helpless victim. Good, good." He kissed her neck.

Disgust boiled in her gut. She spun out of his arm and grabbed the latch. "Don't you dare take liberties. You try something like that again, and ah'll tell Sir Healy the truth. That ah'm here to help you get Meath Hall for your family." She jerked the door open.

Wilfred laughed. "You think he's going to believe that when you're nothing but lies?"

She stalked out of the room, firmly pulling the door shut. Another door down the hall clicked. She headed to the lavvy without looking back.

The following morning Livie was dressed and in the dining hall before any of the other passengers. She used this time to drink the rich coffee, nibble on sweet rolls, and think. So far in their conversations, she'd learned little about Colin and he'd learned more about her than he should. There had to be a way to get him to talk about his childhood, family, and how he came to be the heir to Meath Hall.

"Miss Leatherby, you're up and about early." Captain Whiteside sat across from her with a cup of coffee.

She smiled. Maybe he knew Sir Healy's history. "Ah'm not used to the creaks and groans of the ship."

"I'm sorry to hear that. The sounds put me right to sleep."

"That's because you spend so much time at sea, ah'd think." She leaned across the table. "Wot do you know about Sir Colin Healy?"

The man studied her a minute before a twinkle lit his brown eyes. "You two looked cozy last night at dinner."

Heat fused her cheeks. While that was the plan to show interest in Sir Healy and become "cozy" the idea flushed her skin and raced her heart.

The captain laughed. "Aye, I'd say you are just a bit taken by him."

No sense in concealing an infatuation. If she

wasn't convincing enough to get the information, poor Ellis would rot in Gaol.

"A bit. But ah know nothing about him." She sent the captain a pleading look, hoping to learn something that would help her open up the subject with Sir Healy.

Captain Whiteside glanced over her shoulder and started to rise. "Perhaps you should ask the bloke himself."

Her heart raced faster. There would only be one reason for the captain to say that. Her lips tipped into a welcoming smile. She hoped her fluttering insides didn't show in her voice.

Sir Healy stopped beside the captain. "Good morning, Captain, Miss Leatherby."

Colin stared at Livie's smile and couldn't stop the happiness building in his chest. He'd thought a lot about her circumstances last night. At the strength she must have to head to a new country alone. He now knew why her clothing, while being bright and cheerful were tailored to give only a hint of the woman lying beneath. They were all modestly cut, only showing her long neck above lacy collars. An older woman had made sure that while on her travels Livie didn't collect the wrong type of man. He liked the added mystery of a woman who didn't use her assets to lure a man in and make it hard for him to concentrate while talking with her.

That was yet another exception he'd taken to Miss Gwendolyn Marsh. Every time he visited the Marsh family, Gwendolyn's breasts nearly popped out of her dress, making it hard to concentrate on conversations.

"Sir—Ah mean Mr. Healy, good morning."

Livie's soft voice had grabbed him from the first time he'd heard it. This morning it seemed to hold even more intimacy.

"I've matters to attend. I hope you two take a stroll or two about the deck today. It looks to be a find day for it."

"Thank you, Captain, we'll make sure we get some sun." Colin put his hand on a chair and peered across the table at Livie. "Do you mind if I sit with you?"

"Ah'd enjoy the company. Ah didn't realize ah'd be the first oop. This is later than ah usually get oop." She picked up the porcelain cup and sipped.

He had a hard time moving his gaze from her pink lips to her eyes, which peered at him over the brim of the cup.

"What was your position with the duchess?" Now that he knew her true status, he felt more at ease with her. And enjoyed hearing her speak with the dialect unique to Liverpool.

She took another sip before setting the cup down on the saucer. "Ah was the Doochess' lady's maid. It's awkward having Abigail do for me wot just weeks ago ah did for the doochess." She wrinkled her petite nose with a smattering of light freckles. "Ah don't like being helped. Ah'd rather do things meself."

"Let her go."

Livie's mouth opened as if to say something, then closed. She picked up the cup, sipped, and studied him.

She was stalling.

"You don't plan to keep her when you get to America, do you?"

"No. Ah, well, ah hadn't thought that far ahead." Her hands shook as she placed the cup on the saucer.

"Does she know the truth? That you aren't… privileged as you pretend?"

"No. She believes she is working for Lady Olivia Leatherby." Livie reached across the table as if looking for something to grasp on to.

Colin clasped her seeking hand in his. "Why do you look so unhappy?"

"Ah hadn't thought through wot would happen to Abigail once ah'm on me own." Her wide eyes peered into his. "Ah'll have to see if she wants to stay or return home. Why didn't W—the doochess think of that afore hiring her?"

She'd almost started to say a name. Had the duchess been so informal that they'd called one another by their given names? The woman seemed to have been less constrained by the rules of peerage to have given her servant money to leave the country.

"Why did you agree to leave England? Don't you have family?" Was she an orphan? That would explain the older woman's taking her under her wing.

"Me dar beat me mam and the day he hit me was the last ah saw him."

Colin hadn't taken her for a woman who had been hurt by a man's hands, but now he did see the small details that proved she wasn't completely convinced all men didn't beat women. "Did your mother take you away?"

"No, me mam said me dar must have finally drunk too much and fell in the river."

The steadfast expression and unwavering eye contact told him more than her words. He'd no doubt her mother made sure the man didn't come home again.

"Is your mother the only family you have? No brothers or sisters? Aunts, uncles, cousins?'

She glanced away then back. "Ah've a brother in Gaol. Since he was nibbed no one else in the family wants much to do with me mam and me." She took the last sip of her coffee. "Mam gave me blessings to make a place for meself in America."

"Your mother sounds like a strong person." A lot like his ma.

"She wasn't very strong before me dar hit me, but after, there was a fire to her eyes ah'd never seen afore."

Colin understood the fire. When a person took charge of their destiny, they felt invincible. "I know the feeling."

Her gaze snapped back to his face. "You do?"

"Yes. My da died when I was small. My ma traveled to America and married Mr. Miller." He'd never been able to call the monster by any other name. He glanced around the room. They were still the only people in the dining area. "He beat on Ma. I was too little to help much. One time he beat her senseless. I sat with her all night and she finally came around." His hands clenched into fists. If only he'd been old enough and strong enough to fight back.

Livie put her hands over his fists. Her quiet acceptance allowed him to continue.

"Ma was pregnant with my sister, Shayla. Mr. Miller came home drunk and hollering he wanted his dinner. Ma and me had been out in the mine all day and just came in ourselves." He closed his eyes. The scene came rushing back to him as if it happened yesterday. His gut clenched and his hands felt clammy.

"You don't have to say more."

Livie's soothing voice pulled him from the memory. Colin opened his eyes and stared into her concerned gaze.

"Ma was with child. He hit and kicked her until she lay silent on the floor." He stared over her shoulder. "I hit him with a board, and he stumbled out of the shack. I tended to Ma and the baby coming. The next day we were told he'd been found dead. I spent several years believing I'd killed him."

"Did you?" Her question sounded more curiosity than accusation.

"No. I found out later that a man who believed Ma would marry him if her husband was dead had killed Mr. Miller. The same man nearly killed me and Ethan, Ma's husband now. The man was a friend of my Uncle Clay, Ethan's brother. He also blinded Clay by throwing dynamite at him." He smiled, thinking of the Halsey brothers and how much they had taught him and how they loved Ma and Shayla and himself as if he and Shayla were blood.

"Your mam's new husband is good for her?"

Livie's skeptical tone drew his gaze to her face.

"Yes, he loves her and she loves him. Ethan brought my family to Ireland and England right after they married. That's when I first saw Meath Hall."

Her body straightened and her composure became intent. "That was the first time you saw your estate? How old were you?"

"Thirteen. Ethan and Uncle Orin wanted me to see why I needed to get my schooling."

"Is your Uncle Orin from your mam's side?"

"No, he's my da's cousin, but I call him uncle. Meath Hall was owned by my grandfather's family. They were English. My da's mother was English and when she was the only child to have a son, Meath Hall went to my da, but he died shortly after he received notice Meath Hall was left to him."

"That's quite a story. Are any of your relatives who left you the estate alive?" She asked the question as if she didn't care, but the intensity of her eyes said otherwise.

He wondered at her curiosity. Was she looking to become the gentry she pretended to be? "None on my grandfather's side, but there are several on my grandmother's side who believe the estate should be theirs. They didn't like an Irishman getting it when it passed to my da, and I've had several visits from the same, thinking it should belong to the English side." He'd thought about handing the estate over to the side of the family that lived in England, but he didn't want to let his da down. He'd lost his life to give the estate to his son. Colin felt giving it up would be disrespectful to his da.

"But now you are on the way to America. Who looks after the estate while you are gone?" She moved crumbs around on her plate with a fork.

Movement by the door drew their attention. People started arriving for the morning meal.

"The uncle I mentioned, and his son, handle the estate while I'm gone." He nodded toward the people flowing through the doorway. "This is a topic I prefer to only talk about between us."

She nodded and pushed the empty dishes to the middle of the table. He expected her to rise and leave since she appeared to have already eaten. But she remained seated across from him as the servers placed platters of bread, boiled eggs, bacon, and bowls of porridge down the long tables.

Livie filled her plate and began eating with an appetite few women of gentry would approve. Colin glanced along the table. The women seated at the table had noticed Livie's voracious appetite.

He nudged her with his foot under the table, gaining her attention. When she questioned him with her eyes, he held up his fork overflowing with food and shook his head slightly. He reloaded his fork with a small amount of food and tipped his head toward a couple of the women.

Livie's cheeks reddened, and she resumed eating in a more sedate manner.

After placing the last bite in his mouth, Colin

chewed, drank the last of his coffee, and prepared to leave.

Livie scrambled up from her chair before he could round the table and ask her politely if she cared to go for a stroll.

Chapter Six

Livie was grateful Colin had brought to her attention her bad eating habits. While she wasn't a thin woman, growing up food had been scarce, and she tended to eat all she could when the chance came.

When Colin rose to leave, she hurried to her feet, wanting to learn more about him. The conversation they'd shared before the meal had shown her they had a similar childhood. She was excited she'd found someone who understood living with an abusive parent.

Colin came to her side of the table and offered his arm. A girl could get used to having him to lean on.

Wilfred entered the room. His appearance reminded her why she was cozying up to Colin—to get Ellis out of Gaol. She couldn't let her new kinship with him deter her from her mission to free her brother. Thinking of him as Colin, made him a friend. She must use his formal title and keep her distance. Once he discovered her part in Wilfred's scheme, he wasn't going to want anything to do with her. The thought stung, but she'd promised Ellis and Mam she'd do what it took to get the information Wilfred wanted.

She tipped her nose in the air as she and Colin—Sir Healy— walked by Wilfred. She needed to keep her emotions unattached, but she couldn't think of Colin as a sir or a baronet. He was an American who didn't care about his station. One more thing she admired about him.

Tension in Colin's arm revealed he was ready for a confrontation. Thankfully, Wilfred only glared at them and continued into the room.

Out on the deck, she exhaled the breath she'd been holding.

"I don't like Canfield," Colin said, moving them quickly over to the railing, away from people still entering the dining room.

"He makes me skin crawl." She crossed her arms, trying to stave off the cold she felt when Wilfred was around.

"If he's at the Captain's table at dinner, I'll ask to have us moved to another table."

She peered into his sincere eyes. "You'd do that? Ask to leave the captain's table to make me more comfortable?" No one had ever made such a gesture for her.

"We can talk to Captain Whiteside any time

we want. And it's hard to digest food when you're being glared at." Colin grasped her hand, tucking it around his elbow. "Let's stroll, then I have to go to my cabin and do some reading."

They walked at a sedate pace along the deck.

"What are you reading?" The one thing her mam had insisted she and Ellis learn was reading. She enjoyed reading anything she could find. Wilfred's sister had loaned her two books from the Canfield library.

"Papers about a new type of manufacturing my cousin believes I should invest in." Colin stopped at the front of the ship.

The wind whipped at her hair, but she enjoyed the freshness of the mist from the bow breaking through the water. "Wot kind of manufacturing?"

"Casting metal parts for machines in factories." He studied her. "Are you interested in business?"

"Ah worked in a factory before ah became a lady's maid." She hadn't liked the work or the roaming hands of the foreman. Several women said to be nice to him and she wouldn't have to meet the daily quota. She might be doing something underhanded to get the information to free her brother, but to make her life easier she'd not become a ruined woman.

"What kind of work did you do?" His interest was genuine.

"It was a clothing factory. Ah ran a sewing machine and had a fair hand at fixing the machines when they stopped." She'd been proud the first time she'd unbound a machine next to her to help the woman make her quota and not get docked. After the woman told others, they soon started calling out to her when the machines jammed.

She blushed under Colin's intense stare.

"I had a notion you had a good head about you." He motioned to the other side of the ship. "Let's stroll down that side."

Livie fell in step beside him, this time not linking arms. There was so much she liked about Colin. His looks, his gentle yet strong presence, and his unaccepting attitude of class distinction.

"Why are you going home?" she asked, wondering if there was a chance she'd run into him again, and if after he discovered her duplicity, he'd even acknowledge her.

He smiled and her breath caught. He was even more handsome when his face lit up.

"My sister, Shayla, sent a letter requesting my presence at her fifteenth birthday and her graduation from grammar school." His tone held the pride of a parent.

She studied him. "You and she must be very close?" Her chest squeezed. She and Ellis had been inseparable as children, and then as he started running with the other lads stealing and doing jobs they had no business doing, she and Ellis fought. She became disillusioned with him and believed he'd end up in Gaol, but of his own accord not by someone else's treachery.

"I was there for her birth, helped Ma through the whole thing." He stopped and stared out at the bluish-green water. "I was the man of my family for five years. I worked alongside Ma, helped when Shayla was sick. Ma and I are a lot alike. There's nothing either of us wouldn't do for Shayla."

"She's a lucky girl." Livie meant it with all her heart. She wished she had a brother, a cousin, a father who believed in her.

Colin shifted to face Livie. He heard the wistfulness in her tone and the sadness in her beautiful eyes tugged at his heart. "I know from what you've said about your father, he wasn't there for you. What about your brother?"

She grimaced. "We were like two peas in a pod as children. But as we grew, ah didn't mind working to help put food on the table, but Ellis took to thievery to help out. We fot over that a lot. Mam was knowing where he got the money, but chose to ignore it so we wouldn't go hungry."

"That's how he ended up in prison?" He'd wondered when she'd skipped over his incarceration in an earlier conversation.

"No, he was nibbed for something he didn't do. The real crook had money and paid to find proof against me brother."

Red started infusing her cheeks, and her hands clenched into fists.

"Have you tried to find evidence against the real crook?" He could send word to Orin to hire a solicitor to look into the allegations against her brother.

Livie let loose a very unlady-like snort. "You think the courts would take me brother's word over someone titled?" She laughed. "You haven't been off your estate much have you?"

Her slight annoyed him, but more her acceptance that because she wasn't titled no one would listen to her.

"I can get a solicitor to investigate the—"

"Ah didn't tell ye this to get yer money or 'elp." This time her face became red and blotchy and she stomped her foot. "We don't need the likes of ye coming in like some 'ero and saving the day. Ah'm working on getting Ellis out, and ye'll keep yer noble actions to yerself." She stomped down the deck.

Her true background came out clear and strong when she was angered. Her words came out fast and full of the lower class slang, unlike the way she searched and slowly pronounced words when portraying a titled young woman.

Why did her anger rise at the mention of helping? Was she so proud she'd let her brother rot in prison rather than take a legitimate offer? *But are you being legitimate*? He hated the little voice in his head that always saw through his intentions.

Watching the sway of her green dress and the way she held herself tall and straight, he knew helping her had little to do with getting her brother out of prison and more with having an excuse to stay connected with her. He growled under his breath and watched from a distance as Livie chatted with an elderly couple before taking a seat on a chair beside the old woman.

He started for the stairs to do the reading he kept putting off due to the charming young woman laughing and talking with the couple. A person walked around the far end of the deck. He knew that frame and walk.

Canfield.

The man stalked straight towards the three people sitting in chairs conversing.

Livie's back was to the man's approach.

Colin's feet started to move, but he held back. He believed Livie when she said the man gave her shivers, but he'd also felt there was more to the two than she'd admitted. The man acted more like a jilted lover, her first version of their acquaintance, than a person who cared that she was masquerading as a Lady.

Livie stiffened when Canfield walked up behind her. He said something that made her flinch and the couple scowl. That was all Colin needed to see. Having Canfield ruin Livie's reputation wasn't something he could live with. Not when it was within his power to help.

His stride lengthened, eating up the distance between him and the group. He slowed when Canfield glanced his way. Hatred flashed in the man's eyes before he masked the emotion.

The only reason he knew of for Canfield to hate him was Livie. There had to be more to their relationship than she told.

"Miss Leatherby, I'm glad you're still on deck. The captain wanted to give you the tour you asked him about." He'd made the excuse to intervene in a hurry. He hoped Livie didn't question the request.

"Of course. That would be wonderful. But first,

let me introduce you to Mr. and Mrs. Horace Duffy. They're from New York." Livie stood, beckoning him over and putting her back to Canfield.

Colin had a hard time not giving the man a nod to leave. Instead, he extended his hand to Mr. Duffy. "Pleased to meet you. I'm Colin Healy."

"An American. After spending our vacation in England, we're ready to get home," Mr. Duffy said, patting his wife's arm.

"Yes, we are. I'm glad Horace only has to come over here every five years for business." Mrs. Duffy nodded and her jowls jiggled.

"What makes America so much better than England?" Canfield asked, inserting himself into the conversation.

"We'd better go if the captain is waiting for oos," Livie said, giving them a reason to get away.

"We'll visit with you more later, dear," Mrs. Duffy said as Mr. Duffy and Canfield started a heated conversation about their own countries.

Colin extended his arm, and Livie slipped her hand through. He liked walking the deck with her on his arm. He mentally shook himself. Don't get attached. You don't know where you plan to settle and you don't need a woman, especially this one who had so many contrary things about her.

"Ah'm glad you came along and saved me."

"From who? The Duffys or Canfield?" He hadn't meant for his voice to sound so hard or harsh.

Livie pulled back and stopped. "That tone isn't necessary. You know it was Lord Canfield ah didn't want to be near."

"What did he say?" He watched her face. One thing he'd noticed about Livie, she couldn't hide her feelings.

She faced the railing, staring out to the water. "It wasn't complimentary."

"That's what I thought from the Duffy's expressions." He walked up beside her and cupped her chin, turning her head to peer in her eyes. The melancholy dimming her usually sparkling eyes made him want to put the sparkle back.

"Let's go find the captain and get our tour." He dropped his hand from her chin and offered his arm.

"Ah'd like to go to me cabin. Ah don't feel like performing like a lady right now. Ah need to be by meself for a spell."

"You're sure?" Only a short time earlier he couldn't wait to get to his cabin to read, now, knowing she was going to her cabin with a heavy heart, he didn't think being alone was what she needed.

"Come on, I know somewhere you won't be disturbed and you won't be alone." Colin grabbed her hand and headed to the stairwell.

"But ah want to be alone." She tugged once, and then followed down the stairs to the first cabins.

He turned at the bottom of the stairs and drew her down to the second cabin deck. And turned, taking her down one more set of stairs.

"Where are you taking me?" The excitement and unease vibrated in her voice.

Chapter Seven

Livie trusted Colin, but he continued to draw her deeper and deeper into the hull of the ship. As curious as she was to see what he thought was a good place to hide, she was nervous about being alone with him. What if people found out they were alone down here? It could ruin the reputation of Miss Olivia Leatherby and work against her getting the information Wilfred wanted. Thinking of him only caused her dampened mood to grow glummer.

If he wanted her to remain respectable and keep Colin's confidence then he shouldn't make remarks that put her in a bad light. He'd walked up behind her and said it appeared she found her way back to her cabin last night after visiting him. In front of the Duffys. As if they wouldn't think her seeing him at night wasn't inappropriate.

She'd witnessed the scowls. Resentment burned

in her stomach at the way he treated her and that she had to put up with it until she did her job and Ellis was free.

"This is one of the storage areas." Colin lit a lantern hanging by a door. He motioned for her to enter ahead of him.

Wooden crates of varying sizes were stacked in the area. The only open floor space was five meters straight in from the door.

"What are we doing down here?" She was intrigued that Colin knew the ship so well and had the run of the vessel.

"Do you like to read?" He stood beside a crate.

She dropped her gaze and saw his name written on the crate. "Yes, reading has always been a favorite pastime."

His smile grew. "I was hoping you'd say that. I have a crate of books I'm taking to Shayla. If you'd like to borrow one or two for the trip, you're welcome." He pulled the lid off the crate.

Livie dropped to her knees and fingered the covers of the top books. "Ah've never seen so many books in one place other than the C-doochess's library." She'd almost said Canfield's. That would have ripped this moment and Colin's friendship away.

Colin sat down beside her. "I didn't learn the power of books until Ethan came into our lives. He would visit and bring a book to read to us. Ma could speak fair English but couldn't cipher it, and the community where we lived wasn't friendly to us, so we didn't go to school."

Livie studied his face. Their backgrounds were so similar. "Ah didn't get any formal learning. Mam was learned and taught oos to read. Once it stuck with me, ah'd find anything ah could to read. Newspapers flying in the street, advertisements, and ah'd go into the stores that allowed me and read the labels on things."

He shifted onto his knees and picked up a book. "I think you'll like this one. It's a book of fables."

"What are fables?" She took the book he offered and ran her hand over the cover reading the title, *Aesop's Fables*.

"They are stories with mystical creatures or talking animals that teach a moral. I found several have been helpful in seeing events in my life that I thought were bad, actually brought me to something good."

She peered into his eyes. Was he trying to say she was something good? Her heart raced. But she wasn't. She was here to get information from him and save Ellis. She cleared her throat and stared at the book.

"Are you going to stay in America or return to Meath Hall?" She had to get him talking about himself and his family. Getting the information from him and then hiding out in her cabin was the only way she'd keep from telling him everything and submitting Ellis to a life in Gaol.

"I haven't decided. This trip is to see where I want to live. With family in Sumpter, but I'm unclear what I would do there, or stay at Meath Hall. I enjoy working with the tenants and my Irish relatives." He sighed. "But I miss Ma, Shayla, and the Halsey family."

Her ears perked at the mention of Irish relatives. "Are the Irish relatives the ones who would inherit the estate after you?"

He watched her, his blue eyes intent.

"Being not of the titled, ah don't understand the way things happen."

His intent gaze and slight narrowing of his eyes told her he'd started to question her interest.

"No. Meath Hall will pass down to my oldest son. In the case I don't have a son or something happened to me, it would then go to the eldest male on my English grandmother's side."

Colin peered at her long enough to make her squirm. "Why are you so interested in what happens to Meath Hall?"

"Ah've never known anyone titled who would talk with me about such things." Her insides quivered at yet another lie to a man who had told her so much about himself.

He pulled out another book. "This is the first book Ethan read to us. *Moby Dick*."

Colin's mind went back to the days when Ethan came to their shack on the pretense of checking on them and would read. At the time, he would have argued he didn't like Ethan hanging around his ma. But now, he saw how the man had saved all of them from a life of poverty. He'd not only given them a home and family, he'd given them respect. Something his abused mother had given up on.

He watched Livie open the book of fables. He

saw that haunted look in her eyes when she thought he wasn't paying attention. There was more to her than she told.

"Do you remember your dar?"

He stared at her. Where had that come from?

"I was still very small, but I do have vague memories of riding on his shoulders and Ma being happy. And I remember the night Ma's father hurried us to the ship that carried us to America." When he was young, before Ethan came into their lives and they'd traveled to Ireland and England, he'd dreamed Da would find them and everything would be better.

"Why did he do that?" She glanced up from the book, her brow furrowed in puzzlement.

"I learned later, when Ma thought I was old enough to understand, that Da had been killed that day and grandfather somehow knew it was my English relatives getting rid of the heir to the estate." He fisted his hand as he remembered Ethan walking with him into Meath Hall when he was thirteen. "Ethan took me to reclaim my inheritance when I was thirteen. The Rodericks weren't pleased when our solicitor told them they had one week to leave."

"But you didn't stay?" She sat on her backside.

"No, I was too young to run the estate. I still had a lot of schooling I needed to be prepared to run it. We left Orin, my da's Irish cousin, in charge. I corresponded with him monthly and visited yearly when I was old enough to make the trip on my own."

"That's why you know this ship so well!" Her

eyes lit up. "Ah was wondering how you knew your way around."

"Yes, I've made the trip a few times." He stood, helped her to her feet, and handed his book to her. "It's getting cool down here. We should leave." Colin replaced the lid on his crate and picked up the lantern he'd placed on another crate.

"Ah'm going straight to me cabin and start reading. Ah hadn't thought to bring a book for company on this trip." She stood on her toes and kissed his cheek. "Thank you."

Colin stood rooted to the spot as Livie hurried out the door and up the stairs. He quickly closed the storage room door, blew out the lantern, and followed. She had already ascended the first set of stairs when he started up. He followed, keeping an eye on her as she hurried up the next set of stairs and down the hall to her cabin.

He entered his cabin and stared down at the papers he'd left spread out on the small table. He didn't see the numbers or writing, his mind was back dissecting the questions Livie had asked. Why was she so interested in his background? Was it purely curiosity of a titled person? He didn't know what she was up to, but the kiss on his cheek had sent his mind to thoughts that would only hurt them both when the ship docked in New York and they went their separate ways.

She needed him to protect her from Canfield. Which was another puzzle. What did the man have on her? It was more than exposing she wasn't gentry. What could it be?

Chapter Eight

Livie remained in her cabin until she heard the bell for dinner. Abigail had started dressing her an hour before. If being titled meant changing clothes every night for dinner, she preferred her real station in life. It was exhausting to be fancied up every evening for a meal. She did however like the fact Abigail insisted she lie down every afternoon and placed heated, scented rags over Livie's eyes. That kind of pampering she could get used to.

She patted the side of her hair. Abigail had a knack for putting Livie's hair up in a fashionable bun. Having a lady's maid wasn't so bad.

"Thank you, Abigail." One thing she learned as a maid for the Canfields, the people you worked for rarely thanked you. Unless you did something that was not a usual chore or put extra effort into a chore.

"Thank ye, me lady. Will ye be back directly after dinner?" Abigail stood at the end of the bed her hands clasped in front of her.

Allowing Abigail to server her, made Livie feel like a fraud. *Will Wilfred allow me to return to Liverpool in the same style once he has the information he wants?*

"No, ah'm hoping Sir Healy will care to stroll again tonight." She thought a minute. "Why don't you take the night off?"

"But 'ow will me lady get ready for bed?" The perplexed expression on Abigail's face was comical.

"Ah'll be fine. Please, take a night to yourself."

"Thank ye. Ah will." The young girl blushed.

"Are you blushing because there's a young man you'd like to see?" The thought Abigail may have found love lightened Livie's heart.

The young woman giggled and nodded.

"Then you definitely need the night off. Ah don't want to see you until morning."

"Thank ye! Ah'll be here afore the sun is oop."

Livie smiled and pulled the brown wool shawl around her shoulders. This would be warm enough to walk about the deck without having to come to her room first. She stepped out the door.

The sight of Colin waiting by the bottom of the stairs started flutters in her belly. He was handsome in a dark blue suit jacket and trousers. A gray sweater stretched nicely across his chest.

He spotted her and smiled. The warmth emanating from his eyes took her breath away. No man had ever looked at her in such a way. Guilt landed in her stomach, smashing the flutters. And this man would soon not look at her at all if he ever found out she was working him for information.

The moment Colin's smile faded and lines formed on his brow, she knew her thoughts had shown on her face.

He strode down the hall toward her. "Is something wrong?"

"No, Ah just…" I should tell him the truth, but Ellis. "Ah'm not feeling well tonight. Ah think ah'll skip dinner." She pivoted to go back to her room.

"Why don't you try some fresh air first?" Colin offered his arm. "You look too pretty to stay in your room."

Her heart started a jig in her chest. *He said I'm pretty!* "Fresh air might be wot ah need. Ah've been in me room since you gave me the books." She slipped her hand through the crook in his arm. "The fables are scary and so truthful."

They started up the staircase as Wilfred came around the side.

"My, one would think you two would get enough of one another."

Wilfred's snarky tone made her clench her teeth to keep her tongue from flapping and saying something she'd regret.

Colin's arm tensed.

"When a woman is this beautiful, one can never get enough of her company," Colin said, escorting her up the stairs and down the deck away from the dining room.

Livie's feet felt like they floated across the

wood deck. Not only had he called her pretty but beautiful as well. She drifted on a cloud of euphoria. No one had ever told her she was pretty.

Colin stopped at the front of the ship.

She peered ahead at the ocean stretching on and on before them. They had twelve more days on the ship. Twelve more days to be with Colin before he headed home and she went back to Liverpool with Wilfred. Her good mood dropped like a stone.

"You appeared better when we stopped. Now what has you looking like a girl who lost her puppy?" Colin slipped his arm around her waist, pulling her to stand beside him.

She shouldn't allow him to touch her so freely. But the warmth and comfort of his strong arm was better than having enough coal to keep them warn through a cold winter night.

"Ah think about me brother and feel guilty that ah'm heading to a new life and he's stuck in Gaol." This is what I need to remember. Why I'm here. "Ah should have stayed and helped to prove his innocence."

"Why didn't you?" It wasn't an accusation.

"The doochess said if ah wanted to take her offer ah had to go now. Ah think she feared if she gave me the money to go at a later time, it would get used trying to get Ellis free." Another lie… He is never going to believe a thing I say when I do tell him the truth.

"Would you have used the money to help your brother?"

He didn't look at her, but she could tell by his

fingers pressing firmer against her side, her answer meant a lot to him.

"Yes."

His grip loosened. "But the duchess must have felt your getting free was more important than getting your brother, who you willingly said was a thief, out of jail."

"True, she believed in me but not him." *Bugger!* I'm getting glib at telling lies. I'm no better than me brother.

"Then you shouldn't allow guilt to bother you. Your choice wasn't yours it was made for you by someone who saw good in you." He faced her. "Livie, you are a remarkable woman. I'm sure when you get to America, you'll find a job and make a better life for yourself than you had in England."

During the discussion her conscience had been thinking maybe she should get off in America and not go back. Then Mam's face, alive with hopefulness when Livie told her she had a chance to get Ellis out of Gaol, crossed her mind, and she knew what she had to do. If I get off the ship and don't look back, that act of selfishness will kill me.

"Thank you for your confidence." She slowly spun out of Colin's one-armed embrace. "Ah'm hungry now." Without waiting for him, she started walking toward the dining room.

Colin couldn't figure out the many temperaments of Livie. When she stepped out of her cabin, her eyes had lit up along with a smile that warmed him to his toes. Within seconds, she'd become morose. The encounter with Canfield hadn't helped, but she'd perked up when he called her beautiful. Now, she was running from him moments after she'd gone sullen, again.

He knew women could change moods in a heartbeat at times from listening to the Halsey men talk about their wives. Maybe this was that time for Livie. He'd have to make sure he didn't say anything to upset her.

Catching up, he cupped her elbow in the palm of his hand and escorted her into the dining room. Canfield was at the captain's table. The smirk on the man's face melted when Colin maneuvered Livie to a table near the door with two open spaces.

He'd find Captain Whiteside later and see what he could find out about Canfield. The baron reminded him of the man who killed Mr. Miller.

Livie was quiet during the meal, only answering questions that were directed at her. She didn't wait for desert, but quietly left the table. Colin held back from jumping up and following her. She'd said she didn't feel well earlier.

He finished with an apple tart and coffee. Because he and Livie had arrived later than the others most of the passengers had left by the time Colin finished. He noticed the Duffys at the next table over.

Picking up his coffee cup and saucer, Colin moved to the chair across from the couple. "We met earlier today," he started.

"Yes, you were the nice young man who asked Miss Leatherby for a walk on the deck." The woman smiled and nodded her head.

"I was. And I wondered if you'd tell me what Canfield said to Miss Leatherby before I arrived."

The husband and wife glanced at one another. The woman started to shake her head, but the husband leaned forward. "I can see you care about Miss Leatherby." He cleared his throat and his wife put a hand on his arm, shaking her head, again.

"Mavis, a man has a right to know what others are saying. Lord Canfield made a remark that he was happy to see Miss Leatherby made it back to her room after visiting him."

Colin felt like a cold blade of steel struck him in the back.

Mrs. Duffy reached across the table, touching Colin's fisted hand. "The way he said it, he wanted others to hear. Now, Miss Leatherby didn't deny it, but I could tell she was stricken and puzzled by his declaration."

Colin watched the woman's lips move but barely heard a word for the buzzing in his head. What could the two be hatching? That had to be why Canfield glared at him all the time, he thought Livie was two-timing him. But Livie had a genuine fear of Canfield. His head hurt thinking of all the lies and deceit he'd taken as fact from Livie.

"Thank you. Thank you for your truthfulness. I need to go." He stood.

Mr. Duffy rose and stretched a hand out to him. "Young man. Don't do anything stupid. Take some time to think about who you believe, Lord Canfield or that nice young woman."

Colin nodded. "I need to think." He stumbled

out of the dining room and strode around the deck.

"Are you trying to walk a hole in my deck?"

He stopped and faced the voice calling to him. Captain Whiteside stood on the poop deck grinning like he had a good wind to his sail. "Come on up, boy. There's nothing better for the soul than standing up here and watching the sunset."

He wanted to ask about Canfield and this was a perfect opening to do so. Colin climbed the short set of steps up to the area where the ship was steered and the orders shouted.

"What has you so riled up you're pacing around the deck like a caged lion?" Captain Whiteside asked as he stared out across the ocean in front of them.

"What do you know about Lord Canfield?" He wasn't going to waste breath making small talk to get to the information he needed.

"He's from a prominent enough family in Liverpool. They've been gentry since the middle ages. But too many men in the family prefer women and cards to running their estate and their holdings have been getting smaller and smaller."

"I don't care about the family. What about the man on this ship?" Colin knew about families losing estates. He had his eye on a neighboring estate that was having a hard time paying the upkeep.

"He likes the women and several have complained he's rough, if you know what I mean."

Colin nodded and a knot formed in his gut. No wonder Livie was scared of him. "Go on."

"He's been nothing but a problem for his father

since he come of age. Between drinking, gambling, and the women, he has besmirched the family name."

"Why is he on this ship?" That had been nagging at Colin from the first day he spotted the man boarding the ship.

"Don't know. He paid for his cabin and another." The captain faced him, a solemn expression on his usually jovial face. "I thought Miss Olivia Leatherby was a special friend, if you know what I mean. But she's been spending all her time with you. I don't know why he paid for her cabin."

Another connection she didn't tell him about. What about the duchess she said paid for the cabin and sent her on this trip? Another lie?

"What are you thinking? You're looking like a storm's a brewing." The captain pulled him to the side of the smaller deck. "I noticed you and Miss Leatherby didn't sit at my table tonight and she left early."

"She said she wasn't feeling well." She may have lied to him, but he wouldn't tell this man or anyone about her lies. It would make him look a fool.

He peered into the captain's concerned gaze. "I'm fine, just trying to understand things. I've got some work to do in my cabin."

Colin left the poop deck and casually took one last turn around the deck before heading to his cabin. He had a lot to think about. First how and when to ask Livie to tell him the truth about her and Canfield. This afternoon, his interest in her had taken a turn he'd tried to avoid.

Knowing she'd been lying to him should have dampened his feelings. Unfortunately, all the time he spent with her, he knew deep down, there was something more to her connection with Canfield. After hearing he was rough with women, there was no way in hell he would allow her to be hurt by Canfield's hands. Even if he had to ignore all the signs he was being used to stay close and keep her safe.

Chapter Nine

Livie paced back and forth in her cabin feeling like she was the one in prison and not her brother. I have to tell Wilfred what I found out. But what will he do with the information? It isn't different than he already knew. Colin is the heir to Meath Hall and there is nothing Wilfred can do about it.

She picked up her pin watch and checked the time. It was after ten. Everyone would be in their cabins. She didn't want to wait until tomorrow to tell Wilfred what she'd learned. The sooner she told him she'd failed, she could hide out in her cabin during the day to avoid Colin.

The next eleven days were going to be the longest days of her life. Avoiding a man she had feelings for to keep him from learning the truth about her.

Without Abigail to help her undress, she'd left

her evening dress on, knowing she'd be headed out to talk with Wilfred after everyone was asleep.

Her hands shook as she opened the door and peeked up and down the hall. All was quiet. She slipped out and slowly closed the door to avoid making any noise.

At Wilfred's door, she knocked softly.

The door opened immediately. "I've been expecting you. Where have you been hiding since darting out of the evening meal?" Wilfred smelled of whiskey and was dressed in a long robe.

"If you were expecting me why aren't you dressed?" She didn't like his actions that said she wasn't worth upholding proprieties.

"You know before this trip is over, I'll have you in my bed." He stepped closer.

Too close.

She backed away.

He followed until she was pressed against the cabin wall with his body against her.

"You forget, I am the one in control. If you want your darling brother out of Gaol and not to have the others on this ship think you're a tart, then you'd better do what I want." He stroked a finger down the side of her face.

Livie cringed and swallowed the bile rising in her throat. She'd never willingly get into this man's bed. She'd heard stories from the other maids at the Canfield townhouse. He had been so rough with two maids they had to go to the hospital and were ordered to say they had been raped in the street. She shuddered.

He smirked. "Do as you're told and I'll treat you like the lady you're pretending to be." He leaned in as if to kiss her.

Livie turned her face and shoved on him. "Ah won't be telling you a thing if you keep pawing and trying to kiss me."

He grabbed her arms. The grip tightened as his eyes darkened. "You aren't the one giving orders. I paid for you to be here, and you'll do whatever I want." He shook her so hard tiny lights sparkled behind her eyes.

He stopped shaking her and released his hold.

She slithered to the floor even as she forced her mind to stay alert. She didn't trust what he might do if the vapors took her.

Wilfred stepped over her and refilled a glass next to the whiskey bottle on the small desk.

Her vision cleared and her body responded. She pushed to a sitting position on the floor.

"What have you learned from that imposter?" he asked, standing by the table watching her.

"He is the son of Patrick Healy, who was killed right after he inherited Meath Hall. Worried your family would come after Colin, his Scots grandfather sent Colin and his mam to America. She married a nasty man who beat her. He died and she married Ethan Halsey. He is the one who brought Colin to England and hired a solicitor who reinstated Colin as the baron of Meath Hall."

Wilfred's face grew redder and redder as she spoke.

"It's what I thought. I'll have to take other

means to give Meath Hall to father." He swallowed the glass of whiskey and paced as if she wasn't still sitting on the floor.

"There are no other means. Colin is the legal heir. You can't take that away from him. The estate has been in his family for centuries. There is no way to discredit him."

She didn't like the gleam in Wilfred's eyes or the wicked set to his lips.

"Colin Healy is the last of his line for Meath Hall." The finality of his words sent a shiver down her back.

"Not if he has a son." She didn't like the direction she realized Wilfred was thinking.

"He *is* the end of the line." Wilfred walked over, grabbed her arms, and hauled her to her feet.

"I feel like celebrating." He leaned down to kiss her.

She spit in his face. "Be leaving your hands off me!"

His hand came around so fast she didn't see it before the blow stung her face.

"I paid for you to be here. You will allow me to touch you." He pressed his mouth to hers.

Pain in her arms and the assault of his teeth and pressure on her mouth made her whimper.

He pulled back and smiled down at her.

She raised her right knee as hard and fast as she could. The feel of connecting with his male parts and the expulsion of whiskey breath in her face made her want to retch. She pressed her hands to her mouth.

She was free!

He grasped the juncture of his legs and swore.

Livie threw the door open and ran to the stairs. She stumbled over her skirt but kept moving upward, away from the putrid man and into the clear, clean night air.

Colin stood at the railing staring out into the darkness. He'd read the same page over and over and finally gave up trying to concentrate and came on deck to clear his head. But thoughts of Livie and Canfield swirled through his mind. What was their connection?

He slapped the railing and turned away to head back down to his cabin.

A woman stumbled out of the stairwell and onto the deck. She ran to the railing on the opposite side of the ship, retched over the side, and fell in a heap.

He heard her sobs from where he stood.

Getting involved with one woman had caused him nothing but confusion. He stood at the railing arguing with himself about intervening or staying away from another distraught female. Her vulnerability to the elements and someone less sympathetic propelled him across the deck.

Drawing close, he recognized the hair and then the dress. Livie.

He dropped to his knees beside her. "Livie, what's wrong."

Her tear streaked face appeared moments before her arms wrapped around his neck and she clung to him, continuing to sob.

He rubbed his hands up and down her back. "Everything will be fine. Tell me what made you cry."

The sobs subsided. Her grip on his neck loosened.

He continued to rub her back. Her body relaxed in his arms.

She sniffed and wiped her nose with the hem of her dress.

Her beautiful copper hair had come loose from the fancy pins. They dangled about her head. Colin plucked the pins from her hair. The long tresses fell about her shoulders and down her back. He slid his fingers through the strands, marveling at the silky texture.

She leaned into him.

A shout to hoist a sail, reminded him they were in a public place.

"Let me take you to your cabin. We can talk in private there." He released her, stood, and drew her to her feet.

"We do need to talk." Her voice was raspy from crying.

The apprehension in her voice worried him.

He put an arm around her shoulders and led her to the stairwell.

She pulled back. "No! Not that one. Can we take the one closer to me cabin?"

The fear in her voice confirmed she'd been running from someone. He had a good idea he knew who.

He turned them around and headed for the stairway at the front of the ship. What had Canfield done or said that had Livie so upset? Why had she been with him?

They descended the smaller stairway, pressed close together. At the top he'd tried to draw away. She wouldn't let go of him.

He led her to her cabin, opened the door, and was surprised to see it empty. "Where is your lady's maid?" He'd hoped to have another woman to comfort her.

"Ah gave 'er the night off. She's smitten with someone and wanted to spend time with 'im."

The stress had brought out the true Livie. He liked the way she dropped her h's and had more of a lilt to her speech.

He faced her after shutting the cabin door. A large red welt covered the side of her face.

"What happened?" He tipped her head to get a better look in the lantern light.

Her eyes, swollen from crying, and the red welt still didn't take away from her beauty. It only made her appear fragile. A trait he hadn't thought of in respect to the fiery woman.

Her gaze landed over his shoulder a moment before she met his eyes. She sighed from the tips of her toes and grasped his hand. "Sit. This will take some time." Still holding his hand, she led him over to the desk chair.

He sat and watched her settle on the edge of her bed. Her knuckles turned white as her fingers knotted together.

"Most of what ah've told ye, except for me brother being in Gaol 'as been lies." She sniffed, pulled a white handkerchief out of the sleeve of her dress and wiped at her nose.

Colin held back a grin as she slipped into the dialect of her childhood. Her acknowledging most of what she'd told him was lies, confirmed his thoughts. "I had a feeling."

Her gaze locked with his. "Ah'm a terrible liar. Ah give away everything on me face."

He finally smiled. "Yes, you do. That's one of the things I like about you. I can tell what you're thinking."

She blushed.

"Will this story explain the welt on your face?"

Anger replaced the blush. "Yes." She cleared her throat which still sounded raspy.

Colin retrieved a glass of water from the pitcher by the basin on the wash stand.

"Thank you." She drank half the glass and set it down on the bedside table. "Ah am Livie Leatherby. Not Miss Olivia Leatherby." She cleared her throat and started slowly, using the more refined language. "Ah did have an abusive dar who went missing after hitting me. Ah am from the rookery and worked in a factory. Ah interviewed as a maid when ah heard the Canfield's were hiring. Ah'd been working for them two months when Wilfred arrived for a visit." She swallowed. "He made advances ah didn't care for. But he also could get me tossed out." Her wringing hands stalled. "Ah learned he liked to gamble. Ah told him if he left me be me brother could find him some foon." She shook her head and her expression became more sullen.

"It was smart of you to come up with something to keep him at a distance. I've heard rumors—"

"That he's hard on women? Ah know this to be true. But ah didn't realize the extent he would go to…to…bed me." Her lips quivered. She bit the bottom one.

Colin couldn't stay in the chair. He sat beside her on the bed, placing an arm around her shoulders. "Shh…don't think of that. What happened?"

She leaned against him. "He involved me brother in a scheme that landed Ellis in Gaol but it was Wilfred who should be there. Wilfred told me ah had two choices to help Ellis, either sleep with Wilfred or chum you up for information about your family." She pulled out of his arm. "He's the one who bot me clothes, paid for the first cabin, and told me to act like gentry. All so ah could get close to you and find out if you are the real heir to Meath Hall."

Colin stared at her. He didn't understand why Canfield would care. He understood her need to help her brother and avoid the vile man's bed.

"I don't understand, why does he want to know if I'm the real heir to Meath Hall?"

"His dar has threatened to disown him for all his actions. Wilfred believes if he can get Meath Hall for his dar it will patch things between them." She shook her head. "Ah honestly don't think even that would put him in good with his dar. Wilfred has done too many things to taint the family name."

"I still don't understand. Why Meath Hall?"

"The Canfields are your English cousins." She stared him square in the eyes.

It wasn't making sense. "No. Rodericks are my English cousins."

Her copper hair slid around her shoulders as she shook her head. "Roderick Canfield is Wilfred's father. His Christian name is from his grandmother's side of the family."

"No, I had Orin dig up all the information on my English relatives. I wanted to know who would be circling like vultures to regain the estate." He'd poured over the documents for days, making sure he knew each family member. There was no mention of Canfield.

"Ah don't know the full of it, but that's wot Wilfred told me. He wanted the estate to give to his father, Roderick Canfield." She touched his arm. "You have to be careful."

"Why?" He grasped her hand, twining their fingers.

"Wilfred was talking crazy about you don't have an heir and that makes you the last of that line." She shivered. "His eyes weren't right and he had a nasty smirk to his lips."

Colin understood the man believed he must die for the Canfields to get the estate. He'd ask Captain Whiteside to have his men stay vigilant to Canfield's movements.

He cupped Livie's chin. "None of that explains this welt on the side of your face."

She squeezed her eyes shut as though forcing away a bad memory.

Her eyelids raised and the fear and regret dulling her green, brown-tinged orbs brought out his protective nature.

"Canfield did this, didn't he?" If Livie hadn't been clinging to his hand, he would have stomped out of the room and down the hall to *Lord* Canfield's and give him someone his own size to beat on.

"Ah went to his room after ah thot everyone had gone to sleep to tell him wot ah'd learned about you. He was in a robe and *kaylied* as usual." She cringed and made a distasteful face. "He pushed me against the wall and tried…" She shivered, again. "Ah shoved him back and told him if he wanted information to keep his hands off. But when ah told him wot ah knew, his eyes widened with a crazy look and his lips smirked. He wanted to celebrate. Ah tried to leave and he grabbed me arms. It hurt. Then he tried to…"

Colin shot to his feet. "That no good, poor excuse for a man—"

Livie jumped up beside him, grabbing his hand, and holding him still. "No, don't go. When he tried to kiss me, ah spit in his face, that's when he slapped me. Ah shouldn't have made him mad."

"You did nothing wrong! Don't ever say you deserved to be hit. No woman or child does anything that requires a man to beat them." He grasped her shoulders, careful to not squeeze as he pressed her to understand. All those years of watching Ma get beat and getting beatings from Mr. Miller, he'd become adamant no man should lay a hand on a woman or child.

She shook his arm. "Listen! When he tried to kiss me again, ah raised me knee, like ah'd seen other women in the rookery do when a man was getting too handsie." Her face paled. "It felt awful, but he released me to clutch himself and ah ran up to the deck." Her hands held his to her chest. "And you were there to help me. For a third time."

"You're brave to take him on like that in his cabin." Colin had a new respect for the woman he pulled into his arms. "I want you to stay away from him and out of his cabin for the rest of the trip."

She pushed on his chest, moving out of his embrace. "Ah lied and used you to get Wilfred to vouch for Ellis and get him out of Gaol." She sat on the bed, tears trickling down her cheeks. "Ah promised Mam and Ellis ah'd get him out. By helping Wilfred ah'd get him free." Livie peered up into his face. "Ellis will never get out of that prison. And if ah don't do wot Wilfred says, he'll leave me in New York with nothing and no way to go home." Tears ran down her face.

Colin knelt in front of her. He wiped at her tears with his thumbs. "It is safer for you to stay away from Canfield. I'll buy your passage back to Liverpool, and I'll send a note for you to take to my solicitor asking him to look into your brother's charges."

Her eyes lit up. "You'd do that for me? After ah lied to you?"

"I understand the reason behind your lies. And I saw through most of them and still wanted to spend time with you. Livie, you are a remarkable young woman." He tipped her chin up. "One I hope to learn more about the rest of the trip." Not wanting to bring back the unpleasantness of her encounter with Canfield, Colin kissed her forehead when he really wanted to taste her pink bow-shaped mouth.

He stood. "Go to bed, it's late. I'll call for you in the morning for breakfast. I don't want you roaming the decks alone. I don't trust Canfield."

"Thank you."

Her whispered gratitude and faint smile warmed his heart. He had to leave before he pulled her into his arms and kissed her. An action that would be hard to explain without telling her what he was starting to realize.

He'd fallen in love.

Chapter Ten

Livie enjoyed every moment she spent with Colin. Every day he met her at her door for the morning and evening meals. In between they walked the deck, debated books they'd both read, and enjoyed sitting on the deck watching the other passengers. The last seven days had been a dream. She kept waiting for Wilfred to tell the captain she was a fraud and kick her out of her first cabin. But the captain smiled when she and Colin walked by and always kept two chairs at his table reserved for them. Wilfred no longer sat at that table. He did glare at them when they chanced to pass on the deck or in the hallway, but he didn't confront them.

"What are you thinking about?" Colin asked from his deck chair only a foot from hers.

"Ah can't believe Wilfred hasn't made trouble for me." She scowled. "It's unlike him to let something like this go."

A frown etched Colin's brow. "The trip isn't over yet. We still have five more days before we reach New York."

"Waiting, knowing he's planning something is making me skittish." She slid her feet to the side of the chair and stood. "Let's walk. Ah don't like sitting here worrying."

Colin smiled and stood. "I was tired of sitting anyway. Where do you want to go?" He placed her hand in the crook of his arm.

"Just around. If ah see new sights, ah have less time to brood."

"Dolphins off starboard!" hollered the sailor in the crow's nest.

"Which is starboard? Ah can't remember." She tugged on Colin, wanting to see the creatures. There had been talk at the dinner table the last two nights that they were coming into an area the animals frequented.

"This way." He laughed and led her across the deck to the railing.

A dozen other passengers lined the railing, staring out at the vast ocean.

"There!" a man yelled and pointed.

A shiny gray body leapt into the air and back down. The long nose, sleek body, and wide tail were a sight to behold. Livie held her breath as another fish leaped from the water, arched, and glided back into the depths.

"They're beautiful!" she exclaimed, grasping Colin's hand and squeezing. Never in all her dreams had she envisioned standing on a sailing ship, holding the hand of a man she cared about, and watching such a miracle. This was a long way from the slums of Liverpool.

Several more dolphins leapt from the water. She stood mesmerized by the beauty long after the fish disappeared and the other passengers had moved on.

"Are you ready to continue our walk?" Colin asked.

His voice was so soft and intimate, she folded her body into his arms.

"That was a perfect gift," she said. "Being by your side to watch those beautiful creatures."

"I agree."

The huskiness of his voice drew her gaze to his face. She saw the same awe and admiration in his eyes as she'd felt moments ago.

"Ahoy! Loose Boom!"

Before she could register where the shout came from something hard, heavy, and fast struck her across the back. The blow knock her and Colin over the railing and out of one another's arms.

Livie flew through the air before the smack of water resounded and all became muffled as she sank in the cold salt water. *I don't know how to swim!* She flung her arms and kicked with her legs, wrapped in her skirt, fighting to find the surface and air.

The more she struggled, the more the light on the surface faded. Her heavy skirt dragged her deeper and deeper into the cold darkness.

There was no more air in her lungs.
She couldn't breathe.
Darkness swept her away.

Colin popped to the surface and searched for Livie.

"Livie! Livie!" he shouted and paddled.

God, please don't let her drowned. She has so much to live for. With long even strokes, he made widening circles looking for any sign of her. He was thankful Ma taught him to swim when they bathed in the creek.

Shouts from the ship drew his attention. The sails were down and the life boat was being lowered.

"Livie!" He shouted and tread water searching the surface. He saw two fins.

Sharks.

He searched his memory for anything he'd heard about dealing with a shark. Staring at the two fins, judging when they would get to him, he noticed light green fabric floating in front of the two. *They had Livie!*

Pain seared his chest. He didn't care about himself, he had to save her. He swam toward the fins.

Ten feet away, he realized the creatures weren't sharks. They were dolphins, and they were pushing Livie, face up through the water.

"Thank you!" He shouted and swam at them. The creatures gave her a push toward him and veered away from the life boat heading their direction.

Colin turned onto his back, placing Livie's head on his chest and floated, waiting for the life boat to reach them.

Captain Whiteside himself was in the life boat along with two oarsmen.

"I don't know what happened. A boom came loose and…Lord help us you're both still alive." He reached down, grasping Livie under the arms and lifting her into the boat.

Colin grasped the boat but was weak. "Give me a hand."

The captain helped him in. Colin scrambled to Livie's head. He felt for breath, she wasn't breathing. He turned her over the bench and pressed on her back, trying to force the water from her and get her to suck in air.

She coughed, expelled water, and sucked in a huge breath.

Colin held her unconscious body on his lap all the way back to the ship.

He draped her over his shoulder and climbed the ladder to the deck. His legs shook from all the exertion and from fear of losing Livie.

"I'm taking her to her cabin. Send the doctor," Colin ordered, cradling Livie against him and heading for the stairwell. At her cabin, he kicked the door in.

The lady's maid hurried over. "Oh dear! What happened to me lady?"

"She was knocked in the ocean. Quickly, get her out of the wet clothes and into a nightgown. I'm going to change. The doctor should be here any minute." He started to place her on the bed, but didn't want it to get wet. "Can you undress her on the floor? I'll place her on the bed when I return."

"Yis, ah can manage. Oh Lord, is she breathing?"

"Barely. Be gentle and check for bruises. She took the worst of the blow from the boom that hit us." He placed Livie on the floor and remained kneeling beside her. She had to regain consciousness.

The injuries the massive pole could have done worried him as much as the water she'd swallowed.

He pressed the tips of his fingers to her neck, feeling for life. The pulse was slight, but there. He kissed her forehead and stood.

"I'll be back as soon as I change." He left the door ajar to make his return quicker.

In his cabin, he tore the wet clothes from his body and hastily pulled on dry trousers and a sweater. He didn't bother with socks, shoes, or undergarments.

Colin stepped out of his cabin as the doctor knocked on Livie's door. He hurried over to the man and pushed the door open.

"She needs your attention," he said, ushering the man inside.

In two strides, Colin crossed and knelt beside Livie, scooping her into his arms and placing her on the bed.

"We didn't want to get the bed wet," he said, when the doctor stood rooted by the door, his mouth agape.

Colin's temper burst at the man's inactivity. "Come tend to her. She was hit by an arm of the main sail and knocked overboard. We both were, but she took the brunt of the hit." Colin stood beside the head of the bed.

The doctor approached, placed a satchel on the end of the bed, and reached out taking her wrist in his hand.

"Abigail, did you see any bruising on her?" Colin asked, wondering about the competency of the doctor. He'd watched Aunt Rachel arrive after an accident. She was swift, asking questions and checking the patient.

"Yis, Sir Healy. She be black and blue across 'er back from shoulder to shoulder."

Colin's chest squeezed. If I hadn't stopped to hold her in my arms…But he'd enjoyed standing beside her and seeing her awe and appreciation for the magnificent animals that ultimately saved her life. He would have never been able to find her if the dolphins hadn't rescued her.

"I'm going to have to lower her gown to take a look at the bruising. You should leave." The doctor said, his face blushing.

Colin knew one thing. Until the captain came here and told him this was an accident, he wasn't leaving Livie's side.

"Do what you must, but I won't leave her."

The doctor frowned, but waved Abigail closer to the bed. "Help me raise her up and slide the gown down so I can see the bruising."

Abigail hurried to the bed.

Colin knew he should turn around, but he was curious about her bruises and still didn't trust the doctor.

The lady's maid unbuttoned the front of the white gown and eased it down Livie's shoulders as the doctor raised the shoulder closest to him, turning Livie toward Abigail. Their gentleness staved off some of his concern.

His insides twisted at the sight of the six-inch wide bruising, just as Abigail had said from one lovely shoulder to the next.

"Can you tell if she broke anything?" His question came out on a gush of air. He'd pushed on her back to get the water out of her not thinking she may have had injuries from the pole. *I could have injured her worse.*

The doctor peered at him. "In this area, there is nothing I can do other than tell the patient to not move. That is the only way to mend any bones that might be broken across the back. Without her conscious to tell me what hurts worse…" He shrugged. "Keep her quiet and still. When she is awake, give her liquids and don't allow her to get up until I've seen her."

"What about the water she swallowed?" Colin had heard of men who'd nearly drowned and then become sickly from the water they'd inhaled.

"Time will tell us how badly her lungs were affected. Keep her warm and keep her still."

The doctor picked up his satchel and headed for the door. He stopped with his hand on the latch. "Have Jack come get me when she wakes."

Colin nodded and returned his attention to the woman in the bed. "Go to cabin ten and gather all the blankets off my bed. She's starting to shiver."

The maid nodded and hurried from the cabin. Colin sank to his knees by the bed and grasped Livie's hand. "You're a strong woman. You have a brother to fight for and a long life ahead of you. I promise if you get well, I'll be there for you whatever you need." He kissed the back of her hand and stood as the door burst open.

Abigail sailed in with a bundle of blankets in her arms.

Captain Whiteside stood at the threshold. "May I enter?"

"Yis, me lady is decent," Abigail said, unfolding a blanket and floating it down over the bed and Livie's still figure.

Colin faced the captain. "What did you learn?"

The man nodded to the hallway.

Colin shook his head. "Close the door. I'd rather talk in here where it's more private." He could tell by the downward tilt of the man's usually smiling face that the information was going to be what he'd feared. It wasn't an accident.

The captain stepped into the cabin, shut the door, and stood at the end of the bed. "How is the lass?"

"She has a large bruise all across her upper back. No way to tell if anything is broken until she wakes. She swallowed a lot of water." Colin didn't realize he'd picked up her hand, until the captain raised his eyebrows and stared at their linked hands.

It didn't matter what anyone thought. He and Livie knew who their enemy was and they needed to stick together.

"How did you find her? That was a lot of water to get separated in."

"The dolphins." Colin glanced down at Livie's pale face. "I couldn't find her, was starting to panic, and two dolphins swam toward me pushing her."

"Tis a miracle!" Abigail said, peering down at her lady.

"It was indeed," Captain Whiteside said. "It was no accident that boom came loose. We found the sailor who cut the lines." He shook his head. "He's not tellin' us why he did it. All I know is another sailor saw him and that's the size of it."

Rage burned inside Colin like a coal furnace. He knew why the man cut the rope.

Chapter Eleven

Colin's lower back ached. He stretched and discovered he slept on a chair. *In Livie's room.* Opening his eyes, his gaze settled on the motionless form in the bed. Her eyes remained closed, her face pale. He continued to stare at her chest until he saw the covers rise and fall.

A soft snore pulled his gaze to the rug by the bed. Abigail slept curled up on the rug. They'd stayed awake keeping Livie warm and watching for signs she was waking until they both couldn't stay awake any longer.

After his swim in the ocean, Colin's body was worn out. Sleeping in the chair hadn't helped his stiff muscles. He rose, stretched his back, and moved to the bed.

"Livie? Livie, you need to wake. You need food and water." He grasped her hand and smoothed wisps of hair back from her face. He'd grown fond of her. Too fond. He'd had time to think during the night, and he'd come up with a plan. One that would keep her safe until he could escort her back to Liverpool.

"Is me lady awake?"

Abigail's soft question startled him from his reveries.

"No." He continued to hold Livie's hand but turned his attention to the woman. "Who paid you to come on this trip?"

She peered at him as if he'd asked her to stand on her head.

"Why, me lady, of course."

Then her loyalties were with Livie and not Canfield. That was good. He'd worried last night that the maid was working for Canfield.

"Would you go to the galley and bring back toast and tea. If she wakes, I want to have something for her." His stomach growled, echoing in the quiet room.

"Ah'll bring a tray for ye both." Abigail patted her hair and left the cabin.

Colin knelt by the bed. It had been a long time since he'd got on his knees and asked God for help. The last time was the third time Mr. Miller beat Ma. He'd prayed as he lay in his bed listening to the man's cursing and Ma's sobs. When the fourth time happened, he gave up on God. Now, he wanted Livie's safety as much as he'd asked for his ma's safety all those years ago. He didn't expect a miracle, but he didn't have anyone else to ask for help.

The people he'd depended on the last ten years were in Sumpter.

"Livie, I have a plan. Once you wake up, I'll tell you about it." He kissed her forehead. The skin scalded his lips.

This was what he'd feared. The cold salt water in her lungs would bring on consumption. He couldn't leave her. But he could holler for Jack.

He strode to the cabin door, opened it, and bellowed. "Jack! Jack!"

The cabin boy came running down the steps at the far end of the hall. "Yes, Sir Healy?"

"Fetch the doctor, quick."

The boy didn't even reply. He spun around and ran for the staircase.

Colin closed the door, poured water from the pitcher into the basin, and dunked a cloth. Wringing out the excess water, he approached the bed and placed the cool cloth on Livie's forehead. He knew the fever had to be broken or she could die. "Aunt Rachel, I wish you were here right now."

The door burst open. The doctor hurried in with Abigail carrying a tray right behind him.

"Why did you summon me?" The doctor placed his bag on the end of the bed and reached for Livie's wrist.

"She's hot as a frying pan," Colin said, moving aside to allow the doctor to feel her forehead.

The doctor felt her skin and shook his head. "Not good. Need to break the fever." He peered at Colin. "Go to the galley and see if they can spare a block of ice."

"I'm not leaving her alone." He stood by the bed, his feet firmly planted. "But I'll ask Jack to get it."

The doctor stared at him before returning to his examination of Livie.

Colin went to the door. He found Jack waiting in the hall. "Go to the galley and bring us as much ice as they can spare."

"Yes, sir." Jack took off at a run. Clattering up the staircase in the middle of the ship.

Back in the cabin, Colin remained by the door as the doctor once again examined her bruising and instructed Abigail to remove all but one blanket.

The doctor faced Colin. "The fever has to be broken. If it goes too high there could be permanent damage." He glanced at the tray of food. "You'll need to force her to drink tea. The fever will dry her body."

Colin nodded.

"The next twenty-four hours are critical. If the fever breaks she'll have a good recovery. If it doesn't…" The doctor picked up his bag and walked to the door. "Have Jack get me if there are any changes."

"I will. Thank you." Colin closed the door. He'd never felt as helpless as he did right now.

"Ah'll tend to me lady. Ye should go change and get soom fresh air." Abigail dampened the cloth and replaced it on Livie's head.

"No. I won't leave her alone." He studied the woman. He had to have someone he could trust. "What happened yesterday wasn't an accident."

Abigail gasped. "Who would want to hurt me lady?"

"You'll find this hard to believe." He continued to study the woman. Could he tell her the truth? It would be easier to have her be aware of the person responsible for trying to harm them. The more he thought about it during the night he realized, Canfield wanted him dead for Meath Hall and Livie dead because she would know who caused his death.

Abigail narrowed her eyes. "It's Lord Canfield isn't it?"

"Why do you say that?"

"I saw Lord Canfield 'oldin' onto me lady one day. She didn't look happy, and 'e was stormin' about soomthin'."

"I don't know if Miss Canfield told you, but she came on this trip to get away from Lord Canfield. He'd made her nervous with his advances. He's followed her and has been mean to her." Colin figured using Livie's own story would help to keep the other passengers wary of Canfield and watch out for Livie.

"That scoundrel! Ah wondered if it wasn't sooch a thing." Abigail uncovered the tray. "And seeing ye and her being so comfortable together, 'is jealousy 'as 'im believin' if 'e can't 'ave 'er no one will." She smiled smugly as if she had the situation figured out.

Her idea about jealousy was right, but she was wrong about the type. It wasn't love that made him jealous, it was Colin owning Meath Hall.

"Come sit, Sir Healy. Ye need yer strength to 'elp with me lady." She watched Livie for several moments, then faced him. "Lord Canfield won't come near me lady as long as ah'm watching over 'er."

"Thank you, Abigail. That's what I needed to hear." Colin sat at the desk and glanced at the food. It was true he needed to eat, but it was hard to swallow anything thinking what could have happened to Livie if the dolphins hadn't saved her. When Ethan brought his family to England ten years earlier, he'd heard the sailors talking about similar stories of dolphins helping people who went overboard.

"Eat," Abigail said again, while passing him to dampen and cool the cloth for Livie's head.

Banging at the door shot Colin to his feet. He pulled it open.

Jack stood at the threshold, lugging a piece of ice as big as a horse's head in a large wood bowl.

Colin relieved the boy of his burden and placed the bowl on the desk. He scanned the room for something to chip at the block and make smaller pieces. There wasn't anything pointed and strong.

"Jack, go to my cabin and bring back the knife in my boot sheave."

The boy's eyes widened. "Ah'm not to go in a passenger's cabin when they aren't with me."

"It will be fine. I ordered you to go." Colin waved him off and turned to Abigail. "We'll need something to wrap the small pieces in and put them next to her body."

The woman rummaged around the room and

came back with two sheets.

"That should work fine. We can place the ice in a row, roll it up and place that along her sides." Colin waited for Jack. When he didn't return in the length of time he deemed enough, Colin opened the door.

Canfield had Jack by the back of his jacket. The boy clutched Colin's knife to his chest.

"Canfield, put the boy down, he's on an errand for me." Colin stepped into the hall.

Jack's feet hit the floor, and he ran down the hall toward Colin.

"Why are you in Miss Leatherby's cabin?" Canfield asked. The man's voice was calm and not the least bit inquisitive.

"She was knocked overboard yesterday. But then you know all about that." Colin reached out and took the knife Jack offered to him. "Thank you, Jack." He backed in the room and closed the door. His comment had warned Canfield he knew who caused the "accident". From the way the man's eyebrows lifted, he wasn't pleased.

He started pounding the point of the knife into the block, knocking chunks off. As quickly as he dislodged a piece, Abigail lined them up on the sheet. When they had one about three feet long, he stopped to help the woman place the rolled up ice under the one blanket and up against Livie's body.

"If we took the blanket off that would help allow the heat to escape," he said, feeling her still fevered forehead.

"It wouldn't be proper for 'er to be only in 'er

nightgown with ye starin' at 'er." Abigail crossed her arms and glared at him.

"Do you really think proprieties matter when she's fighting to live?" Colin grabbed the top of the blanket and pulled it down to the foot of the bed. Her white gown covered all of her body from her ankles to her wrists and up to the base of her neck. The only naked part he'd not seen before were her dainty feet. He touched one and grimaced. They were as hot as her forehead.

"Taking the covers off was necessary. Feel her foot?"

He went back to hacking at the ice block. When the other roll of ice was placed by her side, he sat back down to poke at the food on the tray. "The doctor said to get liquids in her. Have you tried?"

"Ah've been slippin' a spoon of tea between 'er lips, now and then. She's been swallowing."

"Good. Good." He repositioned his chair to watch the bed. The next twenty-four hours would feel like a week if the fever didn't break soon.

Livie's teeth chattered and her throat felt like someone had shoved a wool cloth in her mouth. Her heavy eyelids finally opened. It was dark. She was so cold, mainly along her sides. Her chest ached and every breath burned. Between her shoulders on her back dull pain danced like a thousand pricking pins.

A faint light allowed her to see her surroundings. It was a small room. The room swayed. Deep mumbling snapped her gaze to the right. A man sat in a chair with his upper body draped over a small desk.

He was familiar…the bed listed and the man slipped, catching himself before he landed on the ground.

"Wot's 'appening?" a female voice asked from somewhere below her bed.

"We must have hit the storm Captain Whiteside saw coming at us before dark." The man was on his feet.

Recognition hit. She and Colin were standing at the railing watching dolphins. They embraced and something struck her, knocking them both in the ocean.

She reached out a hand. The movement sent shards of pain into her back. "Oh!"

"Livie?"

"Me lady?"

"Wot…" Her voice was scratchy and faint. The effort to speak felt like fireballs traveling up her throat.

Colin stood beside her before she had time to blink. "She's shivering. Take the ice away."

That was why she was so cold. "Why…" Her voice gave out on her.

"Shh, don't talk. You had a fever. The doctor told us to cool you."

Once Abigail removed the cold from her sides, Colin pulled a blanket over her.

"T-thank you." She had so many questions, but her voice wasn't cooperating.

Colin pulled a chair up to the bed and sat down. He picked up her hand, clasping it in his. "The doc told us if the fever didn't break in twenty-four hours we might lose you." He pushed the hair from her forehead, his palm lingered. "It's nice to touch your skin and not feel scalded."

A whisper of a smile tipped the corners of his mouth.

She had questions to ask, but her throat and weakness prevented her from doing more than peering up at Colin's handsome face. Genuine concern sobered his features. But his eyes glistened with an intensity she'd not noticed before. Had there been that glow of—she couldn't place what the emotion was—but the sight swirled warmth through her.

"Me Lady, ye need to take a few sips of tea and then this broth. If ye don't care for it cold, ah'll send young Jack to get it warmed back oop." Abigail stood beside Colin. The grin on her face proved Abigail was almost as happy as the man holding Livie's hand.

She pointed to the tea cup.

Colin stood. "We need to make sure moving you doesn't cause more injury. Can you move everything? Is there anywhere that you have more pain?"

Livie wiggled her fingers and toes, then her ankles and wrists, moving up her body until she tried to sit up. "Ohh. Oopper back. Like working all day."

She eased her body up while Colin placed the pillow behind her.

Abigail handed her the tea cup.

Livie's hands shook, spilling the liquid onto her blanket.

Colin eased the cup from her hands. "Let me help."

He gently held the cup to her lips. She drank all the tea and her throat felt less parched.

Placing the cup on the tray, Abigail held, Colin asked, "Abigail, will you ask Jack to fetch the doctor."

Colin sat down on the chair and laced his fingers with Livie's.

She liked holding hands with him. Feeling his strength and warmth.

When Abigail stepped into the hall, Colin kissed Livie's knuckles.

"When I came to the surface of the ocean and couldn't see you anywhere…" He blew out a breath then drew another back in. "I started to panic. It's a big ocean. I knew I couldn't find you. But then I saw two fins. Two dolphins brought you to me."

She stared into his eyes. He didn't seem to be telling a story. She held up two fingers. "Dolphins?"

He nodded. "I was never so grateful for an animal in my life."

The door creaked.

"We'll talk more later." He placed her hand on the bed and rose as Abigail hurried to the bed.

"Jack is off to fetch the doctor, Sir Healy."

"Good. Once he says Miss Olivia is healing, you can take a break." He held up his hand when Abigail started to protest. "When you get back, I'll go to my room and change."

She smiled.

Livie watched the exchange between the two.

There was something they weren't telling her.

A knock on the door grabbed her attention. A man with graying hair and a head shorter than Colin approached the bed.

"It's good to see you awake, Miss Leatherby. I'm Dr. Gray. That was quite the ordeal you had." He placed a satchel on the bed by her feet and stood by her bedside. His cold fingers probed her wrist then stopped as he stared into her eyes. Releasing her wrist, he asked, "Where do you hurt?"

"My chest. Back stings."

"Any pains inside?"

She shook her head.

Dr. Gray ignored her and faced Colin. "Keep her warm and in the cabin for several days. Give her only liquids until she's up to more. There's nothing you can do about the bruising on her back but let it heal on its own." The doctor glanced down at her. "You're a lucky young woman." He picked up his satchel and left the cabin.

Chapter Twelve

Colin had remained by Livie's side the last five days. Only leaving for short periods of time to change clothes, or see if Captain Whiteside had obtained any new information from the sailor caught slicing the rope. He didn't know what kind of hold Canfield had over the sailor, but he wasn't giving up the person who put him to the deed.

He entered Livie's cabin, happy to see her dressed and sitting in the chair.

"You look well," he said, crossing the room and kissing her cheek.

She flushed as she did every time he kissed her cheek. Which had become a habit every time he was around her.

"Ah was tired of sitting in that bed in me night gown. Half of feeling better is getting back to normal." She poured him a cup of tea. "Ah heard we're docking today." Her eyes lost their luster. "How am ah going to get back to Liverpool?" she whispered.

He understood. She still played a role, and Abigail didn't know Livie wasn't of gentry.

"Abigail, why don't you go visit with your beau a while," Colin said, not taking his gaze from Livie. The maid had told him about the sailor as they nursed Livie.

"Thank ye. Ah won't see much of 'im once we dock and ah go back to Liverpool."

The sadness in her voice gave him an idea. "Where does your beau live?" he asked.

"'e's from America. 'e's 'opin' to only go on two more trips and then 'e wants to settle down and run a shop."

"If he proposed to you, would you marry him?"

Livie arched her eyebrows and studied him. He winked

"Wot about me lady? Who'd 'elp 'er back to Liverpool?"

He glanced at Abigail. Her eyes widened and a knowing smile tipped her pink lips.

"I'll see she has a proper escort back to Liverpool. I think it would be a shame for you to miss out on happiness after all the wonderful care you've given Miss Olivia." He again winked at Livie. She smiled.

"Thank ye, Sir Healy." She bowed. "And me lady. Ah really do love this man, and 'e 'as asked me to stay. Thank ye." She rushed out the door.

Colin sighed. Time to see how his plan was accepted by Livie.

"Wot was that all about? Wot are your plans? You know ah have to go back and find a way to get Ellis out of Gaol."

Her words held conviction, but her pale complexion and sagging body told him she wasn't ready for another trip so soon.

"My plan is to check into a hotel in New York until we can catch a train to Chicago. While here, you'll rest, and I'll send a message to my solicitor in England to make inquiries about the incident that put your brother in prison. He'll work discreetly so Canfield doesn't get wind of it."

She held up her hand. "Ah can't afford a solicitor." Her eyebrow rose, and she tipped her head slightly. "Wot do you mean *we* catch a train to Chicago?"

He reached across the table and grasped Livie's hand. "You're in no shape to travel back across the ocean right now. We know Canfield made one attempt on our lives. I don't want you travelling alone if he tries again."

"Ah have no money. Ah can't repay you for travel expenses or anything." Her cheeks reddened.

"The fees my solicitor charges will be worked off at the estate by your brother when he is released." He stared into her eyes. "Is this agreeable with you? It should keep him out of trouble at least until he's worked off his debt."

A smile slowly formed on her lips. "Being out of the city and putting in a day's work wod be the thing he needs." Moisture glistened in her eyes. "Thank you. Knowing Ellis isn't running with the likes he was before will make me mam's days and nights mooch easier."

"You're welcome. I'll get another hand at the estate and won't feel so bad about leaving Orin and Denis to handle things." Staring into her eyes, he wanted to lean across the table and kiss her lips. He'd dreamed of kissing her the last two nights, but had felt awkward about doing so when she was lying in bed. Now, dressed and looking healthier, he didn't think he could control his need to take their intimacy a step farther.

Unable to stop himself, he stood, drew her to her feet, and stepped forward, placing his body in front of hers. "I've been wanting to do this ever since we watched the dolphins together." He lowered his head and gently brushed his lips over hers.

He squeezed his eyes shut, holding onto the sensation of her soft skin against his lips. He'd never felt anything so soft. Her breath puffed against his chin. He opened his eyes and stared down at her copper eyelashes resting on her flushed cheeks. Her pink lips were slightly parted.

The notion he could delve between those pretty lips and taste, shot heat to his groin. With shaky hands, he held her head gently and covered her mouth with his. Her body slumped against him as he tasted first her top lip and then the bottom. He didn't know which was sweeter or more tempting the plump bottom lip or her upper lip shaped like a bow.

He released her head but continued to kiss her. His hands roamed down her back, drawing her closer. He never wanted to stop kissing her.

She drew her head back, gasping for air. He trailed kisses down her neck.

"Colin, this—"

He cut her off, capturing her mouth and slipping his tongue in for a brief taste. Honey. He'd never tasting anything as sweet as her.

Rapping on wood seeped into his conscious.

"Miss Leatherby? It's Doctor Gray."

The voice slapped good sense into Colin. He released Livie.

She started to sway.

He cupped her elbow, helping her to ease onto the chair.

"Come in, Doctor," Colin called out and poured more tea into the cups.

The door opened. Dr. Gray entered, his gaze assessing the scene. His eyebrows met above his nose, but he didn't say anything.

"Miss Leatherby, it's good to see you up. I take this to mean you're feeling better." Dr. Gray placed his bag on the bed and stood near Livie's chair.

"Yes, doctor. Ah was tired of the bed."

"I see you have good color today."

Colin nearly choked on the tea he sipped. His gaze collided with Livie's.

Her face flushed.

Dr. Gray chuckled. "I believe you're in good hands, Miss Leatherby." He picked up his bag and headed to the door. "We'll be docking in three hours. I'd advise you to rest a day before you travel on to your sister's. Your constitution isn't strong yet."

"Thank you. Ah'll do just that. Ah don't want to be a burden on me sister." Livie stood. "Ah'd also like to thank you for your care."

He waved his hand. "It's why I'm on this ship. I'm just glad we had a good outcome. Good-bye Miss Leatherby and Sir Healy." He ducked out the door, drawing it closed behind him.

Colin peered up at Livie. She stared at the door. What was she thinking?

He captured her hand. "Why the sad face?"

She shook her head and peered down at him. "Not sad. Just…thinking."

He tugged on her hand, bringing her closer. "When Abigail gets you packed, have your bags sent to the Mansfield Hotel. I'll come get you before we dock. I want to be beside you when you see my country for the first time."

Wariness glinted in her eyes. "Ah don't want to owe you more than ah already do. Ah don't know how to repay you for saving me life."

"You don't owe me anything. If you feel you need to repay me, then come with me to my sister's birthday and graduation. When I'm ready to return to Meath Hall, I'll escort you back to Liverpool." He knew asking her to depend on him went against her independent nature.

She slipped her hand from his grasp and walked over to the porthole.

Livie watched the water outside the window. Anger rippled through her. She had little choice but to rely on Colin. She was poor and soon would be in a country she didn't know. There had to be a way to help with finances. She refused to be a burden on anyone, especially Colin. Perhaps, she could sell her fancy clothes and purchase more serviceable clothing. Then she'd have some money to help pay her way. But it wouldn't last very long.

"When will you return to Meath Hall? Immediately after the events?" She knew for certain the longer she remained with Colin the harder it would be to leave him. And she had no choice. He was gentry, she was a street urchin.

"My plan is to visit with family for a month."

She faced the room and Colin. "A month?" That was a long time to remain with him and keep her heart safe.

"This trip started with a request from Shayla, but I'd decided the trip will determine where I eventually end up. Sumpter or Meath Hall."

"Oh." She hadn't thought he would want to remain in America. "If you decide to stay, ah can make me way back home alone."

He stood. Three strides brought him to her. Colin placed a hand on the side of her face. "I would return to Meath Hall to let them know and arrange the running of the estate. You will not travel alone." He kissed her lips. "Not as long as I'm alive."

The door banged open. Colin stepped back and spun toward the door.

Livie peered around his broad shoulders. Abigail carried a tray with fresh tea and small sandwiches.

"Ah'm sorry, didn't mean to scare ye." The

smile on Abigail's glowing face didn't give her apology any strength.

"I take it things went well with your beau?" Colin asked, taking Livie by the elbow and escorting her to the chair by the table.

Livie didn't want to sit but also didn't want to cause a scene with Abigail watching her intently. She preferred to stay standing and facing the porthole. She needed to sort out this new turn of events. Since arriving at her cabin, Colin had kissed her several times. Not that she minded, but this new intimacy with him unsettled her. Did he truly care for her and wish her safe or was he like all men and decided to use her helpless state of affairs to get her into his bed? He kept saying he'd take care of everything. Yes, he'd offered Ellis to pay off the solicitor fees, but what about the money he'd spend on her until she was back in Liverpool? That would be a goodly sum. She sighed.

"Livie?"

She glanced up into his concerned eyes.

"Are you too tired to eat something?"

The gentleness of his question and remembering the gentle way he'd started their first kiss spiraled happiness around her heart.

"No. Just thinking about all you've said." She picked up a sandwich and nibbled.

Abigail flitted around the room folding clothes and packing them in the trunk at the end of the bed.

"Abigail, when you get the trunks packed wod you let the right person know they go to the Mansfield Hotel?" She glanced at Colin.

The smile on his face lit his blue eyes. Could that genuine pleasure be faked? She didn't think so. She'd know for sure when they checked into the hotel. If he paid for separate rooms, she'd feel easier.

Colin stood. "I need to get my things packed and let you rest before we dock." He moved to the door and stopped. "I'll come by and escort you to the deck when we come into the harbor. You don't want to miss the Statue of Liberty."

She nodded and he disappeared.

Abigail stopped beside her. "Ye and Sir Healy looked chummy when ah arrived." Her eyes danced with glee.

"We are becoming friends." She felt her cheeks heat, remembering the more than friendly kisses.

"'e's a good man. Not many wod 'ave stayed with ye like 'e 'as." She leaned close and whispered, "The night ye took real sick, 'e sat with ye 'olding yer hand, kissing yer forehead, and talking to ye about 'is 'all, like 'e wanted ye to love it as much as 'e does."

"Really?" He loved Meath Hall? In their conversations, his attitude seemed more like the hall was a duty, not that he cared for the place.

Abigail nodded. "'e spent 'ours talking to ye and 'olding yer 'and." She turned back to the trunk. "'e was a man willing ye to be in 'is life."

Livie stared at the back of her maid.

I hope it's the truth. Colin has shown he would be a compassionate lord. And selfishly, if he lived at Meath Hall, it would be easier to know how he was doing, especially if Ellis worked for him.

Chapter Thirteen

Colin picked up his Gladstone bag. The only other item he had to worry about was the box of books in the storage compartment. He'd advised the proper person to have them delivered to the Mansfield Hotel. He'd stayed there while waiting for a ship on his last trip and found, that while it was a bit expensive, the amenities of meals and toilet facilities in the room, along with laundry service, made up for the added expense.

He closed his cabin door and walked down the hall. Movement beyond the staircase caught his attention. Canfield was leaving his cabin. The man turned. Colin glared and held back the urge to march down the hall and slam a fist into the man's smug smile.

Knocking on Livie's door, he watched Canfield climb the stairs.

Abigail opened the door. "Sir Healy, she's ready."

Colin could only stare at the vision in front of him. Livie wore the same vivid blue coat and flowered hat as the first time he saw her. But her face glowed and the wariness that had dulled her eyes had been replaced with a sparkle.

"Ready?" he asked for no reason other than to say something.

"Yes." She turned to Abigail. "Thank you for all your help. Ah wish you all the best with your new life."

Abigail flung her arms around Livie. "Thank ye, me lady. Ah wish ye the best as well." She winked at Colin and let go of Livie.

Colin slipped Livie's hand through the crook of his arm and headed up the main staircase.

"I think you'll enjoy watching the ship enter the harbor. The first time I watched, I couldn't speak." Colin remembered the day Ethan led Ma, Shayla, and him to the railing of the ship as they returned from their visit to England. The sight had made him proud to call himself an American. He might have Scots and Irish blood, but his heart belonged to the country that had made him a man.

Once on deck, he led Livie to the front of the boat. All the passengers stood peering at the land growing closer.

He wanted to keep them in the crowd, but give her a good vantage point. Someone tapped him on the shoulder.

He glanced back. Captain Whiteside's assistant

stood behind them.

"The captain would like you and Miss Leatherby to join him on the quarter deck."

"We'd be happy to join him." Colin smiled down at Livie and followed the man the length of the ship and up a small flight of stairs to the quarter deck where orders were shouted and the ship was steered.

"Welcome Mr. Healy and Miss Leatherby." Captain Whiteside shook Colin's hand and tipped his hat to Livie.

"Thank you for the invitation," Livie said. Her gaze scanned the deck.

"I have the perfect spot for you to watch our entry into the harbor." Captain Whiteside led them to the right side of the deck.

Colin was pleased with the spot. The small covered room that housed the officers navigating the ship would keep any masts from knocking into them and the railing was higher than on the main deck, making it harder for a person to be pushed overboard.

"Enjoy the view. I have matters to attend." The captain nodded to Livie and patted Colin on the shoulder.

"That was nice of the captain to give us sooch a nice viewing spot," Livie said, grasping the railing with her hands.

Colin moved up behind her. He placed an arm on either side of her and grasped the railing next to her hands. "I agree."

He scanned the crowd below and spotted Canfield scanning the gathered people. The man moved through the passengers like a slithering snake. He talked to no one and stayed in constant motion.

"Ah can see buildings from here."

The whispered awe in Livie's voice expanded Colin's chest with pride.

He glanced at the landscape. What did people from other countries think when they saw this city for the first time?

"Is that the statue?" Livie asked, pointing to the right.

Colin's gaze followed her finger. He spotted the torch held high and the spiked wreath on the liberty's head. "Yes, that's her. A Frenchman gave this to us in 1886. The first time I saw it, I was about fourteen."

Livie spun, gazing up into his face. "Ah hear the pride in your voice."

"Can you? I'm the first generation American from my mother and father's families. I'm proud of the person this country has made me. Listening to the stories Ma told about life in Scotland and Ireland, I think my grandfather sending us here was the best thing for both of us. We may have had to live through some tough times…" He thought of Mr. Miller. "But we came out stronger and found a good life with the Halseys."

"The Halseys and your family are one of the reasons ah'd like to travel with you to this town you call Sumpter. Ah'd like to meet the people you talk so highly of."

He wanted to kiss her. Her face was inches

from his. I need to keep this conversation going to keep from ruining her.

"What are the other reasons you agreed to accompany me?"

"The most compelling—Ah have no other choice. If ah don't travel with you, ah wod have to find work and save money to get back home." She raised her arms, in a "see all of this" motion. "From the size, ah have a feeling this wod be a lot like Liverpool. The rich and the poor." Her eyes saddened. "Ah wod be a poor woman clawing me way to the middle so ah could go home in five to ten years." She peered into his eyes. "You will return me home in months. And ah have a feeling ah'll not be treated like a pauper."

He wasn't sure if her truthful answer pleased or annoyed him. He was thankful she knew her safest, fastest way home was by staying with him. But at the same time, she made it sound like a bad thing. The answer he'd hoped for was she enjoyed his company.

"I'll see you're treated with respect and returned to your family without a tarnished reputation."

Was that a hint of regret in her eyes?

Commotion on the main deck drew his attention. A scuffle at the railing in the front of the ship gathered a covey of passengers. One man had another by the front of his jacket. Within seconds he recognized the man held by the jacket front was Canfield. What was he up to? Assessing the man who had a hold of Canfield, Colin realized what had happened. The man shaking Canfield was Colin's size, same dark hair, identical cut jacket and brown trousers. Canfield had thought the man was Colin. Had he tried to push the man over the railing?

Colin leaned forward. "I'll be right back. Stay on this deck, in this spot."

Livie nodded and watched Colin take the stairs to the main deck two at a time. He ran to the crowd and pushed through to what looked like two men arguing. The two turned to him as he called out.

She gasped. One of the men was Wilfred. What was Colin doing? She started toward the steps but was blocked by Captain Whiteside.

"Best for you to stay here, lassie. Mr. Healy knows what he's doin' and doesn't need to be lookin' fer you when he gets back."

"Why did 'e go down there?" Livie returned her attention to the three men talking.

"I saw the scuffle start. Lord Canfield tried to send the other man over the railing."

She jerked her gaze to the captain's face. By the affirmation in his eyes, he knew she and Colin believed Wilfred was behind their ocean swim.

"Then Colin, Mr. Healy, should have stayed oop here, where it is safe." She gripped the railing, watching the exchange. What were they saying?

Canfield shook loose from the other man. With stealth she wouldn't have thought him possible of, the lord disappeared into the crowd.

Colin continued talking with the other man. He glanced her direction twice while talking. As if he needed to confirm she was still where he left her.

She scanned the crowd, hoping to catch a glimpse of Wilfred. If she kept an eye on him, he wouldn't be able to sneak up on them. A tall man stood in the shadows of the galley. Squinting didn't help her see any better.

"What are you staring at?"

Colin's voice beside her gave Livie a start.

"Ah was trying to keep an eye on Wilfred, but ah lost him. That might be him along the right side of the galley. Ah can't tell." She leaned to the right.

Colin's arm wrapped around her shoulders, drawing her against him. "The man agreed to post charges against Canfield. That will keep him on his toes until his ship back to England. The police will be keeping an eye out for him."

Livie hated to contradict Colin, but she knew Wilfred. "He'll not go back to England until he's accomplished wot he set out to do."

Colin stepped in front of her. "How do you know that?"

"Ah worked in his family's home for six months. He uses people and believes his title gives him the right to do wotever he pleases. If he pleases to take a woman and beat her in the name of being intimate, he does." She shivered.

"Has he taken you in such a manner?" Colin's voice was low and deadly.

"No, ah managed to stay unscathed, but me poor brother is a sop who can't think for hisself. When Wilfred approached him, Ellis actually thought Wilfred was his friend." She snorted. "Wilfred has no friends. Only people who fear him."

"Not here. There's few who would listen to or want to work for a dandied up Englishman."

She shook her head. "You haven't seen his charming side. He gets wot he wants."

Colin pulled her to his chest. "He won't get you, or me. He'll soon see going home is the best thing for him."

She wrapped her arms around Colin and savored the strength and his conviction. But she knew Wilfred. He would not stop until he'd made Meath Hall his father's or he'd died trying.

Chapter Fourteen

Colin waited for the main crowd to exit the ship before he hustled Livie down the gang plank and onto the dock. He hailed a Hansom cab. The horse drawn vehicle pulled onto the dock. Colin helped Livie in, placed his satchel on the floor, and called up to the driver, "Mansfield Hotel, please."

He climbed into the vehicle and sat beside Livie, facing forward.

She stared out her window.

"I don't know much about New York City, other than it's big," he said, peering out the window on his side.

"There are more waterways than Liverpool. And large buildings." She glanced over at him. "Where do the working class live?"

"I'm not sure, but we can ask and visit if you want." Colin studied her. He was impressed she never strayed far from her roots. She was pretending to be of gentry, and had done a fine job, yet she always knew she was working class. Like he was.

"Is this hotel fancy? Ah'm tired of trying to remember how to act." She sighed and leaned back in the seat.

He had to remember she wasn't fully recovered from her ordeal.

"The good thing about America is you don't have to pretend to be anyone. Just be you. No one will know or care about an English birthright." He captured her hand. "The hotel is nice. It has amenities that I feel are worth paying a little extra."

She closed her eyes. "How much extra? Ah need an idea of how long it will take me to pay you back."

He touched her chin, turning her face toward him. "You don't have to pay me back."

Her eyes opened. The sadness in their depths stole his breath.

"I promise. The only thing I'll ask for in return is companionship." The second the word came out, she pulled back. And he realized his poor choice of words. "Not that way. Men who dally with women in that way are lower than snakes. The companionship I'm talking about is a companion at meals. I hate sitting at a table alone and usually eat in my hotel room or train berth. I haven't seen the sights because I didn't want to wander the streets alone." He pushed a strand of her copper hair behind her ear.

She peered into his eyes.

"I'm asking you to allow me to pay your expenses, so I don't have to eat alone in my room and miss out on the entertainment this city is noted for."

"You are asking very little of me for the large sum you'll be spending."

He glanced at her lips. "I've not realized how lonely I was until you came along." He leaned in and kissed her lips chastely. "Believe me, you are doing way more than you know for me."

The cab bobbed to a stop.

The door opened, and a valet with the hotel stood back. Colin shoved his satchel toward the door and the man snagged the bag.

Colin hopped out and offered his hand to Livie. She held on while carefully stepping down to the ground.

"Wait right here," he said and reached up to pay the driver.

"Thank you, sir." The cabby clucked, and the horse and cab moved on down the street.

Colin faced the hotel and found Livie staring, wide-eyed and mouth open.

He laughed and linked their arms. "Come on, this will be the most fun I've ever had staying in this or any city."

Walking up to the registration desk, he was pleased to see the same clerk as the last time he'd stayed.

"Simon, it's good to see you." Colin extended his hand across the counter.

The clerk smiled and shook hands. "Mr. Healy, it has been a while since you graced our hotel."

"It has. I'd like two rooms, preferably close together." Colin still held Livie's arm.

The man smiled. "I have just the rooms. They even have a connecting door."

Livie's hand squeezed his arm.

"That close isn't necessary," he said, even though it would have made keeping an eye on her easier.

"Then now about across the hall?"

"That would be good," Livie said.

"The name on the other room?" He poised a quill over the registration book.

"Miss Livie Leatherby," Livie said, glancing at Colin.

He smiled. He told her she could be herself here.

"Here are your keys. Rooms three-oh-eight and three-oh-seven." Simon handed him the keys.

"We'll have trunks and a crate coming from the ship. Please bring them to our rooms." Colin slid a silver dollar across the counter.

"It will be my pleasure, Mr. Healy."

Colin captured Livie by the elbow and directed her to the elevator. He stopped in front of the elevator doors.

"Wot is this?" Livie whispered.

The bellhopper, carrying Colin's satchel, grabbed the door, pulling it open. "Which floor, sir?"

"Third." Colin couldn't stop his grin as Livie reluctantly followed him into the small room.

The bellhopper closed the door and pushed the

button marked three.

Livie grabbed Colin's arm as the small room shook and moved upward.

"Wot is this?" she whispered in his ear as she clung to his arm.

"It's an elevator."

The room slowed and stopped. Opening the door, the bellhopper smiled at Colin.

Colin liked riding in an elevator with Livie. Her arm, wrapped around his, held tight. Her body pressed against him snug as well.

"We're here. Come on." He hated to step away, but they couldn't stand in the elevator all day.

She took a tentative step out of the elevator.

"We're on the third floor. Riding up in the elevator is better than walking up three flights of stairs." Colin led her down the hall to rooms seven and eight. "Which one would you like?"

"If I may, sir?" the bellhopper asked.

"Yes?"

"The lady may like room eight better. There is a view of the bay." The bellhopper stood by the door numbered eight.

"Good suggestion. Livie, you get room three-oh-eight." Colin unlocked and opened the door, waving her in. Seeing her reaction to the room and the view, had his insides dancing. He vaguely remembered seeing the sights of New York with Ethan and his family. Seeing them again as an adult with Livie he was sure would be the best adventure he'd yet to take.

Livie walked into the room. She'd never seen

anything like it. Not even at the Canfield townhouse. The walls were covered with floral paper
from the wainscoting to the embossed-tin squares
covering the tall ceiling. A large, dark wood bed had
a fluffy, colorful quilt in the same colors as the flowers on the walls. Beside the bed were matching dark
wood tables, a large wardrobe, and a dainty desk
and chair. She walked across to the window covered
with a delicate lace curtain.

Pulling the curtain aside, she peered down into
a smaller harbor than they'd entered. She could see
the businesses along the waterfront and the small
personal boats moving about.

"This is a beautiful view." She faced the room.

Colin stood by the door smiling. The man, who
carried their luggage, stood beside Colin's door
across the hall, holding his satchel.

"You might want to relieve the boy of your
things." She pointed to the young man.

"Yes, I should. Don't close the door. I have a
couple questions." He spun out of her room.

Livie ran her hand over the smooth wood of the
bed and unpinned her hat. She placed the hat in the
wardrobe. All of her previous clothes would have
only filled a quarter of the space. She had no need
for all the clothes Wilfred had insisted she bring
with her. She hadn't picked a single piece. He'd giv-
en her the outfit she wore the first day and the rest
was all a surprise when Abigail started unpacking
them. On one of their outings, she'd inquire where
she could sell the contents of one of the trunks and
the trunk. That would give her a little of her own

money.

A soft knock drew her attention to the door.

Colin stood at the threshold. "The rest of your things should arrive soon." He hesitated. "May I show you something?'

She nodded. He was being quite proper, unlike the way he came and went to her cabin on the ship.

He entered her room and walked to the door she'd noticed but assumed was a connecting door as the man downstairs had mentioned.

Colin opened the door and stood back. "Your own personal lavatory. Complete with bath tub, sink, and water-closet."

Livie hurried across the room and took a peek. A porcelain claw-foot tub sat at the end of the room. A sink and water-closet stood side by side on one wall.

"Ah've never seen anything like this." She walked in, turned the knob on the sink and water came out. Her cheeks hurt, she smiled so broad. The bathtub had knobs. She cranked on one and water shot into the tub.

"Be sure to turn the hot water on first. It takes a while to get to the room."

She spun toward Colin. "Hot water? Out of there?" She pointed to the water flowing into the tub.

He walked past her and spun the knob. "Yes. You can have a hot bath by putting this plug in that hole and turning on the hot water." He pointed to the knob she didn't turn.

Her next thought froze her actions. This hotel

must be expensive. She peered at Colin. No matter how much companionship she gave him it would never take care of the expense she had become.

Colin grasped her upper arms, making her face him. "What's wrong? Has this day been too much too soon?" He led her back in by the bed. "Sit."

He bent down and slipped her kid slippers from her feet. "Lie down and rest."

"Ah'm not tired," she tried to stop his actions and not lie back on the bed.

Grasping her hands in his, Colin stood in front of her. "If you aren't tired why did the color drain from your face?"

She hated to keep bringing up how indebted she was to him, but she couldn't forget.

"This room moost be expensive. Ah'm an added cost and burden. You wod spend less to poot me back on the next ship headed to Liverpool."

He cupped her chin in the palm of his hand, tipping her face upward. "If I thought of you as a burden, I would do just that." He stared into her eyes.

The deep blue in his eyes calmed her, soothed her worried thoughts. Made her think of long moments wrapped in his arms.

"Let's make this a business arrangement if you can't take my help for anything other than charity."

The business tone he used, jerked her thoughts away from intimate thoughts.

"How can we make this a business arrangement?" She was skeptical. The only business she could think of put her in his bed…which she had dreamed about several times since he rescued her from the ocean. But there was only one way she'd willingly go into any man's bed. He would have to love her for who she is…a lower class factory worker.

"I know you can read. How is your writing?" He scanned the room and walked over to the desk. He pulled drawers open and came back to the bed with a paper, pen, and ink stand.

"Ah can write well enough," she said, seeing a mess about to happen. "Take that back to the desk, ah'll write there. Ah don't want to spill ink on me dress or this pretty coverlet."

He carried the items back to the desk. Livie slid off the bed and padded across the room in her stockings.

She sat in the chair and dipped the pen in the ink. "Wot did you want me to write?"

"Rathburn Melding, Esquire. New line. Lancashire, England. New Line.

Dear Mr. Melding, I've come upon the acquaintance of a Miss Livie Leatherby, who I've appointed my personal secretary."

"Really? You don't think people will question a female personal secretary traveling with you?" She raised an eyebrow but liked that Colin was giving her a job and taking her seriously. More seriously than anyone in her life had before.

Colin smiled. "They will only think I have good sense." He waved toward the paper. "Her brother Ellis Leatherby is being held in Gaol for charges of…" Colin frowned. "You never said what he is being charged with."

Her cheeks heated. "Cheating at the tables."

"They threw him in Gaol for that?" Colin paced to the bed and back. "I guess it must be who he cheated. Is that right?"

She nodded. "Wilfred set him oop. He taught Ellis and a friend how to cheat at gaming and then set them oop to play against a duke who also is a judge. When he lost ten thousand pounds and then found oot he was duped by the likes of Ellis and his friend, the Duke sent the bobbies after them and didn't even give them a chance to explain. Ellis never made a thing off the scam. He gave all the money to Wilfred, who told him he'd save it for the next time they wanted to go gaming."

Colin shook his head. "I think you received the beauty and the intelligence in your family."

"Ellis is a simple minded man, but he is me brother."

"Continue the letter, cheating while gaming with a Duke. There is reason to believe Lord Wilfred Canfield is involved with the cheating and the unjust incarceration. Be advised all investigations must be quiet and discrete. New paragraph. You may send all information you gather through my Uncle Zeke. He will be able to find me as I travel. Regards, Colin Healy, Baronet of Meath Hall."

Livie finished the closing and peered up at Colin. "Ah thought you didn't like to be called by your title?"

"I don't. But I have found that in England, it allows me to get things done easier." He picked up the paper and read through it.

Her stomach knotted, hoping he found favor with her penmanship and spelling. She preferred traveling with him as his personal secretary. It made her feel less like a mistress, even if they weren't sleeping together.

"Your penmanship is better than mine." He slipped the pen from her hand, dipped it in the ink stand and added his signature and the days date. "Is there an envelope in any of those drawers?"

She opened drawers and found an envelope.

"Address it to: Rathburn Melding, Esquire, Lancashire, England care of Captain Dickson, the steamship Stanton."

Livie addressed the envelope. Colin folded the letter, placed it in the envelope, and crossed to the door.

"I'll see this gets to Captain Dickson. His ship is leaving tomorrow. The letter should reach my solicitor in five to six days." Colin opened her door. "Rest. I'll call for you at seven for dinner."

"Ah'll be ready." Livie stood as the door closed. She finally had a job that would allow her to walk among everyone with her head held high. Being a maid at the Canfields had brought her up a notch from factory worker, but this—a secretary. She'd never dreamed she could climb this far out of the slums where she grew up.

A knock on the door sent her scurrying across the floor. Maybe Colin had another letter for her to write.

She opened the door and found two burly men

carrying her trunks. "Oh, thank you. Put them over there, please." She stood by the bed as the men eased the trunks onto the floor.

One walked toward the door. The other stood by her trunk, his hand outstretched.

"Thank you," she said again, waiting for the man to leave.

"I packed that heavy trunk a long ways, lady."

She didn't know what to say. She had to agree it was heavy, but hauling it here was his job.

"Come on, Charlie. The lady's stiffin' us." The one by the door stepped out into the hall.

"Just a minute. I want something for my trouble." The man stalked toward her. "How's about a kiss as my payment?"

"No. Ah don't think so." She backed up against the bed. The only direction to get away from the man was over the bed. She rolled onto the bed and only made one revolution when a hand grabbed her arm, stopping her momentum.

She shrieked and curled up in a ball.

"Lady, I was just want—"

The man's words stopped and the sound of flesh hitting flesh registered.

Livie peeked between her fingers. Panic strangled her voice. She'd never witnessed rage on Colin's face before. The man was larger than Colin, but he was beating the man to submission. She had to do something.

She slid off the bed and stood behind the man Colin was beating. "Colin, stop! Stop!"

Running footsteps and a whistle rang down the

hallway.

"Stop Colin!" She grabbed a pillow and flung it at his head.

His fist stopped mid-air. His eyes peered at her with a far-away glaze.

She grabbed his fist in both of hers. "Stop. You'll kill him," she whispered.

"What's going on here? I'm Officer Chester." A man dressed in a blue uniform stood in the doorway holding a stick.

The man who had stepped out into the hall thumped the officer on the shoulder. "That man started beating on my partner for no reason."

Livie stared at the man. He was lying. She gave Colin a nudge, moving him away from the man moaning on the floor. When he moved, she kept nudging him until he was on the other side of the bed from the man. She pressed her back against Colin to keep him where he was and faced the officer. The other man knelt by his friend.

"Sir, those two…" She pointed to the two men who entered her room. "…hauled me trunks from the dock. That one…" She pointed to the man helping his friend up. "Walked out of the room, but the other one said he wanted a kiss and pushed me oop against the bed." Her cheeks heated retelling the story with so many men in the room. Colin moved behind her. She put out her arms, to stop him from doing anything stupid. "Ah tried to roll across the bed to get away. When he grabbed me, ah screamed." She nodded to Colin behind her. "Me employer came from across the hall. He moost of seen the man looming over me lying on the bed."

Officer Chester motioned for the two men to get out of the room. He shoved the onlookers back and stepped into the room, closing the door behind him.

"What's your name, miss?"

The man was her height with piercing gray eyes.

"Livie Leatherby." She'd learned long ago you didn't give a bobbie more information than he asked for.

He stared past her. "And you, sir, what's your name?"

"Colin Healy."

She felt his presence as he stood protectively behind her.

"How do you know this woman?" the officer asked.

"She's my personal secretary. We arrived from England two hours ago."

"I see." The officer's eyebrows raised as his gaze landed on the two trunks and scanned the room.

"And why did you feel it necessary to beat that man?" Officer Chester's gaze landed on Colin.

Livie peered over her shoulder. Colin's eyes no longer appeared glazed. He was here, in the room with them. Where had he been in his mind when she stopped him from pummeling the man?

"I heard Miss Leatherby scream. I opened my door and could see straight into her room because her door was open. All I saw was a large man leaning over her on her bed. I thought…" He ran a hand over his face. "I thought he was…"

"Ah'm fine, but he scared me." She placed a hand on Colin's arm.

He placed a hand over hers.

"I can see where you might have the wrong idea. But you'll have to pay a fine for disturbing the peace and beating that man beyond what is tolerable. If he wants this written up, you'll have to go to court." The officer wrote on a piece of paper with a pencil. He handed the paper to Colin. "Young man, you better control your temper. It could get you in a mess of trouble one of these days."

Colin accepted the paper. "Thank you sir. I'll remember that,"

The officer stopped at the door. "Will you?" He peered at Colin then opened the door and disappeared.

When the door clicked shut, Colin grasped Livie by the arms and held her in front of him.

"Are you really fine? Did he hurt you in any way?"

The anguish in Colin's voice tore at her heart.

"He only scared me. When ah tried to get away and he grabbed me, me mind went back to the times ah watched dar go after mam and ah panicked."

He pulled her into his arms, hugging her tight to his chest. "I saw Mr. Miller, the man who beat my ma. All I could think is I'm big enough now to stop you." He swallowed. "I couldn't stop hitting him."

His body trembled.

Chapter Fifteen

Colin clung to Livie. Over a dozen years had dropped away when he opened his door and saw the man looming over Livie. His mind had raced back to the days when Mr. Miller beat Ma. He'd had one thought in his mind. Kill the bastard.

He trembled. *I would have killed the man if Livie hadn't captured my attention.* The images of the past and the bloody man he'd beaten, mixed in his mind. Flexing his aching hands, he couldn't remember hitting the man. Only the sight of him bloody and unconscious on the floor after he'd sought Livie's voice and glanced back down at the man at his feet.

"What have I become?"

"Shh… You were only protecting me."

As much as he wanted to seek solace in her arms, Colin couldn't. Not knowing the beast he'd unleashed. He released her and stepped back.

Livie stepped toward him her hand out-stretched. "Don't. Don't go thinking you're anything but the man you were before."

"I need time to think about what I did." He walked to the door.

"Will you still come get me for dinner?"

Her voice asked more than the obvious question.

He nodded. "I don't want you out alone. I'll be here." Stepping into the hallway, he pulled the door closed behind him and stood, flexing his hands.

Never had he thought himself capable of such violence. As a boy, he'd dreamed many a night of giving Mr. Miller the beating he deserved. Since meeting Ethan, the anger had slowly disappeared. "Or so I thought."

He needed to be alone with his thoughts. The elevator doors loomed in front of him. He didn't want to be enclosed in a small space with another person. He retraced his steps and pulled on the door to the servant's staircase. The wood vibrated under his feet as he jogged down to the bottom floor.

He pushed open the door and revealed the clatter and clang of the kitchen.

"Excuse me." He repeated making his way to the outside door that stood open.

Once in the alleyway behind the hotel, he set off at a long stride. With no plan, he walked and walked until the event no longer plagued his mind. Stopping to see where he'd ended up, he scanned the businesses.

A police station.

Snorting at the coincidence, Colin entered the building.

He stopped in front of a desk piled high with papers. "Excuse me, I'm looking for an officer who—" he dug into his pocket and pulled out the paper the officer handed him "gave me this earlier at the Mansfield Hotel."

The man at the desk took the paper, read the citation, looked up at Colin, and handed it back. "That would be Max Chester. He's out walkin' his beat."

"Is there a way I could find him?"

"What for? It looks to me you got off easy for beating a man." The officer behind the desk narrowed his eyes.

"I want to find the man I injured and offer help." Colin had determined, while the man was in the wrong, he, Colin, was also wrong to have lost control.

Skepticism flickered in the man's eyes, but he sighed. "Chester has the beat in Hackensack from Twelfth to the cemetery."

"Thank you. Where are we in relation to that area?"

"Take a Hansom to the cemetery and work your way toward twelfth. That's the best I can tell you. Chester could be anywhere."

Colin nodded and exited the station. On the sidewalk he studied the area. Not a Hansom cab to be seen. People had begun to fill the sidewalks. He pulled out his pocket watch. Five after five. He'd best head back to the hotel. If he was late collecting

Livie for dinner, she'd worry.

The top two floors of the hotel were visible from where he stood. "I walked here, I might as well walk back." He headed toward the hotel.

This time his mind didn't focus on what he'd done, but how he'd cleverly made Livie feel needed rather than a burden. He patted his suit jacket. The letter to his solicitor was tucked in a pocket inside his jacket. When he returned to the hotel, he'd ask Simon to send a runner to the steamship with the letter. He wanted the solicitor to get to work on the problem. Once her brother was free, Livie would no longer have to feel an alliance with Canfield was needed.

Just thinking of her and her brother being used by the greedy baron, started his fists clenching. No matter how badly he'd like to teach the man a lesson, using his fists wasn't the way. Using the law would do more long-term good than bruises.

The valet opened the door to the Mansfield and he entered. Simon was registering an older couple. Colin stood back waiting for the clerk to hand the couple their keys and signal the bellhopper with one brisk ring of the bell.

Colin approached the counter and Simon's eyebrows rose.

"I heard there was an altercation on the third floor."

Colin nodded. "The person delivering Miss Leatherby's trunk tried to take a kiss." He narrowed his eyes. "I intervened. You can spread that around so there aren't others who make a bad decision."

"Indeed. I will. Is Miss Leatherby all right?"

"Yes. She's very resilient." Colin pulled the letter out of his jacket. "I'd like this delivered to Captain Dickson on the steamship Stanton."

Simon took the envelope and tapped the bell on the desk three times. A young, negro boy ran up to the desk. "Samuel, take this to the captain of the steamship Stanton."

"Yes, sir." The boy snatched the letter and took off at a run.

Simon smiled. "I guarantee it will be in the captain's hands in twenty minutes. Samuel is my fastest runner and very persistent when it comes to delivering messages."

"Thank you. Miss Leatherby and I will dine in the hotel restaurant tonight, but I'd like some advice as to a good restaurant for tomorrow night and entertainment to follow."

"I'll send a list to your room tomorrow morning." Simon patted the closed book on the desk.

"Again, thank you."

Colin was glad Simon hadn't pried into the events of the afternoon. Then a thought struck him. "The officer that came up to the third floor."

"Chester?"

"Yes, does he come by here often?" Maybe he wouldn't have to search for the man.

"We are on his beat. He stops in and checks on things when he isn't summoned." Simon gave Colin a fatherly, disapproving look.

"I'd like to speak with him the next time he stops in. Would you please send a runner up to get me when he arrives?"

"That can be arranged."

Colin handed the man a silver dollar. "Thank you."

He entered the elevator feeling he'd accomplished a good deal today. On the third floor, he knocked on Livie's door to tell her he'd be by in fifteen minutes. He'd need to clean up and change.

Knocking on the door startled Livie. She stared at the door, then the state of her undress and the two gowns in her hands.

"Yes?" she called across the room.

"It's Colin. Are you all right?"

The sound of his voice eased some of the knots that had formed from worry.

"Fine. Are you ready?"

"No. I just returned from a walk. I'll be another fifteen minutes."

Relief whooshed out of her on a breath. "Ah'll be ready."

She listened for the sound of his door shutting and returned her attention to the two outfits. The light blue one was pretty, soft, and all one piece that required help buttoning up the back. On her own now, she'd best put it in the pile of clothes to sell. Now, I'll have to go back through the clothes I planned to keep and make sure I can put them on by myself.

The other outfit was an eye-catching spring-green skirt with a white ruffled inset on the matching green wrap top that she could easily fasten herself. The top covered her all the way to her neck but had elbow-length sleeves with three bell ruffles. There were four rows of matching ruffles on the bottom of the skirt.

She'd never owned anything so elegant in her life. The thought it was from Wilfred spoiled the enchantment of wearing the garment.

Once the garment was on, she slid her feet into satin slippers. Next was her hair. Colin would be returning any second. She brushed her hair, making it shine. Rather than bothering with trying to get her fine strands to stay up in a fashionable hairstyle, she used two engraved, wooden side combs to hold her hair away from her face, while leaving the rest to flow down her back. It wasn't as formal has having it up, but quicker and easier. At home she wore her hair in a bun at the back of her head. But tonight she wanted her hair to be loose. This would be her first intimate dinner with a man that wasn't a relative or friend of the family.

They'd shared meals on the ship, but that was at a table with other people present. Tonight it would be just the two of them. That thought sent flutters of nerves in her stomach.

A knock at the door spun her towards the sound.

"Yes?"

"Are you ready?"

Colin's wistful tone made her smile.

She crossed to the door and opened it.

His eyes widened, and his body straightened from leaning against the wall.

Livie noted his dark blue wool suit and white

shirt with a string tie. He'd dressed up as well.

"Ah just need to grab me shawl." She hurried back to the wardrobe.

"You didn't need to unpack both trunks. We won't stay here that long." He'd stepped into the room and was surveying the piles of clothes.

"Ah'm not unpacking, exactly. Ah'm sorting through the clothes ah can poot on meself and the ones ah needed a maid's help. Those clothes ah'd like to sell. That way ah'll have a bit of me own chink for necessities." She swung the shawl around her shoulders and faced Colin.

"I've learned a number of the slang words in and around Liverpool, but I'm not sure what chink means." He was eyeing a pile of clothes that happened to have a lacey pair of under drawers lying on top.

Her cheeks heated, but rather than bring attention to what he stared at, she moved to the door. "Chink is money where ah come from."

"I see." He followed her out the door and closed it behind him. He offered his arm to her.

She hesitated. Now that she'd realized the type of evening that was ahead for them, she'd become timid. Not of him, but of her own fantasies.

He stopped in the hall and turned to her. "I would never hurt you." The words sounded like a solemn oath.

She peered into his eyes. What made him say such a thing?

"Ah know. You are the gentlest man ah've ever met."

He shook his head. "What you saw this afternoon wasn't me. It was a-a memory of my past. It won't happen again."

Livie placed a hand on his chest above his heart. "Ah know. Ah don't fear you."

"You're sure? You were hesitant to take my arm." His eyes peered into hers.

She could have stood in the hall for hours staring into his eyes. Feeling his concern from their deep blue depths. She'd also promised herself no more lies or falsehoods.

"Ah didn't hesitate because ah feared you. Ah feared me."

His brow wrinkled. "I don't understand."

"Ah barely understand it meself." She linked her arm with his. "Let's eat. Mayhap ah'll have an answer for both meself and you by the end of the meal."

Chapter Sixteen

Colin had never enjoyed a meal more than this one. Their table was tucked in a quiet corner of the restaurant. Livie had never tasted half the items on the menu. Helping her decide had been a game and now as he leaned back in his chair, watching her eat ice cream and lick her lips, he had never felt so content. And alive.

He didn't want the evening to end, but knew she needed to rest after her peril on the ship. But to-morrow night…he'd take her to a show after dinner.

"You have a smug smile on your face," she said, wiping her pretty mouth with the white cloth.

"I have reason to be. I'm enjoying a wonderful meal with a beautiful woman and looking forward to many more."

"Meals or women?"

The twinkle in her eye reflected her teasing

tone.

"I don't think I could find a woman more beautiful than you."

Her cheeks turned as red as the waiter's vest.

"Ah'm passable at best. It's only the fancy dress that makes you think ah'm beautiful." She ducked her head and picked at something in her lap.

Thankful the table was small, he reached across and tipped her chin up, giving him full view of her face. "You are more than passable and it's not the clothes." He glanced down at her empty bowl. "Let's take a walk."

He hurried around to her chair before she pushed back and stood. While he told her she didn't have to pretend to be gentry, he did like treating her like a titled lady. Colin settled her shawl around her shoulders and offered his arm.

They walked out of the restaurant and onto the street.

"Which way would you like to go?" he asked.

"Toward the water."

He set out at a casual stroll toward the small bay she could see from her window. While the air wasn't as moist and foggy as England, he found the smoke from the factories hard to get used to. A spring evening in Sumpter would be crisp, cool, and clear enough to see the many stars. The streetlamps and haze above the city dulled the sparkle of the constellations.

They stood on the street above the bay.

"It's not as pretty oop close as from the window." Livie's disappointment rang in her voice.

"The piles of horse manure in the alleys makes my eyes sting from the smell. I'll take you back. Tomorrow night we'll be in a different section of town." He wrapped an arm around Livie and pivoted them to head back.

Two young men stood on the other side of the street. From their intent gaze, he knew they planned to rob them. His protective instincts to keep Lily safe and away from the men warred with his desire to fight.

He whispered to Livie, "Do what I say."

She nodded, her gaze leveled on the two men.

"We don't want any trouble." Colin started to walk down the road. The two men mirrored their movements from the other side of the street. Dragging Livie the length of the city trying to avoid the two wasn't a good plan. His hands still ached from the beating he gave the man earlier in the day.

"I'm going to have to do something," he whispered to Livie. Then said loudly, "I'll give you all the money I have if you leave the lady alone."

He kissed her temple and whispered. "Run back to the hotel when they come to get the money from me."

She shook her head. "Ah'm not leaving you alone."

He didn't have time to argue, the two were crossing the road.

"Let's see what you have." The taller of the two held out his hand.

"Bailey what ya doin'? We can get that after we hit 'em over the head." The stockier fella lunged forward, grabbing Colin's arm.

Colin flung the money on the ground. The taller man dove for the currency.

"Run!" he shouted at Livie and gave her a push with his free arm.

"Get her!" the stocky man yelled and swung at Colin's face.

He countered with a fist to the man's belly, doubling him over.

Colin sprinted after the man chasing Livie. He dove, tackling the man around the legs. They both tumbled to the hard ground. Colin scrambled up the man's legs and body, jerking an arm behind the man's back.

"Ow!" the man wailed.

The hollow footsteps of the other man running their way left little time.

"Why didn't your partner want only the money?" Colin pulled on the arm.

"We was paid to knock you over the head and dump you in the bay."

"By who?"

Colin was knocked off the man and flung several feet beyond. The heavier man grabbed Colin's hair, raising his head up to slam it into the concrete. Colin shoved the heel of his hand at the man's nose, hoping to discourage the man's assault.

C-R-A-C-K! The shattering sound of wood splintering dwarfed the sounds of struggle.

The man fell across Colin.

He scrambled out from under the assailant and stared up at Livie holding a broken board in her hands. Her eyes were wide, one long lank of hair looped across her forehead. Pride welled in his chest that she fought beside him.

The other man struggled to his feet and ran down the street.

Colin spun to give chase.

"Don't!"

Livie's plea pivoted him on the spot.

She tossed the board to the ground. "Let's get back before soomthing else happens."

Colin pointed to the man lying in the street. "We should question him. His partner said someone paid them to toss us in the bay." He reached down to turn the man over.

Livie placed a hand on his arm. "We know who wants us dead."

Colin found it hard to believe Canfield could have discovered where they were staying and bought the assistance of thugs this quickly. "He hasn't had time. Not to mention he'd have to be staying out of sight of the police."

She shook her head and slipped her arm around his, leading him up the street toward the hotel. "Ah told you, when he sets his mind to soomthing he has to go through with it. It's just his nature. Come along. Ah don't want to get cot by soomone else. Watching you in a fight twice in one day is plenty for me."

He hurried her along. Instead of the leisurely stroll that carried them to the bay, he marched her back to the hotel in less than half the time. Walking back to the hotel, he ran the events over in his mind. A smile quirked his lips thinking of how Livie came to his rescue just as he had come to her rescue earlier in the day. The two events felt as if they were staking claim on one another.

Simon raised his brows when they walked through the hotel door.

Colin continued his march straight to the desk. "Did anyone come in here today asking for either Miss Leatherby or myself?"

The clerk nodded. "There was a young lad came in when you were out earlier."

Damn! Colin didn't know whether to change hotels or stay and clue the clerk and the local police in.

Colin pivoted and led Livie to the elevator. Once they were clanging up to the third floor in the enclosed box, he pulled her into his arms and held tight. He had a lot of thinking to do tonight. He was on his home ground. The man wasn't going to take his life or Livie's.

Livie wrapped her arms around Colin. She didn't want him to get hurt saving her; however, whether he tried to save her or not, Wilfred planned to kill them both.

The small conveyance bounced to a stop.

Colin led her to her room.

She dug in her pocket for the key. With a shaking hand, she handed it to Colin.

He opened the door and stood in the hall.

"No, you aren't slinking away to look for that man." She grabbed his hand, tugging him into the room. She shut the door and tossed her shawl onto the desk chair.

"Livie, I need to find the man and see if he knows where to find Canfield."

She wrapped her arms around his waist. "Ah need you here. If you go after him and soomthing happens to you, who is going to protect me? Wilfred wants oos both dead."

His hands rubbed up and down her back, pressing her body closer to his. The action and the touch started her body humming with warmth.

Running her hands over his back, under his jacket, she explored the ridges of muscle. Her fingers tingled. She pressed closer, reaching up his back. Her breasts smashed against his chest.

"Livie."

The word heated her lips moments before his mouth covered hers.

Chapter Seventeen

She'd never felt as alive as she did right now. Colin's hands held her head while his mouth took her to dizzying heights. His tongue slipped between her lips and touched her tongue, sending waves of delight dancing through her.

Her hands explored the heated skin under his cotton shirt, slipping between the buttons. The heat, smooth skin, and ridges of muscle made her light-headed. Or was it the deepening of Colin's kisses?

She swayed.

Colin's strong arms lifted her.

His kisses were far too intoxicating, for she missed them as he carried her to the bed.

She wound her fingers in his hair, dragging his mouth down to hers. She didn't want him to stop kissing her.

In one fluid motion, he placed her on the bed and lay down beside her, never releasing her lips.

When her chest ached for air, she released his hair and leaned back, breathing deep.

Colin trailed kisses down her neck to the lace of her wrap.

Her fingers worked at the knot at the bottom of the garment. She wanted to feel his kisses and touch on every inch of her.

Colin's hand stopped hers. "I could easily give you what you want tonight. But I'm not sure you would think kindly of me in the morning." He kissed her lips chastely and pushed to a sitting position.

Her body ached for more, but her mind sprang awake as if he'd dashed a bucket of cold water on her. Did he have that much control over his needs or did he not find her good enough to mate with? Embarrassment swept through her, heating her cheeks and squeezing painfully on her chest. She'd thrown herself at him like a strumpet and he'd rejected her. No doubt because of her actions. She rolled to her side. Tears heated a path over the bridge of her nose, running into her other eye and onto the pillow.

His warm soothing hand rubbed her arm. "Livie, shh, why are you crying?" He pulled her onto her back and wiped at the tears. "What's wrong?"

Through bleary, tear-filled eyes she peered up at him. He was so handsome, so caring. *And above you in every way.* She shook her head. What could she say? Only words that would make her look more foolish.

"I enjoyed the kisses." He softly ran a finger over her bottom lip. "Your mouth is meant for kissing."

She narrowed her eyes. What kind of scheme was he playing? He'd just turned away and here he was touching her and staring at her mouth like a starving man.

"You just broke off our kisses and pulled away."

"Not because I didn't enjoy it." His gaze held hers. "I enjoy every moment I spend with you. But I won't compromise you by taking things too far." He picked up her hand. "Livie, you are the most desirable woman I've ever met. I'll not sully your reputation by taking care of my desires when you don't know what your future will be."

Her mind understood his gesture. Her body yearned for more. And her heart was unsettled. She was here to help Ellis, but if the man staring into her eyes were to ask her to stay and never go back to Liverpool, tonight, she would agree. Because of this knowledge, she needed time away from him to think about her actions, needs, and loyalty.

"Thank you." She shoved her body to a sitting position against the headboard.

"I'll have Simon send up a tray in the morning. Is eight a good time?" Colin stood, shoving his hands in his trouser pockets.

"That's fine. Ah'd like to find a place to sell me extra clothes."

"Don't leave the room without me. When the tray is delivered send a message to Simon asking him. When you get a reply come get me. I'll be in my room." He walked to the door. Gripping the knob, he studied her. "Don't leave this building without me. We have no idea where Canfield is or who he has working with him."

She nodded.

"I've never had as wonderful a meal as I had with you tonight." His gaze swept over her. "Good night."

"Good night," she said, watching Colin disappear out the door.

Her heart raced. From panic and excitement. Could she forget about Mam and Ellis and live the rest of her life here with Colin? Her body and heart said yes. She could easily give herself completely to him and not regret a day. But she'd come on this journey to get Ellis free. With Colin's help that could happen. In essence if Colin asked her to marry him, she could in good conscience because he would help her free Ellis.

She slipped off the bed and began undressing. Heat crept up from her toes, infusing every inch of her body remembering his hands and lips and how wonderful they'd felt everywhere they'd touched. Donning her nightgown, she turned off the light and slid under the covers.

Remaining locked in this room didn't sound like a pleasant way to spend her day. If I get the clothes sorted and get a list of places to sell them, Colin will take me around. That will get me out of here for part of the day.

I wonder when we'll take a train farther west.

Colin paced his room. He'd undressed to his drawers. That still didn't relieve his heated body. If good sense hadn't come over him, he'd be in the room across the hall lying in Livie's arms, bringing them both the completion they wanted.

Thinking about it only heightened his need.

I should be out on the streets looking for the men who attacked us. Walking the streets, looking for Canfield would be more productive than pacing and thinking about Livie's creamy skin.

He pulled his trousers on. Donned a working shirt and slipped his feet into his work boots. He wanted to blend in with the locals, not stand out as the gentleman he'd been dressed as before.

Opening his door, he stared at the one across the hall. He doubted she'd go anywhere tonight. But in case, he'd have a bellhopper keep an eye on the elevator to make sure she didn't leave. He shoved his cowboy hat on his head and entered the elevator.

On the ground floor, he marched out into the street and headed to the bay. He'd noticed a number of saloons along the street that bordered the water. He visited bar to bar, starting up conversations with the men tending the bars.

He stepped into the Red Dog and stopped. The thin man who'd ran off sat at the end of the bar. His hunched posture and hanging head proved he'd been hitting the bottle since the incident.

Colin took a stool not far from the man and ordered a beer. When the bartender set the beer down,

Colin slid a half dollar across the counter. He tipped his head to the thin man. "He looks a little under the weather. What's his name?"

The bartender pocketed the coin and wiped the counter. "Melvin's his name. Came in here couple hours ago out of breath and mumbling about should've known better."

"I'll go see if I can cheer him up."

Colin picked up his beer and took the stool next to Melvin. "You look like you lost your dog or something." Colin didn't look at the man. Took a sip and watched him in the mirror behind the bar.

"Don't own a dog." The words were slurred, and he didn't even look up.

"Then something else has you drinkin' like a man fresh out of the desert."

Melvin raised his head and peered bleary-eyed at him. "What you know about deserts?"

"They're hot and a man can get up a powerful thirst. They're also dangerous. That could be why a man gets thirsty." He took a swallow of his beer. The warm yeasty drink wasn't a favorite but he'd learned to drink it when the need arose.

"Yeah, danger. I been in danger." He took a swig of his beer. "I need to stay away from fancy fellas. They're all talk about easy money." He snorted. "There ain't no easy money. No way. Not when you're killin' someone."

Colin leaned a little closer. "Who you supposed to kill?"

"A man and a lady stayin' at the Mansfield." He shook his head. "They're both too cagey."

"Why?"

"They beat up my partner and I ran. I wasn't goin' to get beat up along with not gettin' paid because we didn't do the job." Melvin swallowed the last of his beer and wiped a grungy sleeve across his mouth.

"Why were you supposed to kill them?" Colin took another sip of his beer and motioned for the bartender to bring Melvin another.

Melvin stared at him. "Some fancy dressed Englishman offered us fifty dollars to dump the two in the bay."

The bartender placed the glass in front of Melvin.

"Thank you, pal." Melvin picked up the glass and poured half the liquid down.

"Where was this fancy Englishman when he offered you the job?" Colin hoped to keep the man talking before he became suspicious of all the questions.

"He was standin' on the corner across from the Mansfield."

Colin smacked his glass down on the counter, sloshing beer onto his hand. Canfield was watching the hotel. If he went back after the botched attack, he'd know Livie was alone.

He jumped up from his stool and headed for the door of the bar. He'd left Livie unguarded. He'd told the bellhopper not to let Livie leave, but he hadn't told him not to let a fancy dressed Englishman use the elevator.

The run from the bar to the hotel raised a sweat

and had him breathing heavy. He entered the establishment and stopped when the few late night people stared at his entrance. With measured steps he approached the bellhopper.

"Did anyone not a registered guest of the hotel go up the elevator while I was gone?"

"No, sir. We only allow guests to use the elevator. Anyone else has to wait at the desk for the party they want to come down."

Relief calmed his racing heart. "Good. What time does Officer Chester come around?"

"He usually comes mid-morning and mid-afternoon."

"When he arrives in the morning would you send him up to three-oh-seven, please." Colin fished in his pocket and pulled out a quarter dollar.

"Yes, sir!"

Colin entered the elevator. At the third floor he exited and stopped outside Livie's door. He wanted to knock and see that she was indeed in the room and safe. But if she were sleeping he didn't want to rouse her or cause her to worry. He sighed, pulled out his room key, and turned to his door. Tomorrow he'd tell her what he knew. She had to be vigilant with Canfield watching their every move.

He shoved the door open and clicked on the light. Electricity was a wonder. He'd been working with Orin to get a generator for Meath Hall. The building could use some updates.

Colin entered the lavatory. The convenience of running water. He remembered how Ethan had lured his mother into the stamp mill office with living quarters that had running water and sturdy walls. He smiled and washed.

Walking naked back into the bedroom, he had the odd sensation someone watched him. They were three floors up and his window faced the street. *The street in front of the hotel.*

He clicked off the light and slipped to the side of the window. Pushing the lace curtain to the middle, he peered down at the street three stories below. A man stood under a street lamp. The distance was too far to see his features but the clothing resembled the type Canfield wore.

"Tomorrow, Officer Chester will grab you and with the confession from Melvin, you'll be locked up and we won't have to worry about you."

Chapter Eighteen

Livie woke fully rested for the first time in months. Her mind wasn't cluttered with worries for Ellis, her mother, or if she'd keep her job for not allowing Wilfred to have his way with her.

She lay in bed, enjoying a bit of leisure. Working most of her life, she had to be up early to get to work on time, usually with little in her belly. "Ah could get used to this lifestyle."

As soon as the words were out she knew it wasn't true. Having been a worker her whole life, she didn't like to sit idle. She swung her legs off the bed and walked to the wardrobe. The best thing to do was get dressed and finish sorting the clothing. By the time her food arrived, she'd have a note written for Simon. Once he sent a reply, she'd gather Colin and they could head out to sell her clothes.

Picking up the skirt she wore the night before,

she cringed at the sight of a dark stain on the hem. She'd collected someone's blood on the fabric. Giving it a critical once over, she noticed several dark spots. They could have come from her striking the man on the head with the board. Her hands shook as she carried the skirt to the bathtub and started the water. She'd have to get the blood out or the garment would be unfit to wear again.

While the skirt soaked she donned a dark brown skirt and flowered blouse. She'd asked the woman sewing the wardrobe to make her two serviceable blouses for day time use when she didn't need to look like a titled lady. They would come in handy now that she didn't want to wear fancy clothes and draw attention. She sat at the desk and wrote her note to Simon.

Faint tapping on the door drew her across the room. She pulled her watch out of her skirt pocket. Eight o'clock. The staff at the hotel were punctual.

She opened the door and was met by a tall, thin girl with small eyes and a large nose.

"Morning, ma'am. I've brought your morning tray as requested."

"Thank you. Please, set it on the table." Livie crossed to the desk and picked up her note to Simon.

The young woman placed the tray and faced the room.

"Please, give this to the clerk, Simon." She held out the note.

"I will, ma'am. What time will you be out of your room today?"

Livie stared at the woman. "Why wod you need to know that?"

The woman's eyes widened. "Why to come in and clean."

"Oh, yes, of course." Livie's cheeks grew warm. "Mid-day, Ah believe."

"Very well." The woman walked to the door. "Do you want me to remove the tray before then?"

"No, it can wait until you clean. Thank you." Livie walked to the door. Instead of taking the elevator, the woman walked down the hall to a door that opened onto a stairwell.

Once the woman was out of sight, Livie crossed the hall and knocked on Colin's door.

The door opened only enough for Colin to lean his fully dressed upper body into the space.

"Good morning. I didn't expect to see you this early." His gaze traveled from her head to her feet and back up.

"Me tray just arrived. Wod you like to join me?" She didn't want to sound too anxious.

"Thank you. I ate an hour ago. I've been going over ideas I have for the estate." He remained holding the door open only enough for a glimpse of his upper body.

His message was clear. She wasn't welcome in his room. "Ah'd like to take me extra clothes around in an hour. Will you be ready?"

He shook his head. "I'll come over when I'm ready."

"Fine." She pivoted and marched back to her room, entered, and closed the door, loudly.

She wasn't sure why he was so evasive this morning. It couldn't possibly have anything to do with their kisses last night. He'd stopped to save her reputation. Did he really? Could he have been carried away in the moment, then thought better of it? She had little experience with men, and kissing.

Sitting down at the small table, she pulled back the cloth on the tray and discovered a boiled egg, ham, toast, preserves, and a pot of tea. Savoring each bite of the cold, but divine meal, she was struck with a thought. Colin asked me to be his personal assistant. He didn't ask me to allow him to court me.

"Stoopid!" She'd thrown herself at him after the attack, and he, like any man, had taken what she offered. But unlike other men, he had stopped before they'd gone too far.

"Ah'm so bloody stoopid."

Too agitated to eat, she placed the outfits she wanted to sell in the larger trunk. She didn't need two trunks. One was more than sufficient for the few clothes she kept.

A knock on the door echoed through the silent room. She marched over and opened the door.

A smiling bellhopper held out a note. "From Simon."

"Thank you." She started to close the door but heard the elevator doors open. Glancing that direction, she spotted Officer Chester stepping out of the contraption.

"Wot's he doing here?" She tilted her head the direction of the officer.

"He's here at the request of Mr. Healy," the bellhopper said.

"Really? Thank you." She waved the man away and stood in her threshold, waiting to see what Colin had to say when he opened his door to the officer.

A brisk rap on his door, pulled Colin out of deep thoughts. He crossed to the door and opened it.

Officer Chester stood at the threshold. Beyond him Livie leaned against her door frame watching them both.

"Officer, thank you for coming up. Livie, you saved me a trip across the hall. Please, join us."

The surprise on her face made him chuckle. She'd expected him to chase her off. But he'd thought it through and her account of the attack last night would give the officer more than one report. The more they could get against Canfield the better.

He opened his door all the way. Officer Chester waved Livie in first and followed.

Colin removed his discarded clothes from the chair by the table and motioned for Livie to sit. Then he pulled the desk chair to a point half way between Livie's seat and the bed. Colin sat on the end of the bed.

"The bellhopper said you wanted to talk to me." Chester pulled out a small booklet and a pencil.

"Yes. Last night after dinner, Miss Leatherby and I went for a walk to the bay. When we came to the water, we discovered two men. At first I thought they wanted to rob us, but when I offered them money, they said they had to knock us in the head and throw us in the water."

"In other words they wanted to kill you?" Officer Chester studied them both.

"Yes." Colin glanced at Livie. Her knuckles were white and her eyes downcast. Was reliving last night upsetting her?

"Why would they want to kill both of you?"

"They were being paid. We knocked one unconscious and the other fled. After I returned Miss Leatherby to the hotel, I went back out looking for the other man."

Livie gasped. "Ah told you not to go back out. Soomthing could happen to you."

"I'm fine. I had to know who hired them. I found the one who ran away in a saloon. He was drunk and talkative. I struck up a conversation with him." Colin peered into Livie's eyes. "He told me it was a fancy-dressed Englishman who paid him."

Officer Chester stirred in his chair and stared at Livie. "Miss Leatherby, you're English. Does this man have anything to do with you?"

She nodded, but Colin jumped in.

"He was on the same ship from Liverpool. Livie—Miss Leatherby—worked for his family. He employed her to get to know me and uncover information."

"What kind of information?" Chester leaned forward in his chair, his pencil poised over his booklet.

"It's a long story, but I inherited an estate that he, Wilfred Canfield, believes belongs in his family.

When Liv—Miss Leatherby—couldn't discover information to disproof my legitimacy as an heir, Canfield realized the only way his family would get the property is by my death." Colin watched Livie.

Her color paled.

"Why is he also after Miss Leatherby?" The officer turned his attention to Livie.

"Because ah not only know he plans to kill Col—Sir—Mr. Healy, but ah also know he has wrongfully accused me brother of crimes, he, Lord Canfield, committed. He said he'd get me brother freed from Gaol if ah became friendly with Col— Mr. Healy. Lord Canfield asked me to find out all about Mr. Healy's past. Ah did. When it confirmed his place at Meath Hall, Wilfred—Lord Canfield became angry. He hurt me. And later he knocked oos off the ship."

"This isn't the first time he's attempted to kill you?" Officer Chester stared at Colin.

"No. The sailor who cut the rope won't say why he did it. But there were others who saw him talking with Canfield before it happened." Colin wanted to get Canfield locked up. "The reason I asked to see you was to tell you about last night and to inform you I believe from what Melvin, the man I talked to at the saloon, said, that Canfield is watching the hotel. He pointed us out to the two who tried to toss us in the bay. And last night when I came back to the hotel, there was a man standing in the shadows across the street from the front door."

Chester perked up. "Describe this Canfield."

"Slightly shorter than me. Five foot, ten inches,

I'd say." Colin glanced at Livie.

She nodded. "He has blond, shaggy hair; a narrow face; and close-set dark eyes. He is usually dressed in expensive clothes with a top hat and walking stick that has a brass pheasant head."

The officer scribbled in his booklet.

"Captain Whiteside of the *Americana* sent a notice to the harbor police to apprehend Canfield for the attempted murder." Colin rubbed his hands on his knees. "Apparently he slipped by them."

"I'll turn this description into the station and write up a warrant. In the meantime, I would suggest you stick close to the hotel or not go on any walks in quiet places." Officer Chester stood.

"We are going out in a bit and will be attending a show tonight. We're booked on the train to Chicago tomorrow." Colin walked the policeman to the door.

"I'll do my best to find this Canfield. From what you've said, it is likely he'll follow you."

"I'm hoping he does." Colin grinned. He'd already sent off a telegraph to Zeke. "I have an uncle who works for the Pinkertons. I've told him about this man and when we'll be arriving in Chicago."

Chester stared at him. "Sounds like you have more help than the New York Police."

Colin slapped the officer on the back. "That I do. Uncle Zeke will know what to do."

"If I learn anything I'll let you know."

"Thank you, we'd appreciate it." Colin closed the door and faced Livie.

She studied him intently. "Wot is a Pinkerton?"

"They are special investigators. They help law enforcement and people pay for their services to find stolen money, kidnapped people, and to infiltrate organizations that are corrupt." He pulled the chair Officer Chester had sat in closer to Livie.

"And ye have an uncle who does this?"

"And an aunt. Zeke and Maeve married and joined the Pinkertons. Maeve's father was a Pinkerton, but she didn't know that until she and Zeke went looking for him." He leaned forward, grasping Livie's hands.

Since leaving her room last night all he could think about was when he'd get to be with her again. This morning when she'd knocked on his door, he'd been thinking of her and had a bulge in his trousers he didn't want her to see. He'd hid behind the door. He could tell she was annoyed by his rejection of sharing her breakfast. But he didn't want to explain his condition.

"When Roderick, Wilfred's father, was looking for the heir to Meath Hall, he sent a man to America to find me. They didn't know where Ma had taken me or that she had remarried. The man killed several boys, one was a son of a rich railroad man. He hired the Pinkertons to find the man responsible for the killing. Zeke and Maeve followed him to Sumpter and realized I was the boy the man was supposed to kill." He hung his head. "Those other boys' lives were taken when it should have been me."

A small hand stroked his hair. "You're lukey. We're all lukey you were spared."

Livie's soft voice eased a small part of the torture he'd hidden inside him all these years. Why had he lived when he was the intended victim and the others died?

"I've lived with the guilt for eleven years."

"Never feel guilty for being alive." Her tone was strict and strong. She grasped his chin, as he'd done so many times to her, making him peer into her eyes.

"Life is the greatest gift. Many don't get to live as long as we have, nor as long as many others. We are all here for a reason. Soom more significant than others." She continued to stare into his eyes. "You have a purpose. Ah believe it is to help those who depend on Meath Hall and give strength to your mam and sister."

The conviction in her tone and strength in her beautiful eyes made him believe she could be right.

He grasped her hand and kissed the palm. "Thank you. It's been a long time since anyone cared about my thoughts."

"If no one cares, we give oop on our dreams."

Colin studied her. "What are your dreams?"

She looked taken aback by his question.

"Hasn't anyone asked you that before?" He continued to hold her hands. They tensed and she tried to pull away, but he held tight.

"Where ah grew oop one dreamed of a good meal or that they wouldn't be nibbed or assaulted." Her body sagged, and she avoided looking at him.

"You're not there now. You don't have to go back there."

Hope started to grow in her green orbs.

"You must have had dreams. You worked your way out of a factory into a job as a maid." He rubbed his thumbs back and forth across her knuckles.

"Me dream was to get out of the rookery. From there ah hadn't a plan."

Colin smiled at the conviction in her statement. "You're out. You are the only person who can put you back there."

He stood, drawing her to her feet. "Are you ready to sell the things you no longer want?"

"Yes, ah have the list, Simon sent oop." She pulled a slip of paper from her skirt pocket. "He even listed wot each store sells."

"Go to your room and get ready. I'll order a Hansom to take us round and get a bellhopper to help me get the trunk to the street." Colin led Livie to his door. "You did save a nice dress out for tonight, didn't you?"

She nodded. "Ah kept one evening gown ah can poot on meself. Why?"

"We're going to a nice restaurant and a show tonight. I've always wanted to go, but felt awkward going alone." Colin had wanted to see a show after Ma and Ethan saw one and Ma couldn't stop talking about the people singing and acting out a story.

"You don't need to spend money on me. Ah'll never be able to do enough work to pay you back." Her cheeks flushed.

What was she thinking? He'd had thoughts of ways she could thank him, but he'd never stoop that low. Having her for a companion was enough payment for him. Nothing more.

Livie walked across to her room and closed the door without looking back.

Colin hurried down the hall, forcing the images of Livie in his bed to the back of his mind.

Chapter Nineteen

Livie sat in a theatre watching an operetta. Colin had led her to a small balcony that held three other couples. When the group discovered neither Colin nor herself had ever seen an operetta, the oldest couple offered their front row seats. The woman handed Livie what looked to be small spyglasses.

"They're opera glasses," Colin said, holding the smaller end up to her eyes.

The stage and people on it became larger.

"It's wonderful!" Livie leaned with her elbows on the balcony railing and watched in this manner until there was an intermission.

Everyone stood. Livie handed the glasses to the woman. "Thank you. It was a wonderful thing to see the costumes oop close."

"You have a unique accent. Where are you from?" the woman asked.

"Liverpool, England." Livie sensed Colin move closer to her back. Always the protector.

"Are you here visiting relatives?" The woman waved her husband out of the balcony and continued to block Livie and Colin's exit.

"Yes, I'm escorting her to her sister." Colin grasped Livie's elbow. "Didn't you say you were thirsty?"

"Yes, ah'm quite parched." She grasped the woman's hand. "Thank you."

The woman finally moved out of their way.

Colin escorted her out into the upper hallway. People filled the hallway and the staircase to the lower floor.

"Lemonade?" Colin asked, leading her into the crush of men gathering drinks for their companions.

"Please." She couldn't help but notice the other men had left their women in groups to chatter while they wandered over here to get the drinks. Being the only woman on this side of the room, she'd garnered quite a few gawkers, both male and female.

"I think your man wishes to keep you to himself," an older gentleman said, winking at Livie.

She giggled at the reference of Colin as her man, but nodded, not sure how to retort.

Colin faced her holding two glasses of lemonade.

"You're right. Excuse us," he said, once again cupping her elbow and moving her along. Colin stopped when they stood in an unoccupied small area.

"That was rood." Livie didn't think in the time

she'd known Colin he'd ever acted so short with another person other than Wilfred.

He sipped his lemonade, scanning the room. After his gaze had traveled over every person, he said, "I don't want a repeat of last night. We don't know who in this room or the balcony could be bought by Canfield." He touched her cheek with the back of his hand. "Until I know he is in jail, I'll be skeptical of anyone who starts up a conversation with you. They could lure you outside and Canfield could be waiting to get his hands on you."

His knuckles whitened as his hand curled into a fist. He dropped it to his side.

"Ah won't go off with anyone, but you can't stay with me all the time." Her cheeks warmed. "There are certain things ah have to do alone."

He choked on his drink. "Do you need to go now?"

Livie laughed. "Not at this moment, but before we leave, ah'll need to visit the lavatory."

"I'll wait by the door."

The bugle announcing the start of the second half rang out. People began moving in a mass of bodies back toward the seating areas. Colin didn't move. He casually finished his drink and watched the people until only a few stragglers remained.

"Let's go," he said and offered his arm.

Livie was glad to not have to push through the crowd of people to return to their seats. The bodies and noise during the intermission had felt as suffocating as when she nearly drown in the ocean.

Before they'd climbed half the stairs a scream

and collective gasps filled the air. Attendants ran down the stairs and others ran into the lower area of the theatre.

"What happened?" Colin asked, stopping one of the men.

"Someone fell from a balcony." The man shoved on by.

Livie noted the tension in Colin's jaw, and his arm squeezed her arm tighter against him. He continued to their booth. A man stood at the entrance.

"You can't go in," said the man.

"We were sitting here before the intermission." Colin started forward.

"A person just fell from this area. No one is permitted in or out."

Livie's mind spun as her heart stalled to a stop. "Man or woman?"

The attendant peered at her. "Man."

Her heart pounded in her chest. She stared at Colin. Could whoever Wilfred paid have pushed the wrong man?

"Where was the man sitting?" Colin asked.

His tone told her he had the same thought.

"At the balcony. Why are you asking so many questions?" The attendant's eyes narrowed.

"Because we were sitting in there. It could be a friend."

Colin's clipped answer gave her insight to how well he'd taken to his role as baronet of Meath Hall. The words put the man in his place and punctuated Colin's authority.

"I'm sorry, but I'm not to let anyone in or out."

Colin spun on his heels, taking Livie with him.

"You know how ah feel about bobbies, but shouldn't we wait and talk to them?" she asked as he hauled her down the stairs. She grasped the front of her skirt with her free hand, but still had trouble navigating the quick pace.

"Slow down. Ah'm going to fall and you're going to draw attention to our fast exit. They'll think we shooved the man."

She'd no sooner made the comment and two men stepped in front of them at the bottom of the stairs.

"My wife isn't feeling well, I wanted to get her home quickly," Colin said, pulling her tight against his side.

"She don't look sick to me." A large man said, walking up behind the others. "I run this theatre and don't appreciate people who give it a bad reputation."

"We have nothing to do with whatever happened." Colin squeezed her.

Livie assumed it meant to keep quiet, which was fine with her.

"We went to return to our seats and the attendant wouldn't let us in. If we can't watch the performance we might as well leave." Colin stepped to walk around the men.

One stuck his arm out.

The large man stepped forward. "You shouldn't mind waiting until the police arrive. If you're innocent."

Colin didn't believe in coincidences. That a

man in the booth they were sitting in fell meant he had been the target. If they were going to be detained, he needed Officer Chester to vouch for the other attempts on their lives.

"We'll stay, but I want you to contact Officer Chester of the Hoboken Police Station." Colin held Livie close. If they tried to separate them, he'd make sure she never left his sight. As badly as Canfield wanted Meath Hall and the fortune he had behind him, he could have bought half the attendants in the theatre and possibly police.

"Follow Bud, he'll take you to a room to wait for the police." The large man waved his hand toward the blond man who'd detained them.

Colin nodded. He kept his arm around Livie as they walked to a room off the box office. Once inside, Bud closed the door on them.

They were alone. Colin pulled Livie into an embrace. Her body trembled.

"We're not in any trouble. Once they talk with us and the others in the booth tell them we weren't anywhere near the booth when the accident happened, we'll be able to leave."

"That's not wot scares me. Ah know we didn't do anything. But Wilfred." She peered up at him with tear glazed eyes. "He's not giving oop and he's hurting others."

Guilt exploded in his gut like a dynamite blast. More people were being harmed because of him. I should hand the estate over to Roderick and walk away. But he couldn't. He'd heard and seen what some English lords had done to other estates once they got hold of them. They didn't think of the tenants who made a living from the land, only how the lords could profit. He'd grown too fond of the tenants to allow that to happen to them.

"He'll be caught once we get to Chicago." Colin eased Livie down into a chair. He pulled up a chair and sat in front of her, holding her hand. "I booked a private car for us to ride to Chicago. No one will be able to do anything. Zeke will meet us at the station. I'm sure he'll have a plan for capturing Canfield." Having a private car would let them have a few hours of peace, knowing only the conductor would come through the door. He rubbed her cold hands. "We just have to get on that train tomorrow morning."

The door opened and a police officer walked in. "I'm Officer O'Reilly. I was told you were detained because you were leaving the building in a hurry."

Colin stood and offered his hand. "I'm Colin Healy and this is Livie Leatherby." The man looked competent. Colin was getting tired of repeating the past attempts on their lives but it would need repeating again. The more people who knew about Canfield the sooner he would be apprehended.

After shaking hands, he sat back down. "We were leaving in a hurry. The person who fell was from the box where we'd been sitting before intermission. We've already had two attempts on our lives and wished to get back to the Mansfield before something else happened to us."

The officer's eyebrows rose and his eyes narrowed. "You've had two attempts on your lives?

How? When?"

"There is a complaint filed with the harbor police for the attempt at sea." Colin went on to retell the near drowning and the attack they reported to Officer Chester. The more times he talked about the near misses by Canfield, he feared the next time wouldn't be a miss and either he or Livie would die.

The officer nodded his head. "I can see why you'd be jumpy." He walked to the door. "But you can see that I'll have to keep you contained until I can confirm your story."

"I understand." Colin sighed. He'd hoped to get Livie out of here by now.

Officer O'Reilly opened the door. Outside the other patrons were leaving the building.

Colin didn't like the possibility of being left here with minimal people around. "How long will confirming our story take?"

"If it's all been recorded, an hour or so."

"I don't like sitting here where Canfield can find us easily."

"Don't worry, there'll be a guard." O'Reilly closed the door.

"Damn!" Colin paced. Waiting an hour or better didn't sound like a very good option.

"If we have a guard, we'll be safe," Livie offered.

He peered down at her. The usual sparkle in her eye was gone. Her bottom lip was red and had small teeth marks.

"Don't worry." He pulled her up into his embrace. "We'll be out of here and in good care in two days."

Colin inhaled her floral scent and placed his cheek on the top of her head. "I'm glad you agreed to remain with me until I can get you home. If you'd been left alone…"

Her shivers echoed the shivers in his heart thinking of what could have happened to her if left alone. Canfield was proving to be a ruthless, vindictive man. He'd seen more than his share of that type of man in his lifetime. They were dangerous.

Chapter Twenty

Livie could barely keep her eyes open as the Hansom cab rumbled along the vacant streets. It was well past midnight. The information on the filed reports finally came through, then O'Reilly had asked for their accounts of the evening.

Her eyelids finally won. She leaned her head on Colin to ease the jerking of her neck. Her last glimpse was of Officer O'Reilly, who insisted on escorting them back to the Mansfield.

She slipped into a dark oblivion and moments later Colin's low voice entered her dream.

"Livie? Livie, we're at the hotel. Time to wake up."

A slight shake on her shoulder and the movement of the cab stopping, forcing her body forward, shocked her eyes open. Colin held her shoulders and peered into her face.

"Can you walk? It's been a long day when you're not fully recovered."

The lamplight barely seeped into the cab, making it hard for her to see him.

"Ah am exhausted, but ah think ah can manage."

Colin hopped out of the cab and raised his arms to her. She dropped into his hands, knowing he would never let her fall. Once on the ground, Livie leaned heavily on Colin as they entered the hotel lobby.

Her limbs pulled and moved like logs. It was clear she hadn't completely recovered from her ocean ordeal.

In the elevator, she wrapped her arms around Colin's waist to help keep her standing. The last bounce before the elevator stopped was her undoing. Her tired legs gave out.

Colin scooped her into his arms and strode down the hall to her room. "Where's your key?"

She slipped a hand into her reticule to fish for the key. The cold metal touched her fingers. She pulled it out, sliding it into the keyhole and turning.

The door opened and Colin carried her into the room. "Will you be able to get ready for bed?"

The concern in his blue eyes plucked at her heart. Each time he did something to show his concern, she lost another piece of her heart to the man. He was everything she'd believed a man could never be, with only her dar, Ellis, and Wilfred as examples.

"Ah'll manage." She sat on the bed and then

realized the position would be awkward for taking her shoes off.

Colin retraced his steps to the door and closed it. Facing her and the bed, he captured her gaze. "I'll help you with the outermost garments."

She shook her head. *Did I hear him right?*

"You don't want me to help you? I'll only take off your shoes, stockings and your dress. You can do the rest or sleep in what's under the dress." He knelt at her feet and began unhooking the buttons on her shoes.

Too exhausted to care, she lie back, allowing him to remove her shoes. Then his warm hands slid up her legs and relieved them of her warm stockings. She wiggled her toes in the cool air.

Her eyes popped open when Colin eased her to a sitting position.

He leaned close, as his fingers, one by one, unfastened the buttons down the front of her dress.

She inhaled his spicy scent and rubbed her cheek against his chest.

His hands stopped. "I thought you were exhausted."

"Ah am. You smell good and your body poots off a delicious heat."

The chest under her cheek, rumbled and a soft laugh warmed her senses.

"Your honesty is refreshing. So many of your countrymen are false." His fingers continued down her front.

The gown's sleeves slid down, revealing her shoulders.

"Stand." Colin's voice had a husky ring to it. He held out his hands to her.

She placed her fingers in his palms, and he drew her to her feet.

He slid the sleeves down her arms and over her fingertips. The gown slid over her hips and pooled around the hem of her petticoat.

"Would you like this removed?" He ran his finger down the front of her corset.

The softly whispered question, heat in his eyes, and thundering of her heart, made her mouth feel as if she'd sucked on a cotton ball. All she could do was nod her head.

She studied his face, etched with concentration. When the first hook loosened, she peered down at his shaking hands. This intimacy affected him too. She sucked in her chest and belly to aid him in loosening the hooks.

The last one gave way. He caught the garment before it hit the floor.

Perspiration beaded his brow. Livie rubbed a thumb across his forehead and stared into his eyes. She no longer felt exhausted. Her heart raced and her body hummed with anticipation.

"You should be comfortable now." Colin took a step back.

Livie stepped out of the circle of her gown and placed a hand on Colin's chest. She wasn't ready for him to leave.

Colin stared at Livie. He'd never wanted a woman as much as he wanted this one. Taking her stockings off had afforded him the chance to skim his hands down her shapely legs. He'd managed that feat and knew her gown and corset had to come off to make her truly comfortable. But seeing her creamy skin and feeling the fullness of her breasts as he unhooked the corset had pushed him to the limit of his restraint.

He needed to leave before he lost control. But her hand on his chest anchored him to the spot.

Livie closed the distance between them, pressing her body to his and wrapping her arms around his neck. "Don't leave."

Her sultry invitation had him peering into her eyes. Was this something she did often? Use her wiles to get a man to do her bidding? He only had her word she was being used by Canfield. Was she still working for the Englishman? How had he known they would be at the theater or in that booth?

He started to shove her away, when realization hit. He'd kept all the details from Livie. She had no way of knowing where they were going or where they would sit.

There was one way to see if she was still working for Canfield. The only problem was whether or not he could live with himself afterwards.

Colin drew her closer in an embrace and lowered his head, meeting her upturned lips. If she proved to be skilled at intimacy, then he'd know she'd seduced others and was most likely still working for Canfield. The idea he'd fallen for her and she was part of the scheme made his gut ache. He was pulling for her to be as innocent as she'd appeared so far.

Deepening the kiss, he tangled his tongue with hers and eased her body down onto the bed. He'd see just how far she'd allow him to go. He'd been the one to back away the other night. He still didn't like the idea of making love to her. If she was innocent, he'd have no recourse but to marry her and save her reputation. He liked the idea of marriage, as long as she wasn't still in cahoots with Canfield.

She shoved his jacket off his shoulders.

He sat up, giving him a moment to clear his thoughts and toss the jacket to a chair. Peering down at Livie, his gut tightened and his manhood sprang to life. The straps of her shift hung down her arms, the top of her creamy breasts peeked over the top of her shift. The hem of her garment rode up at her knees, exposing her feet and calves. The only other time he'd witnessed so much exposed skin on a woman was the few times he'd visited a house of ill-repute.

He leaned down, untying his boots and kicking them off.

Down to his shirt and pants, he settled onto the bed next to Livie. He'd expected her to reach out for him but instead he heard her softly snoring.

Grinning, he remained on the bed beside her, watching her eyebrows wiggle and her eyes move under her closed lids.

If she was truly out to help Canfield, her exhaustion would have been feigned and she would have seduced him. Livie falling asleep while he undressed was a sign she was exhausted and she didn't have ulterior motives. Her asking him to stay must have been a need for security after all that had happened lately.

He shifted his weight and stood. Pulling on his jacket, he picked up his socks and boots. He leaned over the bed, placed a kiss on her cheek, and crept out of her room.

Back in his room, he sat down and made a list of the day's events. There had to be a clue to how Canfield knew where they would be tonight. He couldn't wait to arrive in Chicago and let Zeke apprehend Canfield.

Tapping the quill on the paper, his thoughts wandered. He'd told several people of their plan to head to Chicago on tomorrow's train. Would Canfield also be on the train? Should they act like they were heading to the train station and stay in a different hotel until the next train to Chicago?

Colin woke to pounding on his door.

"Mr. Healy! Mr. Healy, you asked to have a crate picked up."

The bellhopper's comment shot Colin to his feet. He was still dressed in last night's clothes. His back ached. Crossing to the door, he raised his hands above his head, stretching and working the kinks out from sleeping draped over the desk.

He opened the door and spied Livie peeking out her door. "The crate is at the end of the bed," he instructed the bellhopper and strode across to Livie's room.

She opened the door. Her trunk sat by the door. The valise he'd purchased for her to carry extra clothes in while traveling on the train sat on the end of the bed with her blue coat and fancy hat.

"You look rested," he said, stroking her cheek with the back of his hand.

"You look like you were oop all night."

The concern in her green eyes warmed his insides. "After you fell asleep, I sat down to write a list of the events, trying to figure out how Canfield knew we were at that particular balcony at the theater." He ruffled his hair with both his hands. "I guess I fell asleep in the chair. Anyway, that's where I woke up."

Another bellhopper arrived at Livie's door. "Is your trunk ready, Miss?"

"Yes." She didn't take her gaze from Colin's face.

He waited until the young man could be heard getting into the elevator before closing the door and stepping close to Livie. "Someone had to have told Canfield where we were going and which balcony we were sitting in." He kept his voice low so anyone hanging around in the hall wouldn't be able to hear.

Livie leaned close. "Ah was thinking about that this morning when ah woke. How did he know? We even switched places with that older couple."

Colin nodded. "We shouldn't have been sitting at the balcony's edge. How did whoever pushed that man know that's where I was sitting?"

"Do you think the older couple were bought by Wilfred?" Her eyes widened.

"At this point we don't know who to trust other

than one another." He grasped her upper arms. "You do trust me, don't you?"

"Yes," her breathy reply without hesitation was the answer he needed.

He kissed her and drew back. "When we get to the railroad station, don't question when I ask you to do something, just do it." If anything happened to Livie… "I need you to be safe."

"Ah'll be mindful of your wishes," she said, placing a hand on his chest.

Colin covered her hand with his. "Good." He peered into her eyes.

The clank of the elevator door slapped his mind back to the moment at hand.

"I'll get dressed and meet you in the hall in five minutes." He dropped another kiss on her lips and spun around.

At the door, he pulled it closed behind him and strode into his room. He quickly dashed water over his face and combed his hair. The whiskers would have to wait. Although for the plan he'd concocted when Livie admitted she'd had the same idea that someone had to have told Canfield everything, allowing his whiskers to grow could be part of their disguise.

He pulled on his wool jacket and stepped into the hall. Livie joined him and they entered the elevator. His idea would get them to Chicago without the threat of Canfield, he was sure of it.

Chapter Twenty-one

Livie held her hand out to Colin who helped her down from the Hansom cab and then leaned in to grab their bags. The train station bustled with activity. The throng of tightly bunched people and noise was more suffocating than the ship had been. She hoped she didn't lose Colin in the crush of people.

Colin grasped both bags in one hand and cupped her elbow, escorting her toward the ticket office.

"Ah thought you already have tickets." she said.

"I do." He stopped and studied the train departure board. "Come on."

He led her to the train standing at the loading platform. Releasing her arm, he studied the ticket in his hand, then motioned toward a car near the back of the train. "That's the private car."

She stared at him. "That's bloody expensive."

"I wanted to make sure we didn't have to worry about being killed while we slept." He nodded, and she headed toward the private car.

He climbed the steps onto the car platform and reached down to help her up. They both stood on the platform as he opened the door.

Livie stared in shock at the lavishness of the car. It was larger than the hotel room and more elegant. Two doors at the opposite end stood open. One led into a bedroom and the other to a lavvy.

She walked around touching and wondering at the cost of purchasing a ticket to ride in the car just the two of them. Her gaze traveled to the bedroom and her cheeks heated. Would they share the bed?

Spinning from the sight, she found Colin peering out the windows.

"Wot are you looking for?" She unbuttoned her coat.

He glanced her way. "Canfield. Don't take your coat off. We aren't staying."

"Wot do you mean?" She walked up behind him.

"Remember what I said? Don't ask questions just trust me?"

"Yes."

"This is the trusting." He pushed away from the window. "This will be the last place the conductor will come to collect the tickets and make sure we're comfortable. By then we should be on a train headed a different direction." He kissed her cheek and peered out the windows opposite to the loading platform.

She wasn't sure what he had planned, but she did trust him. Peering out into the crowd of people, she didn't know how anyone would know who boarded the train. Then a top hat came into view.

"Colin."

"Yes?"

"He's here." She wasn't sure whether to move away from the window or stay and let Wilfred see she was on the train.

Colin came to her side. He placed an arm around her. "Good. See how he's staring at this car. He's checking to see if we're on the train."

He spun her in his arms. "Let's give him a show."

Before she could ask how, his mouth covered hers and sent her thoughts spiraling to things other than the man outside the train.

She sunk into his arms and the kiss, opening her mouth and inviting him to take her to dizzying heights. Her hands fisted in the front of his coat, keeping her from melting at his feet.

"All Aboard!" shouted a conductor out on the platform.

Colin eased out of the kiss. Her eyes fluttered open. The smile on his face and heat in his eyes mirrored the emotions swirling in her.

"He knows we're on the train." Colin grasped one of her hands, leading her to the door. "We're going to get off as soon as the train starts moving."

He picked up the bags in one hand and nodded

for her to open the door. Out on the small platform of the car, he maneuvered her to the steps on the side looking out at the station yard.

"See the second train over?"

"Yes."

"That's the train we want to get on. When this train starts rolling, step off and head that direction, I'll be right behind you."

Livie glanced at Colin over her shoulder. The determination in his eyes and steady smile on his lips eased her trepidation. She trusted him. He'd never leave her stranded in a train station.

The train creaked and jerked forward.

"Now."

Livie clambered down the steps and started walking toward the space between two cars on the next track. She didn't look back until she was standing between the two cars.

The train was moving faster.

She didn't see Colin.

What happened?

Her heart froze.

Did Canfield or one of his rampers catch Colin before he could get off? She started to step out from her hiding spot when she caught a flash of color.

Colin stood. The last car passed by him, and he started jogging her direction.

When he ducked into her hiding spot, she threw her arms around his neck and kissed him.

"Ah thought Wilfred or one of 'is rampers cot you."

"I wanted to wait until I was positive no one

saw you and they couldn't get off the train if they saw me." Colin kissed her back. "Come on. We'll purchase a ticket on the next train. I don't want to chance Canfield has someone watching the ticket office."

He helped her crawl over the car couplings, and they walked over to the next train.

"According to the departure sign, this one will be leaving in thirty minutes." Colin motioned for her to climb on board.

This train wasn't as fancy as the last one.

Livie took a seat in the back. Colin sat down beside her, placing their bags under the seat in front of them.

"Not quite the same as the last train but safer." Colin held her hand. "I'm sorry, we couldn't travel in lavish conditions."

"You forget where ah come from." She waved her hand. "Just being on a train is lavish to me."

He kissed the hand he held. "That's what I like about you. Adventure doesn't frighten you."

Most girls or women she knew wouldn't have taken his comment as flattery, but she found it the highest praise he could give her. Having lived in the Liverpool slums her whole life, she wanted nothing more than adventure.

"Thank you. Where are we headed?"

"Dunkirk on Lake Erie. We'll spend the night there then take another train to Chicago. I'll telegraph Zeke tonight when we arrive at the station and let him know the change."

The train rocked.

"What are you doing on here?" a male voice asked.

Colin stood and faced the conductor walking down the aisle. He hadn't prepared to be found before people boarded the train.

"I'm sorry, my wife is grieving and we didn't want to wait around in the crowd of people."

The conductor glanced at Livie and his eyebrows raised.

Colin mentally smacked himself. Her bright blue coat and flowered hat didn't project a woman who was grieving. "We received the telegraph about her mother an hour ago and came straight here. She wants to get home for the rest of her family."

He smiled benevolently at Livie and discovered her crying into a handkerchief. She was a quick thinker.

Colin held out what he knew was double the fare. "May I purchase our tickets now and just stay here?"

The conductor stared at the money held out to him, then at Livie sniffing and dabbing at her eyes, and back at the money. He snatched the money and nodded, moving on through to the front of the car.

Exhaling, Colin sat on the bench seat beside Livie. He draped an arm around her shoulders. "Nice job. I hope you don't have to cry all the way to Erie, you'll be exhausted when we get there."

Her shoulders shook and merriment twinkled in her eyes when she glanced at him.

"It's been a good while since ah've had to shed fake tears. When ah was younger ah did it all the time to make Ellis and his friends leave me be." Her smile dimmed. "He and his friends were out to bother people even then."

Colin dropped his arm from her shoulders to her waist, pulling her closer. His hand fit perfect at the curve of her waist. "I'm sure they were just like any other boys. When my sister was old enough to tease I played tricks on her I'm not proud of now."

She shook her head. "No, Ellis has always followed others too easily. Soom say he's simple. But he has this need to be liked by everyone. And if that means doing things he knows are wrong but will get him accepted by the people he thinks are his friends, he'll do it. Ah think that's why it was so easy for Wilfred to make Ellis his scapegoat. Ellis thought being friends with Wilfred he'd be accepted in gambling houses he wasn't allowed in."

Her body sagged with the expulsion of a deep sigh.

Colin drew her tighter against him and kissed her temple. "Some people have to go through a tough time before they figure out things. Maybe Ellis' stay in Gaol will turn him around."

"Ah hope so. Mam will need him as she ages." She snuggled into his side, resting her head on his chest.

Holding her and taking on her concerns felt natural. The car lurched. Livie remained cuddled against him as the train pulled up to the platform and the other passengers entered the car. He nodded to the men who came on and ignored the curious glances of the women.

He couldn't tell if Livie had fallen asleep or if she was just snuggling for the sake of being near him. Whichever it was, he didn't mind.

"All aboard!" came the shout from outside the train and soon the car was moving. Faster and faster until the scenery outside the window rushed by at a steady speed.

Colin tipped his hat over his face and rested his cheek on Livie's head. They'd lost Canfield and could relax. Telegraphing Zeke tonight should give him the notice he needed to search the incoming train they were supposed to be on and apprehend Canfield. The rest of the trip he could enjoy Livie's company and not be always on the alert.

Livie squirmed. "Ah need to use the lavvy," she whispered in his ear.

Colin sat up and led her to the back of the car. He only knew the workings of the second class car from exploring the trains when he was a child. From his first train ride with Ethan and his family, he'd always traveled in first class.

At the back of the car, he opened a small door on the left before leaving the car. Inside the small space was a small toilet.

Livie gave him a meek smile and entered the room.

Colin closed the door and remained at the back of the train making sure no one tried to enter the small room.

When Livie emerged, he motioned for her to head up the aisle. He followed, noting the car was only half full. The short trip and standing was a relief from the hard wood bench seat.

The train made many stops along the route. Passengers shuffled on and off. Mid-day the conductor came through letting them know the next stop would be long enough to get off and get something to eat.

"Ah never thought ah'd be so happy to get out and walk around," Livie said, straightening her hat and sitting up straight.

"I agree."

The train slowed. Steam and black smoke wafted past the windows and the car came to a stop. Many passengers rose and grabbed their belongings.

"Wot about the bags?" Livie asked.

Colin had debated if they should take them or leave them. He glanced around at the people still seated. The only ones he felt might be trustworthy were an older couple. He couldn't see them stopping anyone from taking the bags.

"We'll take them with us." Colin leaned down and grabbed the handles of both bags. He stepped into the aisle and motioned for Livie to go first.

She hurried down the aisle and off the train. On the platform she stopped, waiting for him.

Colin caught up. "That looks like a place to find food." He pointed to a small café sitting not far from the depot.

He grasped Livie's elbow, escorting her across the platform and across the street.

The small building was packed with people. A bench sat in front of the building with the porch roof shading it.

"Sit here with the bags while I go in and get us something to eat."

"Do ah have to sit? Can ah just stand?"

Colin chuckled. "You may stand. Just don't wander off."

"Ah'll be right here. There are enough people to watch to keep me entertained." Livie placed a hand on his arm. "Ah'll eat anything. Comes from growing oop poor."

He kissed her cheek. "I'm glad to hear you eat anything. We may have to take whatever is quick."

Entering the building, he had the sensation someone watched him. He stopped inside the door and scanned the packed room. People sat at tables and stood in line at a counter. No one seemed interested in him. He did notice a man staring out the window. Colin followed his gaze and noted Livie standing with her back to them.

While in line, Colin made sure he kept an eye on the man who continued to gaze out the window. Was he watching Livie? Could he be working for Canfield and have followed them on the train? Standing in line, waiting and wondering had him jumpy as a wild horse.

Finally, he could order. "I'll take two sandwiches, two apples, and two cookies."

The woman behind the counter placed the wrapped items and apples on the counter. He paid, gathered up the food, and turned to leave.

Livie no longer stood in front of the window. His gaze shot to the table where the man sat. He was missing too.

Chapter Twenty-two

Colin shoved the food into his pockets and pushed his way through the people lined up behind him.

At the door, he scanned the area. Their bags sat on the bench. He grasped the handles and studied the area between him and the train station. Not a sign of a bright blue coat or flowered hat.

He peered down the street.

Nothing.

Then up the street.

Nothing.

How could they have disappeared so quickly?

His heart raced. Where should I look? Should I contact the police?

A flutter of blue in his peripheral vision spun him around.

Livie walked around the corner of the building,

spinning a small white flower between her fingers.

He dropped the bags and captured her in an embrace, holding her to his racing heart.

Her arms circled him, hugging back. "Ah don't mind being hugged but wot's this all about?"

"I saw a man staring out the window as if watching you. Then I turned around and you were both gone. I thought…" He kissed the top of her head.

"Ah'm sorry. Ah walked to the corner and saw these pretty wildflowers. Ah wondered if they had a scent and picked one." She raised her face and kissed his chin. "Ah'm sorry to have caused you worry."

"I'm just happy you're safe." Colin released her. "Come on. We can eat on the train."

They walked back to the train hand in hand. Colin didn't want to feel that sense of loss he'd felt when he'd turned and didn't see Livie or the man.

He peered up at her as she climbed the steps onto the train. He now understood the emotions Ethan and Ma felt toward one another. He'd watched their attraction grow with a cynical and jaundiced view. All he'd ever known until Ethan Halsey came into their lives was violence between a man and woman. He hadn't liked it and didn't think it would be possible for his mother to love a man. But Ethan's calm ways and dislike for violence had warmed Ma and himself to the man. Ethan had taught him violence was wrong and you never raised a violent hand to a woman or child.

Livie stopped at the door and glanced back at

him. A smiled graced her pretty mouth.

His heart thumped twice and happiness sung through his body. Once he visited family and they returned to Liverpool, he'd ask Livie to be his wife. He couldn't ask her any sooner or she'd think he did it out of duty rather than his affection for her.

He scrambled onto the train and directed her to their same seats.

Livie's body was still heated from the vise-like embrace Colin had given her when she'd walked around the corner of the building. She'd only been out of his sight for a minute, but considering his reaction, she'd best not do anything like that again. Although hugging him had been a wonderful treat.

He shoved the bags under the seat in front of them and pulled wrapped packages out of his pockets along with two apples. "Your meal," he said, handing her two of the packages and an apple. "Save the apple for last. I don't think there is water on this train."

"Thank you." She unwrapped the largest parcel and found a beef sandwich. It was a bit dry and hard to swallow, but her grumbling stomach didn't care.

"All aboard!" came the shout to re-board. People hustled down the aisle and settled in the seats. The train chugged forward, gaining speed.

She finished the sandwich as the town disappeared and the countryside flashed by the window. Unfolding the paper on the other parcel, she found a sugar cookie. The sweetness helped chase away the dryness in her mouth. But the big red apple was the best to eat last. The juicy sweetness was the perfect ending to the meal.

Colin skimmed a finger up her chin. Removing his finger from her face, he slipped the finger in his mouth. He smiled. "You had apple juice on your chin."

His gaze remained locked on her mouth as she licked at the juice clinging to her lips. Heat scorched her cheeks and the tips of her ears. If they hadn't been in public, she would have leaned and allowed him to lick the juice from her lips. His kisses so far had been dizzying, but imagining his tongue brushing across her lips, swept delicious shivers of anticipation through her body. By the heat in his eyes, she didn't doubt that his thoughts mirrored her own.

She folded the papers that had wrapped their food and slipped them in her coat pocket. Peering out the window, she drifted into a daze. Green pastures and hillsides dotted with wild flowers made an abstract painting as the train chugged past. Her thoughts bounced from Colin to Wilfred to worries for Mam and Ellis.

Even though they were dodging a man who wanted them both dead, she didn't feel threatened. Not with Colin taking charge and asking her opinion. They were tackling the challenge together. She'd never felt like an equal to someone as learned and titled as Colin. He treated her like her thoughts and opinions mattered, and he believed in her intelligence. She'd always known learning to read and write would get her out of the rookery, but she'd never dreamed beyond that. Now, here in America, she could be anything she wanted and no one would care where she came from.

The freedom that knowledge gave her heart and her mind made her light-headed. But to stay here would leave Mam alone if Colin's solicitor couldn't get Ellis out of Gaol.

"Why the frown?" Colin's soft voice whispered over her shoulder.

She didn't turn. The heat of his body pressing against hers alerted her to the fact they'd be lip to lip should she swivel her head. As much as she'd welcome a kiss, they were bouncing along in a railroad car full of people.

"How do you know ah'm frowning?"

"I can see your reflection in the window."

His body heat receded, giving her space to move without their lips meeting.

Livie shifted her body and attention toward Colin. How did she tell him she wanted to stay in America but worried for her mother and brother? She didn't want to sound selfish. But that's what she thought of herself.

Blowing out a breath, she peered into Colin's eyes. The interest and concern in their blue depths gave her the courage to speak her mind.

"Ah like the person ah am since arriving in America. No one cares that ah lived in the rookery or knows that ah shouldn't be among them."

"You can walk among anyone, even in England."

She found his declaration endearing and smiled.

"That is because you grew oop here. Not believing in the classes and titles." She sighed. "Ah grew oop being told every day that ah belonged in the slums. That ah'd never get out because ah wasn't born of titled blood. To stop dreaming."

"No one should ever be told to stop dreaming." Colin twined his fingers with hers.

"Ah agree, but that isn't how ah was raised. Ah wod like to stay here and not return to England. To Liverpool."

Colin's eyes widened.

"Ah know that's a selfish dream. Ah must go back to make sure Ellis is freed and can be there for Mam." She ducked her head. If she saw recrimination in Colin's eyes she'd never be able to continue with him.

Colin grasped her chin, tipping her face up to his. "It's not selfish. Never think wanting more out of your life is selfish. We'll return and get Ellis out of prison. Once your mother is taken care of you can decide what is best for you." His gaze slid to her mouth and back up to her eyes. "I'm hoping I'm part of that decision."

Her heart stopped, and her breath stilled in her chest. *He wants to be part of my future*. Dizziness shocked her body into breathing again. She gasped.

Colin released her hand and patted her back. "Are you all right?"

"Yes. Yes. Ah just forgot to breathe for a moment." Her mind wouldn't stop spinning his statement around in her head. She had to be dreaming.

The clatter of the wheels on the tracks and the

rush of air caught her attention. Colin's hand stilled on her back.

She glanced up.

A man in a black coat and derby walked through the door at the end of the car and down the aisle his gaze drifting over the passengers. He smiled now and then and tipped his hat to the women. When he was just in front of their seat he smiled and tipped his hat to her.

Colin's hand still holding hers gripped tighter.

"Ow," she said in a low voice.

"Sorry." Colin released her hand and faced her. "What's that man doing?"

"He went in the lavvy."

Colin shook his head. "That's the man I saw watching you at the last stop." He cracked his knuckles and stared out the window. "He had no reason to come in here to use the lavatory. There is one on every passenger car." Colin's gaze collided with hers. "He came in here looking for someone."

Livie wiped her clammy hands on her skirt. "Us?"

"That's what I think." Colin faced the front of the car and reclaimed her hand. "He can't do anything as long as we stay in this car. We know he's following us. We'll have to be careful when we get off in Dunkirk."

A door in the back banged. Moments later the man sauntered back down the aisle and took a seat about midway in the car.

Livie glared at the back of the man's head. Having him in the same car would make it harder to sneak away when they reached the depot.

Chapter Twenty-three

Colin eased Livie's head off his shoulder. She'd fallen asleep twenty minutes after the last stop. The man they believed was following them had left the car then. Whether he left the train or changed to another car, Colin didn't know.

Watching the world outside the train window slowly dim, Colin determined the best action would be to get off the train as quickly as possible and blend into the crowd waiting for the train.

As the train slowed its approach to Dunkirk, he shrugged his shoulder, jostling Livie.

"Livie, wake up. We're at Dunkirk. We need to be the first ones off." He kissed her cheek. "Wake up, sleepyhead."

Her lashes fluttered up, and her dazed eyes stared at him.

"Sit up. We need to make a quick exit." He

leaned down and grasped the handles of the bags as the train whooshed and steam wafted by the windows, vaporizing in the beams of the electric lights of the depot station.

He glanced at Livie, satisfied she was awake and ready to go, he stood and moved to the back of the car. They would be the first out the door.

Livie clutched the back of his jacket.

The train whooshed and the clacking cadence of the wheels slowed.

Colin swayed forward. Livie pushed against him as the train came to a stop with a great whoosh of steam.

He shoved the door open and scrambled down the steps, turning long enough to help Livie down. Once they were both on the platform, he grasped Livie's hand and noted the platform had only a few relatives waiting for passengers on this train. He hadn't planned on this being the final destination for the train tonight.

With a fixed determination to not be seen, he ducked into the shadows of the station depot and walked to the end of the building. Across the street he spied a hotel. But would the man look for them at such an obvious place? And he still needed to get a telegraph off to Zeke. The place to do that was here at the station.

"Let's stay in the shadows until the platform is empty." Colin put his arm around Livie's shoulders. "The man I believe is following us left the car at the last stop, but he could have rode the rest of the way here on another car."

"How will we know?"

She asked a good question.

"We won't unless we see him. I'm waiting on the hope he goes looking for us at a hotel. I'll slip in and send the telegraph to Zeke and ask about a boarding house. It would be the least likely place he would look for us."

Livie nodded and sighed heavily. "When ah accepted Wilfred's terms to be friendly with you, ah never expected we'd be running for our lives." She placed a palm against his cheek. "Ah'm sorry."

Colin kissed her palm. "This isn't your fault. I'm glad it was you. Some other woman may have gone along with Canfield's plans, and I'd be dead while she reaped the benefits alongside Canfield." He was glad it had been Livie. It was as if fate brought a woman he could understand and showed him the course he should take for his future.

They stood in the darkness ten minutes before Colin decided he should make a move.

"Stay here. If the man's out there, we don't want to be caught together. It gives the other a chance to get help." He dug into his pocket and pulled out the folded money he'd prepared in case it looked like they would get separated. Grasping her hand, he placed the money in her palm. "If we get separated, this is enough money to get you to Zeke in Chicago. It's wrapped in a paper with his ad-dress. You can tell him and Maeve the whole story. They'll continue getting Ellis free and either come to my rescue or bring Canfield to justice."

"No, we aren't going to be separated." She

shoved the packet back at him.

"We have to be practical. I don't plan on leaving you alone, but in case, tuck that where no one will get it." He wrapped her fingers around the packet and captured her lips.

He needed the kiss and promise of a possible future to shore up his resolve. Drawing out of the kiss, he left Livie leaning against the wall and slipped up the side of the building.

At the end, he scanned the area. All he saw were train employees unloading the freight from the baggage car. He stepped into the light of the lamp and walked into the station. A conductor stood by the telegraph operator's desk, visiting.

Colin walked up to the desk and smiled at the two. "I'd like to send a telegraph to Chicago."

The telegraph operator nodded. "Where to in Chicago?"

"The Pinkerton Detective Agency." Colin took the piece of paper and pencil the man handed him.

"That's a popular place tonight," the man said.

Colin stared at the man. "What do you mean?"

"I had another fella in here tonight sending to the Pinkertons."

What was going on that a Pinkerton was telegraphing from here? He jotted down the message to Zeke that they would be in tomorrow night from Dunkirk. He didn't go into detail.

Colin passed the note across to the man. His eyebrows rose, but he didn't say anything.

"Is there a boarding house close by?" Colin asked as the man tapped out his message.

The conductor nodded. "Maisie Borden has a house west of here toward Van Buren Point. She fills up fast, but has clean rooms and the best cooking."

"Thank you. Is it hard to find in the dark?"

"Stay along the lake shore road. You can't miss it. She has a sign on the road."

"Thanks." Colin shoved a half eagle across the counter to the telegraph agent.

He stepped out the door, made sure no one was paying attention to him, and ducked into the shadow along the building. Halfway down the side, a body launched at him. He hugged Livie tight.

"Everything's fine. I found a place to spend the night where we shouldn't be found. Most people who ride the trains stay at the hotels near the station." He led her to the spot he'd left Livie and the bags. Grasping the bags and her hand, he turned west, slowly working his way over to the shoreline road.

"How far is this place?" Livie asked, wondering if Colin had been given wrong directions. They'd left the town fifteen minutes ago.

"See the light up there? That has to be the place." Colin continued on, switching their bags to his other hand and moving to her other side and capturing that hand.

"Ah can carry me bag," she offered.

"I'm fine."

Another fifteen minutes and they stood on the porch of The Point Boarding House.

Colin knocked.

Mouthwatering aromas wafted out the door as it opened.

"Can I help you?" a woman maybe ten years older than Livie asked, wiping her hands on a white apron.

"My wife and I came in on the train and would like a room for the night."

Livie tried not to react to Colin calling her his wife. The outcome of that remark would put them in the same room all night. She wasn't sure if she welcomed it or feared it.

"You're in luck. I have one room left. Come in." The woman opened the screen door inviting them inside.

Colin placed a hand on Livie's back, ushering her forward. She stepped into the welcoming home but wasn't sure what to say. Did he plan on using fake names as well?

"I'm Maisie Borden, welcome to The Point." She extended a hand.

Livie shook the woman's hand. "I'm Livie."

Colin grasped the woman's hand. "Colin Healy." He sniffed. "We haven't had a real meal all day. Is there a chance you have some leftovers?"

Livie's stomach growled at that moment.

Maisie smiled. "I do happen to have some stew and biscuits left." She glanced down at the bags. "Leave those at the bottom of the stairs and follow me."

Livie walked to the stairs with Colin. "Why did you tell her we were married?" she asked in a whisper.

"Because I don't want you out of my sight and anyone asking about us won't ask for a married couple." He cupped her elbow, escorting her down the hall to the kitchen.

Livie inhaled the wonderful scents of cinnamon and yeast.

"Sit at the table." Maisie dished up two bowls of stew and placed a plate of four warm biscuits on the table between them along with a bowl of butter.

Livie scooped a bite of the stew into her mouth. Her taste buds exploded with happiness.

"Where are you two headed?" Maisie asked as she sprinkled cinnamon on the dough rolled out on the far end of the table.

"Chicago," Colin said.

Livie glanced at him. He was enjoying the stew as much as she was from the look of rapture on his face.

"Going to see family?" Maisie rolled the dough into a long log and began slicing it into two-inch wide pinwheels.

"Yes, my brother and his wife." Colin picked up a biscuit.

"Ah've not seen this type of sweet roll. Wot is it called?" Livie asked when her curiosity got the better of her. She loved to bake but rarely had the time or the ingredients to do so.

The woman tipped her head. "That's an interesting accent you have. Is it British?"

Livie glanced at Colin. *I should have kept my mouth shut.* My talking will make us stick out.

He smiled and nodded.

"Yes, ah'm from England." If she wasn't specific or told her London, maybe whoever might be following them wouldn't give it another thought.

"How did you two meet? You aren't English." Maisie's gaze landed on Colin.

Livie couldn't help but notice the way the woman's gaze traveled over Colin's handsome face. All of a sudden the woman's food didn't taste as good.

"I was in England on business. Livie caught my eye, and I knew I couldn't come home without her." Colin grasped Livie's hand and kissed the back of it.

She peered into his eyes. The green jealousy bug slowly dissolved as she realized he hadn't looked at any other woman on this trip as he did when he watched her.

"You two are lucky. Not many find their true love so easily or keep them." The melancholy in the woman's voice drew Livie's attention.

"Are you married?" she asked.

"I'm a widow." The woman spun to the washboard and began washing dishes.

Colin squeezed Livie's hand. She glanced into his eyes. She witnessed the same curiosity glowing in his gaze. He shrugged and finished eating.

Livie did the same.

When they finished, Colin cleared his throat. "We're ready to be shown our room," he said.

Maisie wiped her hands and headed back down the hall. Colin and Livie followed. Colin picked up their bags at the bottom of the stairs and motioned for Livie to go ahead of him.

"Everyone else retired to their rooms right before you arrived," whispered Maisie. "Your room is this one at the top of the stairs. A lavatory is at the end of the hall. Be sure you lock the door, Mrs. Turley doesn't knock before entering."

She opened a door to the right of the stairway. The room was small, but clean. The bed was covered with a colorful patchwork quilt.

"The train to Chicago leaves at nine in the morning. Would you like me to knock on your door at eight?" Maisie stood in the hallway.

Livie wandered into the room. The bed wasn't as large as she'd hoped.

"Would you wake us at seven? We'd like breakfast and it will take us nearly an hour to walk to the station." Colin placed the bags on the floor.

"Rastus will give you a ride. He works in town and will be leaving at eight."

"Still get us up at seven, and we'll accept the ride. Thank you." Colin pulled out a small pocket purse. "How much to we owe you for the room and the food?"

Livie wandered back to Colin. She wasn't sure how domestic he planned to be tonight.

Maisie's gaze glided from Colin to Livie and back to Colin.

Livie could feel the woman's sadness. What had happened to her husband? She was so young.

"Five dollars for the room and the meals."

Colin handed the woman a coin and closed the door. He heaved a deep sigh as his gaze drifted to the bed.

Livie didn't know whether to grab her bag and run to the lavvy to change into her nightgown or wait for Colin to leave the room.

"Do you need to use the lavatory?" he asked, slipping out of his jacket and tossing it across a chair.

"Yes," she squeaked, bending to pick up her bag.

Colin placed a hand on her arm. "I promise to be a gentleman."

She straightened, staring into his eyes. "You don't have to be." Livie didn't wait to see his reaction. She opened the door and headed to the lavatory at the end of the hall.

Chapter Twenty-four

Colin stared at the door. He couldn't have heard Livie right.

His decision to say they were married was made to keep her close. If they didn't separate, the man following them wouldn't be able to capture her.

Standing in this bedroom, seeing the size of the bed and knowing he would like nothing better than to feel all of Livie's silky skin, he had to make another decision. Strip to his drawers and slide under the covers or stay fully dressed and sleep on top of the covers.

His body heated, his hands itched to touch her, and his manhood pulsed. Doing what his body and heart wished wasn't the best decision.

However, when the door handle rattled and Livie walked in wearing her white nightgown, Colin was in his drawers and settled under the covers.

He'd decided it was best to keep his lower half hidden from view since he couldn't seem to find anything to rid him of his rigid shaft.

He'd turned off all the lights but the one on the table by the bed.

Livie placed her bag on the floor beside his and draped her dress over the chair back. She faced the bed. Her gaze drifted across the room, traveling from the top of the covers resting across his bare belly, up his torso to his face. Hesitant steps carried her across the room to the side of the bed.

"Do you want that side or the wall?" His voice came out huskier than he'd planned. The sight of her walking toward him, her cheeks splashes of deeper color, and her hair glistening in the lamp light nearly made him groan from the pressure building in his nether regions.

"This side is fine."

She raised the covers and slid in, leaving so much space between them Colin wondered she wasn't falling off the bed.

Livie reached out and clicked the switch on the lamp.

The room dove into complete darkness. Heavy drapes on the window didn't allow any moonlight to enter.

Colin remained where he was, afraid if he moved, Livie would fall. Or she'd move and touch his hardness. He was pretty sure she was an innocent when it came to intimacy. The last thing he wanted to do was scare her.

His back started to ache from the way he was

propped against the headboard. Shoving his body down onto the mattress made the bed bounce.

Livie let out a startled yip.

Colin reached out, wrapping an arm around her waist to keep her from tumbling off the bed. She rolled toward him, pressing her body against his with her arms crossed over her chest.

Embracing her to him, he sighed. This was what he'd wanted since he first laid eyes on Livie. To gather her close, inhale her scent, and feel her curves.

Her arms relaxed.

Her fingers slid back and forth across his chest, tickling the scattering of hair. This exploration gave him the courage to run his hands up and down her back and cup her backside in his hands.

He nuzzled her neck, dropped kisses over her jaw, and sealed his lips to hers. Dipping his tongue between her lips, he filled his senses with her heat and sweetness.

Her body melded with his. She moaned and pressed, rubbing her mound against his hard member.

Colin pulled out of the kiss, angling his lower body away from her torturous heat. He released her. "Livie, roll over and go to sleep."

"After you've set fire to me body?" Her soft whisper added more flames to his nether regions.

"We can't do this. You need to sleep. I need to think of anything other than what I want to do with you." He gently pushed on her shoulder, trying to get her to turn away from him.

She rolled to her back and his arm landed across her breasts. The soft pillow they made for his arm sent another round of heat coursing to the appendage that was about to burst.

Her hands fisted in his hair, pulling his face to hers. "Colin, make love to me. Me body's on fire. Ah've heard enough to know there is only one thing that will poot me fire out." She kissed him with ardor and innocence. Sucking on his lips, tentatively dipping her tongue into his mouth, she seduced him as thoroughly as any experienced woman.

He couldn't fight his desire any longer. Colin slid out of her grip and clutched her nightgown in his hands where it already bunched around her waist. She sat up, helping him slip it from her body. He cupped her face, kissing her with reverence. She was giving him a gift. One he wouldn't forsake.

His hands slid down her slender neck and cupped both breasts. They were a good handful. The weight and softness intrigued him. He held one up, licking and sucking on the nipple.

Livie's hands glided over his chest and down his belly. Her fingers dipped under the band of his drawers.

He sucked in air as her fingertips touched his manhood.

He released her breasts and shucked his drawers off, before slipping his hands under the waistband of her drawers.

Her hands helped shove the garment down her legs and over her feet. He wanted to turn the lamp on and see the beauty his hands had explored. That could wait for another time. Right now he was pretty sure if he didn't make love to her, he would make himself impotent for the rest of his life.

Lying on the bed naked, the cool air washing away the heat of Colin's touch, Livie wondered at her brash words. She knew of many girls in the rookery who laid with a man once and became with child. *What have I done?*

She started to voice her second thoughts when Colin's mouth covered her breast, eliciting delicious ripples through her body. And his hand, with spread fingers, pressed gently on her belly giving her the feeling of being his and only his.

His teeth tugged on her nipple. The sensation tugged at the woman parts between her legs. His hand on her belly glided downward, until he cupped the throbbing area.

Pressing her curls into his hand, she couldn't speak or think for the new vibrations heating and sparking in her body. When she'd gathered enough voice to beg for something, anything, he slipped a finger into her body as his mouth captured hers.

She raised her hips, pressing against his hand, wanting more and not knowing quite what. His kiss deepened, sucking her air, making her dizzy and blissful.

Colin eased out of the kiss. He brushed the hair back from her face. "Livie, I need release. Will you allow me to make love to you?"

His voice came from somewhere far away as her body rode on a cloud of heightened senses. "Ah thought we were making love."

"We are. We are." He kissed her again.

This time his entry into her body wasn't as slow. The pressure of something larger, pushed at her opening. She wiggled, welcoming the sensation she'd heard about but didn't understand.

He drew out of the kiss. "I'm almost there. I'll try not to hurt you."

Hurt? What did he mean? She placed her hands on his shoulders, trying to squirm out of his arms.

He captured her in a kiss, once again. She relaxed, fell head long into the abyss of bliss.

Pain seared between her legs.

"Ahh!" Tears trickled down her face.

Colin stilled. "Did I hurt you? Livie, I would never." He started to pull out.

"No! Please, stay still." She bit down on her bottom lip to keep from making any more noise.

Colin kissed her cheeks, her eyelids, her mouth. "I'm so sorry. I've heard some women have more pain than others the first time. I would never intentionally hurt you."

"Shhh… Ah know." She felt his remorse and loved him even more for it.

He drew back. There was less pressure.

The sensation sent vibrations from her center to her toes. "Oh!"

"I'll stop." His tone held recrimination of himself. His head dropped to her shoulder as his hand gently stroked her cheek.

"No. Ah liked it. It doesn't hurt now." She wiggled her hips. The sensation rippled again. "Love me."

"Are you sure?"

The tortured warble in his voice made her chest ache.

"Yes, love me."

He drew her to his chest and eased in and out.

Livie couldn't believe the wave of sensations that rolled through her. She thrust, pressing her woman parts to his maleness. Soon he picked up the pace, thrusting, drawing back, and thrusting again, until her body tingled from head to toe and shattered into a million tiny stars.

"Livie…" Colin squeezed her tight and pulsed deep within her. His body relaxed, and he sprawled across her.

She relished the feel of his wide shoulders shielding her. Running her hands up and down his back and enjoying the tight muscles of his buttocks, she grinned. They'd made love. She'd never experienced anything like it. Now she understood the whispers and stories the older girls in the factory told.

Colin rolled off her, but he draped an arm over her, pulling her backside to his front. "Sleep. Morning will come soon."

She wasn't sure she could sleep. Her whole body still tingled, and then there was the possibility they'd made a baby. She didn't want Colin's sense of duty to cause him to offer to marry her. She wanted him to ask her because he loved her.

He snored softly into the back of her head. It was obvious their coupling hadn't kept him awake.

Knocking on the door roused Colin.

"Mr. and Mrs. Healy. It's seven." A female voice called.

Mr. and Mrs.? Why did the— a soft body was tucked against him. And that body was naked and snuggling her backside into his growing shaft.

Colin opened his eyes and stared into the beautiful copper tresses of Livie. His mind woke fully. He'd told the landlady of the boarding house they were married. And he'd made love to Livie last night.

The whole event came back to him in vivid detail. As he'd expected, she was all he'd ever imagined sleeping with a woman he loved would be. He held her close. Remembering her cry of fear and discomfort ripped through his happiness. He'd hurt her.

Just like Mr. Miller hurt Ma when he'd force himself on her.

Colin released Livie and slipped out over the end of the bed. He'd been just as monstrous as the man he loathed. He quickly dressed and walked over to the bed.

"Livie. Livie, wake up. I'm going to the lavatory then down to breakfast. Get dressed."

She grabbed his hand, holding it under her cheek. "Can't we sleep a little longer?"

He reached out to brush the hair off her face, but stalled. He couldn't allow himself to fall any harder for her. He'd only bring her more pain.

"No. We need to catch the train to Chicago.

Come on, get up." He started to pull the covers back, but the sight of her creamy shoulder and back, spun him toward the door. "Get up." He left the room, shutting the door firmly behind him.

What have I done? His inexcusable actions last night could have produced a baby. After witnessing the pain he brought making love to her, he couldn't marry her. His insides twisted. If making love brought her pain what would having a child do to her?

Guilt sliced his heart.

Since becoming an adult he'd always weighed all his actions. Making love to Livie last night was the first impulsive thing he'd done, and the regret binding his chest made it hard to breathe. He wouldn't bring pain to any woman, especially one he cared this deeply for. He preferred the pain of a broken heart to physically hurting her.

He finished in the lavatory and stopped at their door. Listening, he didn't hear any movement. Colin opened the door.

Livie remained sound asleep.

He entered, closed the door, and crossed the room.

"Livie, get up. We have to eat." He pushed the hair from her face and desire struck him as forcefully as the regret had.

Her eyelashes fluttered up. Her green eyes with brown around the pupil peered back at him. A slow smile tipped the corners of her bow-shaped lips.

His heart lurched and stuttered at the love shining in her eyes.

"Morning." She reached out, capturing his hand. Tugging and rolling, she pulled him down on the bed with her.

"We don't have time for hijinks." He tried to push off her, but that only pulled the covers down exposing her beautiful breasts and making his mouth water remembering their taste.

"Is that wot you call it over here? Hijinks. Ah like it." Her eyes sparkled as she raised up, wrapping her arms around his neck and kissing him.

His body responded, kissing her back. She moaned.

He jerked out of her embrace and stood. "Get dressed. There isn't time for this." He strode to the door. "Get dressed and come down to breakfast."

Chapter Twenty-five

Livie stared out the train window wondering what had happened. Colin was polite and helped her like a gentleman should, but he was distant. She didn't like this stiff, unemotional man. He reminded her of Wilfred, except, she knew Colin would never hurt her. Not intentionally. Though his actions had stung her heart.

The night before he'd made her body sing with happiness, and today, he sat straight forward, never even once reaching for her hand or giving her a warm smile. Did asking him to make love to me, drop me in his esteem?

Her insides knotted. Had she proven her lowly upbringing by seducing him? I caused him to put the distance between us. I acted like a tart and this is my comeuppance. Tears burned behind her eyes. She'd put this wall between them.

"Are you hungry?" Colin's voice interrupted her despair.

"No." The warble in her voice added to her embarrassment. *I should have shook my head, not tried to speak.*

Colin placed a hand on her arm. "What's wrong?"

Keeping her face toward the window, she swiped at her eyes. "Nothing."

"I can see your reflection in the window. Why are you crying?"

The joking tone and caring question was the Colin she'd known before her stupid blunder of asking him to make love to her. Livie shifted, facing him. "Ah'm sorry f-for last night. Ah'm not a tart. Ah don't know wot… Please don't hate me."

Colin wrapped his arms around her and leaned his head close, whispering in her ear. "My feelings for you are far from hate." He kissed her temple.

Livie whispered. "Why are you so distant if you don't hate me?"

His arms tightened before he released her. "That's a discussion we'll have when we get to Chicago and have more privacy." He picked up her hand, playing with her fingers.

She dabbed at the single tear on her cheek with her handkerchief and smiled. At least he was talking and holding her hand. *What about last night had him thinking so hard?*

Her stomach rumbled.

Colin peered at her and raised an eyebrow. "I thought you weren't hungry?"

"That was when ah thought you were oopset with me." She ducked her head, picking at her coat button with her free hand.

Colin laughed and released her hand. He leaned forward, pulling the cloth bundle of food from his bag that Maisie had given them before they left the boarding house.

"It was good of Mrs. Borden to pack food for us." He handed Livie a wrapped sandwich.

"She was nice. But ah felt sorry for her. Ah wod have enjoyed getting to know her better." Livie bit the sandwich and chewed.

"Why?" Colin unwrapped a sandwich and watched her as he ate.

"There was soomthing lonely and wistful about her. She'd been married, yet, seemed to yearn for love." She glanced over at Colin. "She was most wistful when she looked at you."

He stopped chewing and stared into her eyes. "Me?" He shook his head. "No, you must have been seeing things. She was only being a courteous host."

Livie knew what she saw. Maisie had been interested in Colin. Her heart did a little flip that he hadn't noticed the woman's interest.

She continued eating her sandwich and washed it down with the jar of water, Maisie had also provided. Livie was pretty sure it had been because Colin mentioned not having anything to drink on the previous day's trip. Then she unwrapped the delightful cinnamon roll the widow had also packed for them. Livie had enjoyed one with her breakfast and was pleased to see this one.

With her belly full, the sun warming her through the window, the drone of the clacking wheels on the rails, and the swaying of the car, Livie fell asleep with her head on Colin's shoulder.

Colin eased Livie's head off his shoulder and into his lap. She'd be more comfortable, and he could sit more comfortably. The passenger's walking by to use the lavatory raised eyebrows and some women frowned, but he didn't care. She'd had little sleep last night due to his poor judgment.

During the morning as he sat in silence contemplating his time with Livie and the repercussions of their actions last night, there was one thing that kept nagging him. He would never be able to make a life with any other woman. She'd embedded herself in his heart and mind.

But he couldn't love her fully, not the way she deserved. Not knowing his actions could physically harm her. He twirled a wayward strand of her hair around his finger as he stared out the window, thinking about something other than how he couldn't have Livie.

The best part of the day was the fact they hadn't seen the man who followed them yesterday. He wasn't sure if the man coming into their car after seeing him watch Livie was a coincidence or they'd actually lost him. Colin had watched for the man as they entered the depot and stood on the platform waiting to board. He hadn't shown himself.

Once they caught up with Zeke and filled him in on everything, Colin was contemplating finding an older woman to escort Livie back to Liverpool.

It was obvious the more time he spent with her, the harder it would be for them both to part.

His heart pricked with pain every time he thought about sending her home. But it was for the best. Last night was proof. He never wanted to hurt her and making love to her last night had brought her pain. Only because his ardor had been lessened by her pain had she endured the rest of the event. The thought she'd become pregnant from last night and have to suffer through the pain of a birth...He wouldn't be able to bear knowing he brought that agony on her. The best thing was to send her home. Soon.

Livie woke an hour before they clacked and whistled into the Chicago station.

Colin had never felt as nervous seeing his aunt and uncle as he was bringing Livie along. He knew they would make her feel at home, but they would also expect he planned to marry her given the way they were traveling together. He cracked his knuckles as he contemplated how to introduce them.

The train screeched and steamed to a stop.

Livie turned to him. The anxiety on her face, pushed his own away.

"Don't worry. Zeke is the least judgmental of the Halseys. And Maeve, while she looks kind of stern, is really a nice person." He leaned over and kissed her cheek. "I promise. Things will be fine." If only he didn't feel like a hypocrite knowing he planned to send her back alone.

Colin picked up the bags and stood. Livie gripped the back of his jacket and he smiled. He wasn't sure if she was afraid of getting separated or liked the connection with him.

Waiting their turn to move, he attempted to peer out the windows, hoping for a glimpse of Zeke. Instead, he spotted the man from the day before walking along the platform. His eyes narrowed. There would be more eyes to watch for an attack. Zeke and Maeve were more skilled at observing people than he.

Finally, they could move. He walked to the front of the car and descended the steps. He set their bags on the ground and held up a hand to help Livie descend. Once they were both on the station platform, Colin led her away from the train and into the large station.

How am I to find Zeke in this crowd? And the man is here somewhere as well.

Colin grasped Livie's hand and started toward the street entrance of the building. He had Zeke's home address. If he couldn't find him in a reasonable time, he'd head straight to Zeke's place.

They stepped out of the station and Colin's gaze landed on a tall man with a dark-haired woman on his arm. It was Zeke and Maeve walking up the street.

Colin started to raise his hand and holler when the man who had been following them stopped and shook hands with Zeke.

What was happening? How did Zeke know the man? Wanting answers, Colin strode forward, stopping just behind the man's shoulder.

Zeke's brown gaze landed on him, and his

smile stretched from ear to ear. "Colin! Boy are you a sight for sore eyes."

Before Colin could say a word, he was picked up in a hug and slammed back down on his feet. Maeve hugged him with less exuberance, but that was her way. The twinkle in her eye was how she showed her emotions.

Colin stepped back from Maeve and faced the man who had followed them. "How do you know this man? He's been following us for two days."

Zeke placed a hand on Colin's shoulder. "This is Pinkerton agent Peter Standish. I asked him to watch you two until you arrived after I received your telegraph in New York that someone was trying to kill you." Zeke's hold squeezed. "Your ma would have Ethan beat me if anything happened to you."

The Halsey brothers were all equal in size, stamina, and loyalty. But if a wife said jump, they jumped. He'd missed this Halsey closeness and having one another's back.

"Is this the young lady you mentioned in the telegraph?" Zeke released Colin's shoulder.

"Yes," Colin reached back, slipping his hand into Livie's.

"Zeke and Maeve Halsey, this is Livie Leatherby." Colin paid close attention to their reactions.

"Welcome to Chicago," Maeve said, extending her hand.

Livie shook her hand. "Thank you."

As he'd expected, Zeke pulled Livie up into one of his hugs. "Welcome to the family."

Colin coughed and didn't miss the narrowing of Zeke's eyes.

Zeke set Livie back on the walkway. "I think it's best we get back to our place." He extended his arm to Maeve and pivoted.

Colin held out his arm to Livie, but he didn't stride out as fast as his uncle. He knew there would be more than talking about Canfield tonight. He would get a tongue lashing about treating a woman with respect.

Chapter Twenty-six

Livie walked beside Colin, staring at the backs of the couple in front of them. Zeke had given them both a warm welcome. Her ribs still ached a little from his hug. Seeing the way his face lit up and he hugged Colin, the two were close. But Maeve was the complete opposite of Zeke. They made an intriguing pair.

Her cheeks heated. Zeke had thought Colin was bringing her home to marry. After last night, she wanted that. But it couldn't happen until her family was cared for. And from the welcome Colin received, he might not return to England. She didn't know the relationship between Colin and his Irish side of the family, but she doubted it was as close as what she'd just experienced.

Her thoughts turned to why they had stayed at the boarding house as husband and wife. The man they'd thought was following them was sent by Zeke.

"You had no idea that man was a Pinkerton?" she asked.

"None. It makes sense that he was watching us and didn't make an attempt to harm us." His gaze landed on his uncle's back. "But it would have been nice to know he was friendly. I could have saved you a long walk last night."

She rubbed a hand up and down his arm. "Ah don't mind walking with you."

Colin peered down at her and smiled. "I don't mind walking with you either."

He picked up the pace to keep from losing sight of the couple ahead of them.

"They appear to like walking as well." Livie giggled. They'd traveled nearly five blocks by her calculations.

The two stopped in front of a large building and watched as she and Colin approach.

"We have an apartment in this building. I'll introduce you to the doorman. That way he'll let you in if you happen to be out without us." Zeke walked up the steps, leading Maeve.

A man in a fancy uniform, not much different than the bobbies back home, held the door to the building open.

Zeke stopped and ushered she and Colin forward. "Marcel, this is my nephew and his fiancée. If they happen to be without us, let them in."

"Sure thing, Zeke. Pleasure to meet you two." Marcel nodded.

Livie couldn't help but wonder at the tightening of Colin's hand on her arm when Zeke called her his fiancée.

They entered the building. Another man in the same type of uniform stood by the elevator.

"That was a quick trip," he said, opening the elevator doors.

"We met them outside the station. Burt, this is my nephew Colin Healy and his fiancée, Livie." Zeke once again mentioned her as a fiancée.

By the glint in his eye and the way he stared straight at Colin, there was something going on. Something she didn't get but the smug smile on Maeve's face said she did.

"Welcome to Chicago," Burt said, as they all walked into the elevator box.

Livie pressed close to Colin. She still wasn't convinced this contraption was a better way to go up than stairs.

"How long do you plan to stay in Chicago?" Maeve asked, as the elevator bounced to a stop.

"We're not sure. It depends on several things," Colin said.

Again his hold on her tightened. She studied his profile but was at a loss to what he was thinking.

They all stepped into the hallway. Zeke led them to the end of the hall. He opened the door.

A shriek startled Livie. She clung to Colin.

Zeke crouched down and moved forward like a lumbering bear. "Where's that tasty little boy?"

Maeve sedately removed her shawl and turned to them. "Place your hats and coat on the pegs." She walked on into the parlor where shrieks, giggles, and growls emitted.

Colin helped her out of her coat. "I'm sorry Zeke keeps calling you my fiancée."

His tone struck her. She spun and peered into his eyes. "Why? It's no different than you telling Maisie we were married."

For the first time since meeting Colin, his face turned a bright red.

She'd understood his actions last night, saying they were married, but why should his uncle mistaking them being engaged make him uncomfortable?

"I've tamed the wild beasts, come on into the parlor," Maeve called from the doorway.

Colin cupped her elbow, escorting her the short distance down the hall.

Zeke sat on a couch holding a boy of about five on his knee and another boy, close to seven, stood by Maeve.

"Colin, you remember Brendon from your last visit." Zeke nodded to the boy by Maeve.

"I do. You're growing, Brendon. Pretty soon, you'll be as big as your pa," Colin said, escorting Livie to a chair.

"And this is Christian." Zeke lifted the boy over his head, making Christian chortle with glee.

"The last time I was here, he was still in diapers." Colin held out his hand to the littler boy. "Pleased to meet you, Christian."

The boy smiled and grabbed Colin's hand, giving it one hard pump.

Colin sat in a chair across the room from Livie.

She couldn't figure out why he put space between them, when there was a perfectly suitable chair beside hers.

A domestic woman stepped inside the parlor door. "It's time for the boys to eat their dinner."

Zeke placed Christian on his feet and nodded to Brendon. "Go grab your grub. I'll come tell you a story when you're in bed. Thank you, Myrna"

Livie found it interesting that Zeke didn't talk or act like the men of wealth in England. From the looks of the apartment and Maeve's clothes, the Halseys would fit right in with the titled. Instead, Zeke rollicked with the children, hugged his nephew, and now said he'd tell the children a story. He seemed to be the loving, more maternal of the two. The glow on Maeve's face when she talked to or looked at her children showed she cared for the two, but she didn't exude the same abandon and love.

The minute the boys disappeared, another side of Zeke emerged. "Tell me about the man who is out to kill you." He leaned forward, his elbows on his knees, peering from Colin to her and back to Colin.

"It all goes back to the attempt on my life when Ma was marrying Ethan." Colin preferred talking about Canfield to the expectations Zeke had about his intentions with Livie.

"You've had someone after you all this time and you didn't say anything?" Zeke stared at him like his brains were oozing out of his ears.

"No, but it's the same family. For some reason Roderick's son, Wilfred Canfield, decided he wanted to give his father a gift of my estate." Colin shook his head. He still couldn't believe the man was so arrogant to think he could get away with killing him and Livie and then get his hands on the estate.

"How does Miss Leatherby fit into this?" Maeve asked, studying Livie.

"Livie, go ahead and tell them the whole thing." Colin sent her a supportive smile.

She stared at him a moment, cleared her throat, and peered at him again before turning her attention to Maeve and Zeke.

"Ah worked in the Canfield townhouse as a maid. Wilfred tried many times to get me alone." She swallowed and peered at him.

Colin nodded for her to go on.

"When that failed, he brought me brother into a scheme which landed Ellis in Gaol, an English prison. Then Wilfred told me that if ah helped him get information on Sir Colin Healy, he'd tell the authorities Ellis was innocent." She shook her head. "Ah should have known better than to make a deal with the devil.

"When the only proof ah could bring Wilfred was that Colin was the true heir to Meath Hall, he became angry. He hit me and was going…" She trailed off and stared at the bookshelves.

Colin's rage at the way the man had treated Livie, shot him to his feet. He crossed the room in three strides and sat on the arm of her chair, holding her hand. "He threatened her several times, but what Livie didn't get to…Canfield decided the best way to get the estate was to kill me. Because I don't have any male heirs, it would revert to his father."

"Why is Livie in danger? Unless…" Maeve left the thought hanging in the air.

After last night, there was a good chance he did have an heir. But he wasn't going to tell that to anyone. "He's after Livie because she refused his advances and is siding with me against him. She knows of his plan to kill me. That's why she isn't safe."

"I see. And there was already an attempt?" Zeke's gaze remained on their clasped hands.

"Three attempts. One on the ship." Colin couldn't keep his gaze from traveling over Livie's face. He'd nearly lost her in the ocean. "The other when we were walking in New York. Two men jumped us saying they were going to toss our bodies in the river. We escaped, and I thought I saw Canfield hanging around the hotel. Then the next night we went to a play. After the intermission, we dallied in the atrium and some man who sat in my seat was thrown over the balcony." He stared at Zeke. "It wasn't an accident. The man happened to have wandered in to visit with other patrons in that balcony and sat in the seat where I had been before the intermission. I don't know if the police caught the person who shoved him or not."

Colin squeezed Livie's hand. "I wanted to get out of New York and to you for help before anything else happened."

"We need a description of Canfield and anything you know about him." Maeve walked over to a desk and came back with a large writing pad and a pencil.

Livie knew the man better. Colin nodded to her. "You start and I'll fill in what I know."

She nodded and began telling Maeve about Canfield.

Maeve asked pointed details which Livie filled in. Within minutes Maeve held up a sketch that was nearly a ringer for Canfield.

"How do you do that?" Livie asked, staring at the sketch.

Colin felt her tremors and wrapped his arm around Livie. The likeness was uncanny. Maeve even managed to get the cynical sneer to the man's lips.

"That's a damn good likeness," he said. "The harbor police in New York, the Hoboken Police, and the Central District all know about the attempts and have descriptions of Canfield. He's slipped by all of them. He has the money to buy as much riffraff as he wants to kill us."

Livie snuggled closer. Colin knew holding her sent the wrong message to Maeve and Zeke, but she needed his comfort.

Maeve stood. "Come along, Livie. You must want to get freshened up before dinner. I'll show you to your room."

Livie leaned closer a moment, before she drew away and he helped her stand.

"It will be good for you have some time to yourself without fear," Colin said, releasing her hand.

Livie peered at him over her shoulder as she exited the room behind Maeve.

He knew she was safe here, but he'd become so used to being with her, Colin had a hard time keeping his feet planted in the room.

"Tell me more about Canfield."

Colin shook his thoughts free of Livie and faced his uncle, who reclined on the sofa. His relaxed posture wasn't evident in his intent stare.

Colin sat in the chair Livie vacated and ran a hand over his face. "He's a mean bastard. I stopped him from beating Livie twice. She told me stories about maids in the household who left because he'd hurt them so badly while taking their bodies." Anger burned from his toes to his hair. He shot out of his chair and paced the room. "He seems to know how to find the dregs of society and use them to his advantage. He can be charming when he's dealing with wealth and officials, but the charm is only skin deep, the rest of the man is as vile as the devil."

"He may be hard to catch." Zeke's quiet statement stopped Colin.

He'd been thinking the same thing. The man knew how to manipulate and intimidate people.

"Who do you think he wants dead the worst? You or Livie?"

Colin faced his uncle. "What do you mean?" He had a hunch his uncle had a plan and it was going to be dangerous.

"It strikes me that the two of you have been traveling together. That makes you a double target. Two birds, one stone." Zeke sat up and stared at his hands. "If you two were to split up. Who would he follow?"

"He would have more to gain by killing me. But I wouldn't put it past him to send someone after Livie. That's why we stayed together. It was easier for me to keep her safe." Colin knew this was his chance to send Livie back to England. She'd be safer headed home than with him. "Can you find a reliable person to travel back to Liverpool with Livie?"

Zeke shot off the couch. "Back to England? I planned on keeping her here until we caught Canfield." He stood in front of Colin. "What are your intentions with Livie?"

Colin stared at his uncle. He'd never been on the other end of one of Zeke's inquisitions. The man's eyes appeared hard as stone, his face void of emotion, and his tone deadly.

Chapter Twenty-seven

Livie followed Maeve down the hall and into a small, but elegant, bedroom.

"This is our guest room. The door on the right at the end of the hall is the lavatory and bath. Feel free to use the bath if you wish. Dinner won't be ready for another hour. Not until Zeke puts the boys to bed." Maeve stopped by the bureau.

Livie noted her satchel sat on the floor at the end of the bed. Her best dress hung on the front of the wardrobe.

"Thank you. You are all being so kind to a complete stranger." Livie picked up her satchel and being conscious of the beautiful coverlet on the bed, placed the bag on a chair by the bureau.

"You won't be a stranger for long from the way Colin looks at you." Maeve walked over to the hanging dress and shook it. She lingered as if hunting for information.

There was only one way to stop the interrogation. "We haven't even talked marriage. Colin has been wonderful helping me stay alive and sending his solicitor instructions to get my brother out of Gaol. But our social stations are too far apart for anything to come of our feelings." She looked up from shuffling her clothes around in the satchel.

Maeve's eyes narrowed and her brow creased as if deep in thought. "Social stations? You think Colin cares about that?" She snorted. "You don't know him very well if you think that will keep him from marrying you." Maeve walked to the bed and sat down. She patted the mattress next to her. "Let me tell you something about Colin Healy."

Intrigued to hear about his past from someone other than him, Livie sat down.

"When Ethan went to Colin's mother to purchase some of their land, he found a woman and two children hiding away in a smelly shack, digging and clawing at a mine to find enough gold to buy food. Their clothes were falling apart and didn't fit. They didn't know how to read or write." Maeve thought a minute. "I believe Colin was twelve." She patted Livie's arm. "So don't use social standings as a means to not marry Colin. He's lived in poverty and rose above it."

Livie wanted to confide in the woman. Needed someone to talk to. But was this woman as unbiased as she seemed?

She cleared her throat. "Ah-ah could wish for nothing more than for Colin to ask me to marry him. But ah can't until ah know Ellis is free and able to take care of Mam. Ah can't stay in America as mooch as ah wod like to. Ah have to return to Liverpool. Ah'm all Mam and Ellis have."

Maeve cocked her head to one side. Her black hair was neatly drawn up into a bun on the back of her head. Her blue eyes stared at her intently. "From what I've seen, Colin will wait for you."

The thought he would, sent a flutter of happiness tickling her insides. Livie smiled. "Ah hope so. Ah have never met a man who makes me feel like an equal."

Maeve's blue gaze drifted over Livie's shoulder and her lips turned up in a wistful smile. "The Halsey men have a way of doing that with the women they love."

Love. That is the word I want to hear from Colin's lips. If he declared his love, she would have a hard time leaving him to help her family. He had become equally as important to her as the people who helped her survive the rookery.

"Ah don't want him asking me to marry him out of duty. Ah've watched him and listened to him talk about family and Meath Hall. He has a strong sense of duty. Ah won't become his wife simply because he feels he should because of all the time we've spent alone." She couldn't stop the heat rising into her cheeks and ears.

Maeve's gaze fastened onto her burning face. "How much time have you spent alone? Not in a train or with other people?"

She knew what the woman asked. Livie's mind

drifted to last night. Heat scorched through her as her lower regions burned with need.

"Have you two been alone in a bed?"

Maeve's question jerked Livie from her reveries.

"Why do you ask?"

Colin's aunt smiled. "I know that expression. It's a woman who's experienced the touch of a lover."

"It shows?" Livie blurted out and slapped a hand over her mouth.

Maeve laughed. "Yes. There is a radiance a fully-loved woman shows. Were you careful?"

"Careful?" What was the woman talking about? "We told the woman at the boarding house we were husband and wife."

Maeve's deep laugh rippled through the room again. "Not that kind of careful. Did you do anything to prevent becoming with child?"

Livie stared open-mouthed at the woman. Her mother had never spoken this bluntly about the acts between a man and a woman. She'd only heard bits and pieces working in the factory, on the streets, and later at the Canfield townhouse. Usually in connection with Wilfred.

"You can't prevent getting with child." She placed a hand over her belly. Had Colin's seed already started forming a child in her?

Maeve nodded. "Yes, you can. I learned a few tricks from some prostitutes and Rachel, Clay's wife who is a doctor, told me some more. I'll write them down for you. If you don't plan to marry Colin soon, you better find a way to keep from getting with child."

The woman stood and patted her knee. "And I wouldn't worry about your family or yourself. When Colin sets his mind to something, he follows through."

Maeve walked to the door and exited while Livie still contemplated all the woman had said.

Colin wasn't a boy anymore and he'd never allowed anyone to bully him. The man looming over him had always been a kind and loving uncle, but the hardness of his glare showed the man who hunted down criminals for the Pinkerton Detective Agency.

"My intentions are to help Livie's brother get out of Gaol and see that her family is well." He had to keep his love for the woman hidden or Zeke would be more against sending her back to Liverpool.

"That's all?" Zeke sat and motioned for Colin to sit. Zeke reclined back on the couch, but his gaze remained intent. "I can tell from the way you two act you've done more than keep her safe. If you've touched any of her skin hidden under her clothing, you better do more than send her away to keep her safe."

His uncle's insinuation stung because it struck the truth. He'd touched her where only a husband was to touch a wife. He'd seated himself to her soul and she to his. Rage at his inability to keep his hands off Livie shot him to his feet. He paced, seething with self-loathing.

His actions could have made a baby. She would need money to care for the child. A child he'd yearn to see and couldn't…not without wanting to be in its life. He couldn't live with himself if making love to Livie brought her pain.

"Stop pacing and talk to me."

Colin stopped. He swung his gaze to his uncle and sat in the closest chair.

"You made love to her didn't you?"

Zeke's soft statement caused Colin's internal fears and doubts to come forth.

"I tried to remain a gentleman. Tried to do right by her. But last night…I thought the Pinkerton agent was working for Canfield. To lose him, we walked to a boarding house. I told the woman we were husband and wife." He peered up at Zeke expecting to see censure but instead he saw sympathy. "I planned to not undress and sleep on the covers, but I-I was weak and crawled into bed. When we touched, I couldn't stop myself." Colin's anger re-emerged. "I was no better than Mr. Miller. I took what I wanted and caused her pain." Tears burned. He'd thought he was a better man than his vile step-father, but he wasn't.

Zeke knelt next to the chair. "You are nothing like Mr. Miller. If you had treated Livie like that she wouldn't be clinging to you or watching you with love in her eyes."

"But when we…she cried out in pain."

Zeke chuckled.

Colin peered into his uncle's face. "Why are

you laughing? It's not funny."

"The fact you are so worried about Livie is proof you love her and you should be with her." Zeke stood. "I have to put the boys to bed. Every woman has some pain the first time. Did she tell you to stop and shove you? Cry when you continued?"

Memories of Livie's body moving under his, drawing him deeper, and her cry of passion hardened his shaft. "No."

"Then you didn't hurt her like you think." Zeke headed to the door and stopped. "Get married and arrive home with a wife." He slipped out the door.

Colin sat in the chair, staring at a painting of running horses. If what Zeke said was true…he sent his thoughts to how Livie had threw herself into making love after the first thrust and the love shining in her eyes when she woke. The idea of marrying Livie and spending more passionate nights with her simmered in his mind. He liked the idea, if he didn't believe she would be safer headed back to Liverpool while he and Zeke drew out Canfield.

After dinner Colin escorted Livie into the parlor behind his aunt and uncle. Livie had been quiet and pre-occupied through the meal. He'd had to grab her attention several times to draw her into the conversation. What could she be thinking about?

Once they were all seated, Zeke and Maeve on the couch and he and Livie in the chairs facing them, Zeke announced, "Colin and I have decided on a plan."

"What is the plan?" Maeve asked.

"We'll use Colin to draw Canfield out. He'll stay here for a week, start a routine of places he visits every day. We'll bring Marcel in on the plan. He can tell anyone who asks Colin's schedule."

"Marcel? How would he know to do this?" Colin asked.

"Pinkerton agents live in this building. Marcel and all the employees of this building are part of the agency." Zeke glanced toward Livie. "Colin has suggested we find you an escort to take you back to Liverpool."

Colin wanted to strangle his uncle for saying it so bluntly and not giving him a chance to break it to her gently.

Livie's gaze latched onto his. "You're just going to send me away. As if ah have no say in any of this?"

"It's for your safety." Colin didn't want to get into their intimacy in front of his aunt and uncle, even though Zeke knew more than he cared to have anyone else know.

"Safety? How can sending me away from the people who know the danger ah'm in keep me safe? Wot will keep Wilfred from sending soomone after me? He doesn't want me coming back and telling the authorities ah knew of his plan to kill you." She stood and faced the fireplace.

Colin stared at her back then glanced at his aunt and uncle.

Zeke smiled, grasped his wife's hand, and walked to the door. "We'll see you two in the morning and finish making plans."

Thankful his uncle had the sense to leave them alone, Colin wasn't sure how to approach Livie. Her shoulders were slumped and her posture was that of defeat.

He stopped behind her, rubbing his hands up and down her arms. "I want you safe. Surely, you can understand."

She shook her head.

Colin spun her to face him. He tipped her face up. His stomach twisted at the tears trickling down her cheeks. "Livie."

He drew her into his arms, holding her tight. Breathing in her rose scent and feeling her curves, he knew it would take all his strength to send her away. But it was for her safety.

"I don't want to send you back. Not without me by your side, but it's selfish of me to keep you here when you would be safer away from me."

"You can't be certain ah'd be safe. Wot if you do catch Wilfred, but he's already sent soomone to kill me. How will you stop that person? And How will ah know you're safe? Ah would rather die beside you than live the rest of my life wondering if you were killed or found this a good way to get me out of your life."

Colin held her at arm's length. She still didn't believe he cared for her. Peering into her eyes, he leaned down, capturing her mouth with his.

Chapter Twenty-eight

Livie didn't want to fall head long into the kiss, but her body overruled her mind. Colin's lips seduced and enticed, making her dizzy and wanting more. Her body burned for his intimate touch. She slid her hands down to the waistband of his trousers, her fingers wrestled with the button.

Colin pulled out of the kiss. "No, we can't do this."

She slid her hand down the front of his trousers. His need for her was hard. "Please, if you insist on sending me away, ah want another night to hold in me memory."

His eyelids closed, and he moaned as he pressed his hardness into her hand. His eyes opened. Agony-filled dark-blue eyes stared into hers as he cradled her head, holding her still. "Did I hurt you last night?"

"There was brief pain at first, but ah barely remember the rest was so wonderful." She dipped her fingers under both his waistbands and touched the tip of his hardness. "Please, love me. Ah need to believe you won't forget me."

He growled and captured her lips in another searing kiss that left her weak-kneed.

Pulling out of the kiss, he captured her hand. "Where are you staying?" He led her to the parlor door and out into the hall.

She pointed to the door down the hall.

"Where are you sleeping?" she asked, as he led her to the room and pulled her in.

"We were just in my room." He tossed his jacket to the chair.

"You're sleeping in the parlor?" Even as the words came out, she realized this was an apartment with only the one guest room.

"Not tonight." He drew her closer to the bed and began unbuttoning her dress.

She liked watching his hands work the small buttons loose. He shoved the dress down her body, and she stood in her corset, shift, drawers, stockings, and shoes. She reached out to work the buttons free on his shirt. He captured her hands, kissing each one and placing them to her side.

"I want to enjoy unwrapping you," he said, working the hooks on the front of her corset free.

He tossed the corset to the chair. Grasping her hands, he raised them over her head. In one long caress, he slid his hands under her shift, gliding them over her drawer-clad hips, onto her skin, up her sides, brushing against her breasts, and along her arms, until the shift floated through the air toward the other clothing.

The lamp on the bedside table cast a subtle golden glow around the bed. Last night they'd made love in the dark. Tonight, she could see the pleasure and hunger in his eyes as he undressed and touched her.

Colin held her breasts, one in each hand, hefting them as if judging their weight. He leaned down and kissed each nipple before stroking the pads of his thumbs back and forth over the nibs.

The sensations drew Livie up onto her toes. She closed her eyes, immersing her whole being into the caress. She'd never felt so weightless and tingly.

Opening her eyes, she noted she *was* floating. Colin had her in his arms. He placed her on the bed and hooked his fingers in the tops of her drawers, pulling them down her legs and over her feet.

Feet still wearing her shoes.

He tossed the drawers and stood beside the bed, his gaze traveling slow and deliberate from her head to her shoes. "I wanted to see you this way last night." He moved to the end of the bed and picked up her right foot.

Her right shoe came off.

Then her left shoe.

In slow motion, he placed his palm on the outside of her ankles and ran his hands up her legs until he hooked a finger in her stockings. Inch by excruciating inch, he exposed her skin, dropping kisses on the insides of her thighs all the way down to her instep.

Livie fanned her face with a hand. The kisses on the tender insides of her legs sent vibrations to her woman parts. She wanted to cross her legs and apply pressure to stop the throbbing.

"When are you going to take off your clothes?" she asked, hoping it would speed up his love making.

"I think it's only fair since I undressed you, you should do the same for me." He arched an eyebrow.

The thought of touching him as he touched her started her heart racing. She sat up and swung her legs over the side of the bed, motioning for him to step between them.

His gaze hovered on her copper curls before he stepped within her womanly vee.

Livie pulled his shirt tail out of his trousers and started unfastening the buttons of his shirt. When his skin appeared in front of her face, she didn't hesitate to drop kisses on the warm skin. The scattering of dark hair tickled her nose. She loved his masculine scent and muscled body. Leaning, she kissed his belly just above his waistband and watched the bulge in his trousers move.

The reaction showed her the hold she had over him and his body. She could make him spring to life and want her so bad, he'd never send her away. Tonight, she would love him so fully, he'd have to be heartless to send her back to Liverpool without him.

Unfastening his trousers, she slid her hands onto his hips. With one motion, she slid to her knees on the floor in front of him, taking his drawers and trousers with her. Her hands remained in his clothing at his ankles as she peered at the part of him that had brought her such pleasure the night before. Staring at the length and breadth, she wasn't surprised it had caused her pain the first time.

She drew her hands from his ankles and took the appendage in her hands. The silkiness of the skin and heat and firmness of the flesh aroused a primal instinct. Without a thought to propriety, she kissed his hardness from the base to the silky tip.

"Livie."

The strained sound of his voice made her glance up. His face was scarlet and cords of muscle and veins bulged in his neck.

"What's wrong?" She stood, taking his face into her hands. The contrast of his silky smooth hardness and the scruff of whiskers on his chiseled cheeks sent her insides fluttering anew.

Colin had barely been able to say her name. Livie's soft touch and hot wet breath as she kissed his shaft nearly had him spilling his seed. He slid his hands under her arms and lifted Livie to her feet. To keep her hands from claiming him again, he held her close, inhaling her rose scent.

To make love to her again would increase the chances of making a baby, but like Livie, he wanted one more night to remember until he could return to England and make her his wife.

She leaned backwards, and he tumbled with her onto the bed. Her soft giggles and hands caressing his backside while his shaft pressed against her mound of curls was a delicious agony. He kissed her lips thoroughly, keeping his mind on seducing her rather than how wonderful her body felt under him. Trailing kisses down her jaw, her neck, and suckling her breasts, his weighted feet reminded him his trousers and boots shackled him.

Colin nipped and twirled her nipples with his tongue. Sweet sighs, moans, and pants escaped her kiss-swollen lips. His body continued to slide down hers until he stared at her gorgeous copper curls.

There was one more part of her he wished to taste.

He dipped his tongue into her velvet folds.

"Oh!" was her breathy reply.

When she didn't admonish or try to pull him away, he drank in her musky scent and lost himself in the intimacy of making love to her with his tongue.

Her body bucked and squirmed. He grasped her backside in his hands, holding her up to suckle and enjoy.

"Ah need more. You. Inside," she panted.

Colin flicked her engorged nub with his tongue and enjoyed the way her body vibrated in his hands.

He released her and stood, kicking off his boots and clothing. Standing beside the bed, peering down at Livie's flushed body, copper tresses spread out around her head, legs splayed open revealing her swollen center, Colin knew he'd never be able to send her back to Liverpool. This posture proved she offered him her body and soul. He could never push her away.

Scooping her into his arms, he settled her on

the bed correctly and lowered his body over her. "Livie." He kissed her with all the emotions raging in his heart and his body. The need he had for this woman made his heart ache in a pleasant way.

Her fervent response to the kiss heightened his need.

As if knowing the time had come, her legs wrapped around him. With great care he eased into her hot, welcoming body. He pushed deep, seating their bodies, and felt her body squeeze. His mind blanked and his heart opened.

She grasped his backside and pulled him tighter.

He gently thrust in and out, until her hands on his backside guided him faster, harder. Her eyes glistened and glazed over as she gasped. Her hands fell away as her body clamped down on his shaft.

He renewed his pace and soon she was panting and clinging to him. Just as he thought he'd be able to take her on one more ride before he exploded, she grabbed his hair and raised up, kissing him senseless and taking away his sense of control.

He moaned into her mouth as he shot his seed deep. Her body responded with a volley of spasms and Livie sucking the air from him.

Colin collapsed, pushing Livie into the mattress. He knew he was too heavy to lie there for long but he had to gain strength and his senses. They'd spent both their bodies, believing it would be the last time they would make love for some time.

When he had the energy to roll off Livie, Colin

lay on his side and pulled her bottom snug up against his spent manhood. He brushed the moist curls from her neck and kissed her.

"Sweet dreams, we have a lot to plan tomorrow." He smiled when she sighed and snuggled deeper into his body. She didn't know it yet, but after tonight there was no way he could send her back to England without him. He would make damn sure she was under Pinkerton protection until Canfield was caught.

Chapter Twenty-nine

Livie woke feeling refreshed and lighter than she'd ever felt in her life. The juncture of her legs hummed. She placed a hand on her maiden curls and flashes of Colin's touch and intimacy heated her body. She'd been thoroughly loved last night. Of that she had no doubt. Surely, with last night fresh in Colin's mind he wouldn't send her away.

She moved her hand across the bed. It was tepid, and she was alone. Opening her eyes, she scanned the room. Colin's jacket no longer draped over the chair and his clothes weren't scattered around the room.

Scooting to a sitting position, she pulled the covers up under her armpits to cover her naked body. He'd probably slipped out early so no one would know they spent the night together. How would she keep her hands off him and her cheeks from flushing when she thought of the wonderful things his marvelous mouth had done to her?

Small feet running in the hall, propelled her out of bed. The household was up. She didn't want Colin and Zeke coming up with plans without her.

She quickly donned her underclothes and a day dress. Brushing her hair, she stepped out of the room and into the hall. She needed to use the lavvy and pull her hair up into a respectable style.

A click of a latch spun her attention to the parlor door.

Colin stood in the hall. The glint in his eyes and wide smug smile, told her he carried the same memories as she.

He strode down the hall toward her. "Good morning," his deep voice crooned.

"Indeed, it is a very good morning." She wanted to stand on her tiptoes and kiss his lips. Feel the heat they'd shared last night.

To her surprise, he leaned down and caught her lips in a scorching kiss that took her to the dizzying heights she loved.

A throat cleared. "Breakfast is ready if you two can unlock your lips long enough to eat." Zeke's voice was filled with mirth.

Colin released her and whispered, "You're the only food I need."

She blushed. "Ah need to use the lavvy. Ah'll see you in the dining room." Stepping away from Colin was hard. She wanted to remain by his side. If he still wanted to send her to Liverpool, she'd fight him and use her female wiles to get him to change his mind.

At the door to the lavvy she glanced over her shoulder. Colin stood in the hallway watching her. If his expression had been wistful her stomach would have dropped, but he watched her with intense heat and possession.

Her heart thudded with excitement as she took care of business and swept her hair up into a soft pile on her head. He wanted her. That need would be her chum.

When she opened the lavvy door, Colin stood in the same spot she'd left him. She smiled, walked up to him, placed a light kiss on his cheek, and entered her room to put her brush and toiletries away.

Colin remained at the door. From the heat in his eyes, she had no doubt, if he stepped into the room, they wouldn't make it to the family breakfast.

Out in the hall, he captured her hand, twining their fingers and pressing his palm to hers. The contact was as heart-stopping as his naked body pressed against her. Her breath caught and tingles careened through her body.

At the dining room, Colin led her to a chair and took the seat beside her. Glancing about the table as she wished each family member a good morning, she couldn't stop the heat rising up her neck and scorching her cheeks at the knowing smiles and glint in Zeke and Maeve's eyes.

The boys sat across the table from her and Colin. Both were smiling and eating as they chatted together, ignoring the adults at the table.

"When the boys go to school, we'll start planning in the parlor," Zeke said, ruffling Brendan's hair.

"Are you and Ma leaving on an assignment again?" Brendan asked, his smile vanishing.

"This time it's family business." Zeke leaned toward his son. "You'll be going along, but you'll have to do as you're told. We don't want anyone getting hurt because you boys didn't listen."

Brendan's smile returned twice as bright. "We'll be good and listen. Won't we Christian?"

The younger boy nodded.

"Are you sure this is a good idea?" Maeve asked, her worried gaze traveling over her sons.

"We'll take Myrna with us. She can keep the boys out of trouble. It's about time we visited the family." Zeke picked up his coffee cup and took a sip.

"When was the last time you were in Sumpter?" Colin asked.

"We were through there last year, but we were on an assignment and didn't have the boys." Maeve placed Christian's glass of milk above his plate. "It would be nice to visit with everyone. I've missed Rachel and Darcy. And we haven't met Jeremy's wife."

"Who's Jeremy?" Livie asked when she noted Colin perk up at the name.

"Jeremy is Aunt Darcy's brother. He's three years older than me." A wistful smile appeared on Colin's face. "He was in Alaska working as a packer when he saved a woman and married her. I haven't met her, but from his letters, she sounds like she fits into the family."

Livie couldn't help wondering if the same scenario would happen for her and Colin. He'd saved her more than once, and she knew her love for him was more than because he championed her.

"Wot do you mean fits into the family? Whose family?" She was still uncertain about the Halsey family Colin always referred to.

Maeve smiled and patted her hand. "There are five Halsey brothers. Zeke's brothers. They all married independent women."

"And feisty," Zeke cut in and winked at his wife.

Maeve smiled. "You men call it feisty, we call it getting what we want." She shifted her attention back to Livie. "By saying she fits in, Jeremy's new bride is independent and believes she has more to give to society than cooking, cleaning, and raising a family."

"There's nothing wrong with that." Livie stared at the woman. "Most women ah know who cook, clean, and raise a family also help their neighbors and church."

Maeve nodded. "I'm not saying those aren't good qualities. Just you'll find most of the Halsey wives have jobs other than being a wife and mother."

Colin's hand rested on her knee. She glanced over at him.

"You'll fit right in." The gleam in his eyes made her smile.

Then his words clicked.

"Wot do you mean ah'll fit in?" Her heart raced. Had last night pushed him to realize he couldn't send her back?

"I was going to wait, but since the topic was brought up…" Colin faced her, put a hand on her opposite knee, and swiveled her on her chair to face him.

"Livie, I've been thinking that sending you back to Liverpool could endanger your life just as much as keeping you here. And if you're always by my side it will be easier to keep you safe." He grasped her hands. "To keep you with me and not catch my family's wrath, I'd like to marry you. To-day. Here in Chicago."

He's not sending me away! As quickly as her heart burst with love it deflated with sorrow. But he's marrying me out of duty.

Her expressions must have registered on her face. One minute Colin's grin covered his face and the next his brow was furrowed.

What do I say? She wanted to be with him, but she didn't want to be a duty. She wanted to be an equal and feel as loved every day as she was last night and again this morning when he kissed her in the hall.

Colin's heart bobbed up into his throat watch-ing the uncertainty flicker in Livie's eyes. He didn't understand her apprehension. He'd expected her to jump into his arms. She didn't want to go back to Liverpool alone and last night she'd given herself to him completely. He was sure she loved him.

Her hands trembled in his.

He swallowed twice, shoving the knot out of the way so he could talk. "Why do you look so scared and upset?"

Chairs scraped the floor and footsteps left the room. One quick glance noted they were alone. He pulled Livie into his arms, held her to his beating heart.

"Ah don't want to be a duty."

Her muffled words made him replay what he'd said.

Every sentence made it sound like he had to marry her, not wanted to marry her.

He cradled her face in his hands and kissed the salty tears at the corners of her eyes.

"I don't want to marry you out of duty." He whispered before hovering his lips above hers.

"Then why?"

Her warm breath against his lips felt as intimate as their love making the night before.

"I need you near me, and I need to know you're safe because I fell in love with you the first time I saw you in that alley." There had been something about her that had settled into his heart that moment he'd stepped in to save her from the men.

"You love me? Really?" Her russet eyes peered into his, searching.

"Really." He couldn't resist placing a light kiss on her lips. "And I believe you might love me?" He said it as a question, willing her to admit her feelings.

"When you saved me from Wilfred and ah learned you were the man he wanted me to friend, ah had hoped we could start an alliance that would help oos both." She kissed his chin. "The more time ah spent with you me heart opened."

"And last night, you showed me your heart." He captured her lips and kissed her with the abandon they'd shared last night.

They were both gasping for air when the door opened.

"I see you've figured things out."

Colin stared at Zeke.

"The boys left for school. We need you in the parlor," Zeke said, pivoting and leaving the door open as a reminder they were to walk through it.

Colin chuckled. Zeke, and for that matter all his uncles, were never subtle about anything.

"Come on. If we don't get to the parlor soon, he'll come in here and haul us out." Colin twined his fingers with Livie's and led her out of the dining room and into the parlor.

Maeve sat at the small desk with Zeke standing behind her, leaning against the wall.

"We know a justice of the peace who can marry you this afternoon," Maeve said. "We can put a call through to him if you want."

Livie squeezed his hand.

Colin peered into her eyes. "Will this afternoon work for you? We can travel on to Oregon as husband and wife. Unless you want your family present?" He knew some women had an idea of what they wanted their wedding to be like, and he didn't want to take that dream away from Livie. She said she only dreamed of getting out of the rookery, but she had to have dreamed about getting married. Shayla did as a small girl.

Her eyes glistened. "This afternoon is fine. It wod be near impossible to have me family for a wedding, considering..."

Colin raised their clasped hands and kissed her knuckles. "Call the justice of the peace."

Colin led Livie to the couch, and they sat down. "What are your thoughts on Canfield?"

Zeke pushed away from the wall and sat in the chair across from them. He stared at Livie. "By marrying Colin it makes you even more of a target. It means there could be an heir that Canfield will have to get rid of."

Livie leaned against Colin. "Ah know. He already wants me dead. Ah might as well be happy in case he succeeds."

Anger slashed through Colin. "He won't succeed. I'll make sure of that."

"We don't know who he's paid to kill oos." Livie put her hands on his chest and peered into his eyes. "Promise me, you won't get yourself killed trying to save me."

Colin stared at her. What was she asking? Of course he'd do whatever it took to keep her safe. He loved her. "I will do everything I can to keep you from harm. I told you that before."

"You two will have to discuss this later. We need to make plans."

Zeke's voice reminded Colin they weren't alone, and the more people included in the murder attempts, the more eyes they had looking out for them.

"What's your plan?" He clasped Livie's hand and studied his uncle.

"We'll get you married today and get the notice in tomorrow's paper." He nodded to his wife. "Maeve already has the announcement written up. In it she is mentioning a honeymoon trip by train to Oregon. That will let Canfield know your plans."

"Ah thought we'd stay here and catch him?" Livie's voice wobbled.

Colin released her hand and put an arm around her shoulders. "We'll have Zeke and Maeve and their colleagues to keep an eye on us."

"It will be easier to spot anyone making an attempt if we are traveling. If someone seems too interested in you or follows you, we'll know they are up to no good. Here in the city there are too many people to keep track of." Zeke stood. "I'll go to the station and get tickets for the train to St. Paul with connecting tickets on the Northern Pacific."

"We appreciate your help," Colin said. "I'll settle up with you when you get back."

Zeke shook his head. "Nothing to settle. This is our wedding gift to you. Keeping you safe."

Maeve stood. "I'll make the call to the justice of the peace, then Livie and I will go shopping for a dress and other items she'll need for the trip."

"Ah'm fine. Ah have a nice dress that will work." Livie pushed against Colin as if she didn't want to leave his side.

"Nonsense. Every woman needs a new dress for her wedding. Be ready in ten minutes." Maeve left the room, her back straight and her shoulders thrown back with determination.

Colin couldn't contain a grin. Maeve might be a Pinkerton agent but she still wielded her authority like a teacher. He glanced over at Zeke who also had a grin on his face. But it revealed his pride in his wife.

"You'd better get ready to go. When Maeve makes up her mind it takes a whole lot to change it." Zeke unfolded his long body from the chair.

"Mind if I tag along to the railroad station. Otherwise I'll be sitting here with nothing to do." Colin stood, bringing Livie to her feet as well.

"I don't mind. It'll give you a chance to tell me about your life as a baronet." Zeke ambled out into the hall. "Get your hat and meet me downstairs when the ladies leave."

Colin nodded and escorted Livie to her room. At the door, he should have released her arm and walked away, but he followed her into the room and closed the door. He could tell buying a dress didn't set well with her.

"I'm sure you'll have a good time with Maeve," he said to start the conversation.

"She's rather stooffy, don't you think?" Livie plopped her satchel on the chair and rummaged through the bag.

"She was a school teacher before she became a Pinkerton. I have never figured out how she and Zeke get along so well. He's always joking and having fun and she's so steadfast." Colin walked up behind Livie and wrapped his arms around her waist. "Buy a new dress. It's Zeke and Maeve's gift. A welcome to the family."

"That's the problem. Ah can't pay any of you back. Ah've not a quid to me name. All the money from selling the dresses and trunk belongs to you for all you've paid for since New York."

"I told you before, that doesn't matter to me. I enjoy your company. And I'm not marrying you for your money. I'm marrying you because I can't live without you." He spun her in his arms and placed his lips over hers before she could come up with a retort. She had to get over her lowly childhood and realize a person's true worth was in their character and not in their belongings.

A quick rap on the door, reminded him they both had places to be. He eased out of the kiss.

"Go with Maeve and forget all your troubles. This afternoon you'll become my wife and your past will only be a cornerstone to making you who you are." Colin waved to the door. "Go, before she storms in here and forces you."

Livie grimaced and headed out the door with her reticule in her hands.

Colin stared into the small selection of clothing in Livie's satchel and hoped Maeve talked her into buying a few extra dresses and a riding skirt or two.

He left the room and headed straight for the door, grabbing his hat and jacket from a stand to the left. Placing the hat on his head, he went to put his jacket on and noticed one side pulled heavy. He shoved a hand into the pocket and found a small revolver.

Zeke must expect trouble.

Colin retraced his steps to the parlor. Opened his bag and pulled out a shoulder holster he'd had made in England. He never rode about the estate without a gun. Deep down he knew the day would come when his English relatives would try to reclaim Meath Hall.

That time had come.

Chapter Thirty

Livie had to admit, once she ignored the niggling notion she was a charity case, shopping with Maeve became fun. She'd never shopped for clothing. All the expensive clothes Wilfred gave her had been ordered and packed for her. Being able to choose from ready-made clothing and listen to Maeve comment on the cloth and cut was a new and very pleasant experience.

Now, they sat in a tea room in a fancy hotel. Maeve had thought it would make her feel at home. Livie didn't have the heart to tell the woman she'd never been in a tea room. Instead, she watched what Maeve did and mimicked her.

"You made good choices on the dress for the wedding and the others." Maeve's conversation didn't reflect the way her gaze scrutinized the other people in the room.

"Thank you. But one dress just for the ceremony wod have been sufficient." Not only had Maeve insisted on four dresses and a riding skirt, but she'd also purchased two sets of underclothing and a thin cotton nightgown that had no sleeves along with a matching dressing gown.

"Nonsense. You're going to be the wife of a baronet. You need to dress the part."

Maeve's gaze landed on Livie.

The woman's blue eyes narrowed. "A person has to be blind to not see you and Colin are smitten. But are you marrying him for him or for the estate you hope to get and give to this Canfield?"

Livie shoved back from the table and the woman's steely gaze. Bile rose in her throat at the thought of being a part of Wilfred's attempt at killing Colin. "Ah am not Wilfred's pooppet! Ah love Colin and wod never want 'arm to come to 'im." She clenched her hands and glared at the woman. "As soon as ah understood Wilfred's intentions ah told Colin, pootting risk on ever getting me brother out of Gaol and me own life."

She stood and tossed the cloth the waiter had placed on her lap onto the table. She took a breath, calmed, and remembered to talk a bit more refined. When angered she dropped into the lower class habit of dropping the h at the beginning of the word. "Ah won't be called a tart by the likes of you. And you can keep the clothes. Ah'll be just fine as Colin's wife in the clothes ah have with me."

A genuine smile lit Maeve's eyes, one she only reserved for her children and Zeke. "Sit. You just showed me your true feelings. I won't prod again."

Livie's hands shook as she sat back down. That's a nasty way for Maeve to prove my loyalty to Colin.

"I had to see if you were clinging to Colin to help this man or if you really love him. When you hesitated this morning when he proposed to you, I started having doubts." Maeve poured more tea into her cup.

"This morning he asked me to marry him speaking only of dooty. Ah wanted to know he loved me." Livie cocked her head sideways. "Would you have married Zeke if he only talked about your marriage as a dooty?"

Maeve laughed. "If you knew how long and hard that man worked to break through the armor I'd built around my heart, you'd know he never used the word duty."

Livie watched the woman across from her. She could see where Zeke would have had a battle proving to the distrustful woman he loved her.

"Finish up your sandwiches, and we'll head back to the apartment. You'll want to rest a bit before you get ready for the wedding." Maeve chewed the last bite of her food. Her gaze once again scanned the room and its occupants.

Livie finished her food and tea. "Ah'm ready."

Maeve reached under the small table, clutching Livie's hand. "I think we have a person following us. He was outside the last dress shop, and he entered here about fifteen minutes ago."

She squeezed Livie's hand when she started to

twist her neck to look around.

"Don't try to figure out who. He'll know we've spotted him." Maeve smiled. "Stand up and follow me out. Be chatty and act natural. I'm going to walk past our apartment and nod to Marcel. He'll pick up the man if he's still following us."

Livie nodded and picked up the parcels on the floor by her chair. Even though Maeve told her not to look for the man, she couldn't stop her gaze from wandering about the room as they made their way to the door.

There were three men sitting at tables alone. She wasn't certain, but one of them held a strong resemblance to the Pinkerton on the train. Knowing he also followed them was a small comfort. What tied her insides in knots was the realization they had now drawn Maeve and Zeke into this cat and mouse game with Wilfred. If something happened to Colin's aunt and uncle she'd never forgive herself. They had two small boys who needed them.

Out on the street, Maeve continued down the street at the same leisurely pace they'd kept all day roaming from store to store.

Livie's heart raced with apprehension. What if the man tried to get them before they reached the apartment? There was nothing to keep him from pulling out a gun and shooting her right here in the street. The more she thought of all the possibilities, her feet wanted to move faster. Twice, Maeve placed a hand on her arm, to slow her pace when she started to move past the other woman.

Finally, the apartment building loomed ahead.

She didn't know if her racing heart could stand the tension anymore.

As they strolled by the front doors, Marcel stepped up to the large glass door. Maeve gave a slight nod and kept on walking.

"Don't look back," she ordered.

Every muscle in Livie's neck wanted to spin her head around and see if Marcel caught the man. What were they to do? Walk around the block until…what?

At the corner, Maeve crossed the street to their right. This gave them a chance to get a look behind them.

"Don't stare. I see Marcel is gaining on our friend." Maeve linked her arm with Livie's, striding back down the street they traversed on the opposite side.

At the end of the block they crossed traffic again and witnessed Marcel escorting the man that had followed them into the apartment building.

Maeve squeezed her arm. "We lured him in. Let's hope my husband can get information out of him." Her voice held a giddy quality.

Livie didn't know how Maeve could live with this kind of tension. She was exhausted.

Inside the apartment building, Maeve left Livie to take the elevator to the apartment while she hurried off to see what she could learn about the apprehended man.

Livie buzzed the apartment, and Myrna opened the door for her. Livie dropped the packages she carried, and the ones Maeve had thrust into her arms downstairs, onto the floor.

"Ah'm sorry. Ah couldn't hold them any longer."

"I'll pick them up miss. You look like you could use a nice soak. Go to your room and put on a dressing gown. I'll have the bath ready for you."

Livie stared at the woman. She'd never taken a bath in the middle of the day. Not even when she and Colin stayed in the fancy hotel in New York. After the day she'd had, the thought of relaxing in a hot tub overcame her shyness.

"Thank you." She scurried down the hall to her room and slipped out of her clothing all the way down to her skin. If she'd brought the package with the nightgown and dressing gown into the room she could have used her new purchase to wear to the lavvy. Instead, she pulled on the one she'd packed in her satchel. Before getting new clothes, she'd thought wearing the clothes Wilfred gave her to make her respectable was a nice slap in his face. Now, they just made her feel soiled.

Picking up her small bag of toiletries, she hurried out of the room and down the carpeted hall. The feel of the wool under her feet was one more treat she would never take lightly. The only wool her feet had ever touched before were the wool stockings her mother knit for her.

The lavvy door stood open. Myrna turned off the running water. A wonderful floral aroma rose with the steam.

"These are your towels. Lock the door when I leave, or you might get a visitor you don't want."

The woman smiled and exited.

Livie latched the door. She draped the dressing gown over the hook on the back of the door and stepped up to the tub. Dangling her fingers in the water, a giggle slipped out. This experience was new and sinful.

She stepped into the water. A sigh welled up from her toes and mingled with the delicious steam moistening her face.

Colin strode alongside Zeke on the way to the train station. They stepped up to the ticket booth and purchased seats in the Pullman Car. Colin wanted to purchase a private car, but Zeke wanted to be close by to keep an eye on any unwanted visitors.

"You must be running that estate fine if you can afford a private car," Zeke said, as they left the depot. He turned the opposite direction of the apartment.

"Orin and Denis have been good teachers, and I've implemented some American agricultural ways as well." Colin didn't want to boast, but he had made a good life for himself and a family at the estate.

"That's good. But I assume with the estate doing well and marrying a Brit you'll be headed back after Shayla's birthday?"

Zeke's tone caused Colin to stop and face his uncle.

"Is there something I need to know about Ma or Shayla? Something they haven't been telling me?" His stomach twisted thinking they hadn't told him the truth to keep him from worrying.

"No. I know they both miss you a lot. I just wondered if you planned to settle here or in England."

"I'd like to live both places if Livie doesn't mind traveling several times a year." Colin hadn't mentioned it to Livie since he'd only decided to marry her last night. And they hadn't had a whole lot of time alone to discuss where they'd live.

"From the way she looks at you, I expect she'll go anywhere you go and not complain." Zeke swung into a small, dark saloon.

Colin followed, standing inside the door a moment to allow his eyes to adjust.

While the outside of the building appeared to be a low-class drinking establishment, the occupants inside were all well-dressed and looked a lot like the Pinkerton that followed them to Chicago.

"Gentlemen, I'd like to introduce you to my nephew, Colin Healy. Colin, these are the men who will be traveling with us until we capture Canfield."

Colin shook hands with six men. All had non-descript faces and were all the same size and shape.

"I see you're sizing them up. I picked these men specifically because they can blend in and they aren't any resemblance to the description you gave of Canfield. I don't want you to worry if you notice someone following you and you only get a glimpse of them. You will know they aren't Canfield."

"He's used other people before. What makes you think he won't this time?" Colin didn't worry for himself, but for Livie. She wouldn't know who to trust and who not to trust.

"Every person he's paid to do the job has failed. From the information we gather on repeat criminals, when they can't depend on someone else to get the job done, they take it on themselves. It not only saves them money, it proves the job will be accomplished."

Zeke's casual accounting of the criminal mind snaked shivers of revulsion up Colin's back.

"How can you continue to do your job knowing there are men like Canfield planning to kill someone?"

"If I can get them locked up, my family, my friends, and other people can live safer." Zeke nodded to the bartender and two beers appeared on the counter.

Before Colin could raise the glass to his lips a young boy burst through the doorway. "Mr. Halsey! Mr. Halsey!"

Zeke caught the boy and held him at arm's length as the child sucked in air. "What's up, Arnold?"

"Mrs…Halsey…said… come…home…." Arnold gulped air and continued. "She…has…a… man…in…the…basement."

Colin stared at the boy. Why would Maeve have a man in the basement?

Zeke roared with laughter and wiped at the tears trickling down his face. "Leave it to Maeve to set a trap." He swallowed two long drags of beer and tossed coins on the counter. "Come on, Colin. I think my wife has caught a snitch."

Colin still wasn't sure what was going on but as long as Zeke wasn't worried, he wouldn't either.

Zeke's pace back to the apartment building was double the stroll they took to the railroad station. Colin followed his uncle to the back of the building and down a flight of stairs.

A light shone through an open doorway.

Zeke headed down the hallway to the light. He stopped in the doorway and faced Colin. "I want you to look at this man, then head up to the apartment."

"I'd prefer to ask him questions too." Colin noticed a transformation come over his uncle. He was no longer the joking man he'd known growing up. The man standing in front of him had a blank expression and a hard glint in his eyes.

"If this man doesn't talk, I'll not be easy on him."

Colin wasn't sure he could keep his hands off the man if he did acknowledge working for Canfield. "I'm not squeamish. I've seen my share of violence."

Zeke nodded and entered the room.

Marcel stood in front of a chair. Tied to the chair was a young man a bit older than Colin but smaller in build. He had red hair, freckles, and was dressed in a cheap suit.

Zeke strode up to the man and kicked the scuffed-up toe on his right boot. "Who are you?"

The young man's eyes grew large and round. His lips moved but no words came out. Zeke was double the size of the young man tied to the chair.

Colin stepped between Zeke and the man. It was clear the young man was scared. "We aren't going to hurt you. We need to know why you were following the women and who you are.

Zeke backed up. He must have sensed the young man's fear.

"I'm Tommy O'Toole. I wasn't doin' anythin' wrong. Just walkin' along followin' the ladies I was paid to follow. He told me it were only to find out their routine so he could surprise his fiancée." Tommy squirmed in his chair and glanced at Marcel. "This fella, he came outta nowhere and dragged me down in this basement."

"What can you tell me about the man who paid you?" Colin was pretty sure he knew the answer.

"He said if I tell anyone I won't get the other half of my money." Tommy stared down at the ropes wound around his body. "I need the money."

Colin smiled. "What did the man offer you for this job?"

"Twenty-five dollars. He paid me half and said when I brought him the information, he'd pay me the rest."

"I'll give you twenty-five now for the name or description of the man." Colin pulled his pocketbook from the inside pocket of his jacket. "And you can go back and tell the man what my friend here has to say and get the rest of your money."

The young man's eyes narrowed, but when he saw the bills in Colin's hand, he licked his lips and began. "The man is staying at the hotel next to the train station. He's tall, thin, and talks to everyone like they're dumb. He never said his name."

Colin glanced over his shoulder at Zeke. They didn't need a name. The description fit Canfield close enough considering he had this man following Livie.

"What specific did he want to know about the women's routine?" Zeke stepped forward.

"He wanted to know if there was a time when the younger one, his fiancée, was alone."

Colin's heart stilled. Was he planning to get Livie alone, kill her then come after him? He turned to Marcel. "Did Miss Leatherby make it back to the apartment?"

"Yes."

While he wanted to be relieved, he knew he couldn't until they had Canfield behind bars.

"Go on up and ease your mind. I'm going to give Tommy instructions for his money." Zeke held out his hand and Colin placed the twenty-five dollars in his palm.

He jogged down the hallway, up the stairs, and over to the elevator. Marcel may have seen her return, but until he saw Livie was safe with his own eyes, his worries wouldn't ease.

Chapter Thirty-one

Livie stepped out of the bath tub and grabbed a towel.

"She is in the tub. You can't go in there!" Myrna's hysterical voice chilled Livie's skin.

Who would be trying to get into the lavvy? Not Wilfred. He wouldn't be able to get by all the Pinkerton agents.

Banging on the door made her jump.

"Livie? Livie, are you in there?"

Colin's urgent plea, lured her across the room. She unlocked the door and opened it enough to peek through.

"Ah'm here. There's no need to shout like a ruffian."

The fear in Colin's eyes faded and was replaced by the hot passion she'd witnessed in his eyes the night before.

"Colin, go find soomthing to do while ah get dressed."

His hand pushed on the door.

She was no match with wet, bare feet. Colin stepped through the opening he'd made and closed the door with his foot as his arms wrapped around her, pulling her flush against him with only the towel between her and his clothes.

"Colin, we'll be married in a few hours. We can explore one another then. Right now, you in here…" tears burned behind her eyes. She didn't want Maeve, the staff, or even the little boys to think she was a tart by allowing the man she was going to marry into the lavvy with her when she was clearly not dressed.

"Shhh… I just had to see with my own eyes you were safe. The man following you was sent by Canfield. He told the man you were his fiancée. Livie, I have to hear you say Canfield means nothing to you."

Livie stared into Colin's eyes. How many times and ways did she have to tell him she didn't want anything to do with Wilfred?

"Ah cannot believe you are asking me this." She put her hands on her hips, forgetting she was naked under the towel. The fabric fell away, leaving her upper body bare.

Colin's gaze settled on her breasts a moment before he tore his gaze back to her face.

"You saw how he treated me. Why wod you even think for a minute that ah wod want to be with sooch a violent man?" She waved her hand. "Get out. Ah don't want to see you until the wedding."

She opened the door and shoved hard on Colin's chest, shoving him out the door.

Myrna stood in the hall and gasped. No doubt, at the vision of a naked woman shoving a fully clothed man out of the lavvy.

Livie closed the door, clicked the lock, and sat on a stool. She crossed her arms over her bare torso as tears trickled down her face. *Why is he doubting my love? Will he still doubt me years from now?* Her heart was ready to wed Colin, but her head… her head wondered if he would find fault with her at every turn. If he could so easily think she still worked or ever cared for Wilfred… *What kind of a woman does he think I am? That I would give him my body and then turn to the one person who has done nothing but abuse me.*

She had a lot to think about. The grandfather clock in the parlor chimed two. And only an hour to make a decision that could either change her life or toss her back in the rookery, *if* she even made it back to England.

~*~

Colin stood in the parlor listening to the ticking of the grandfather clock. He shouldn't have asked Livie such a question. Going over his wording in his head, he'd as much as called her a harlot and a liar. The fact Canfield called her his fiancée had dug into Colin's mind. He couldn't let the notion go as he'd sped up to the third floor and the apartment. He'd had to see Livie and ask her if she was playing with his emotions. He wanted to marry her, be her husband and provider. *I may have ruined everything with my jealous rant.* His stomach soured at the thought he'd pushed Livie away.

The clock chimed three. He heard voices coming toward the parlor. *That must be the Justice of the Peace. And I'm not dressed.* Colin glanced down at the same suit he wore this morning. Zeke had loaned him a dark wool suit for the wedding. The clothing draped over the back of a chair, exactly where his uncle had left it.

The door opened.

Maeve's shocked face didn't help the guilt building in his chest.

"You aren't dressed! It's three. Time for the wedding." She picked up the clothing and grabbed him by the arm. "Come change in our room."

Maeve hustled him down the hall to the room across from Livie's. She shoved the clothes into his arm and him through the door. "Get dressed!"

Colin caught a glimpse of Maeve raising her hand to knock on Livie's door a moment before he shut the bedroom door. He shucked out of his jacket and started to kick off his boots, when the door opened.

"Livie isn't in her room or the lavatory. Her wedding dress is laying across the bed." Maeve's eyes narrowed. "Did you say or do something? She was so excited about the wedding this morning."

Colin slammed his feet back into the boots and grabbed his jacket. "I was an idiot. When the guy you caught said Canfield called Livie his fiancée, I became jealous. I said some things I shouldn't have." He pushed by Maeve, headed for the apartment door.

"Where are you going?" Zeke asked, stepping into the hallway.

"To find Livie. She's in danger if she's walking around alone. Canfield will find her." He opened the door.

"And what will he do with her?" Zeke asked casually.

Colin's face scorched with rage. "He'll beat her and—" He couldn't voice what other atrocities the man might do.

"He'll also use her to lure you out. Remember, he needs you dead. She's only the pawn he's been using all along." Zeke stopped beside him. "I'll send out some men. See what we can find. We know where he's staying." He motioned to Maeve. "Keep Colin until we hear from Canfield or the men."

She nodded.

Colin stared at his uncle. How could he sit here and do nothing when he caused Livie to leave?

"Come with me." Maeve grabbed his arm, pinching his muscle through the thickness of his jacket.

"Ow! You've got strong fingers!" Colin jerked his arm away from his aunt and stared at the parlor fireplace.

"Don't get any ideas about leaving this room. We can't help you or Livie if you're both traipsing around Chicago." Maeve left the room. He expected to hear the lock click. At least she realized he'd see they made sense now that his anger and fear for

Livie was ebbing.

His anger had caused all of this. Just like when he was a boy. His anger had caused him and his ma more problems than he could count on both hands.

"Damn!" He slammed his fist into a chair and slumped down onto the cushion. Livie was out there all alone and who knew what idea she'd gotten into her pretty head.

Chapter Thirty-two

Livie couldn't stay in the room of the apartment. She needed fresh air and a good walk to think things through. When she heard the door open and close several times and voices in the parlor, she slipped out the door and took the stairs down to the laundry room and exited the building in the back alley.

She stayed to the alley for several blocks before walking out into the street. Even though Colin had accused her of still being part of Wilfred's scheme, she loved him. She'd told him so many lies from their first acquaintance it was no wonder he questioned her loyalty. But it still hurt. After all they'd been through since Wilfred's first attempt on their lives, she thought Colin finally trusted her.

The clock on the train station chimed, pulling Livie out of her thoughts. She spun her attention to the station. The entrance swallowed and spit out people two streets down. In her haste to get away and think, she'd wandered without knowing where she was headed. Thankfully, she knew her way back to the apartment from here.

I need to stay here, in this area so I don't get lost. She stopped to stare at fancy dishes in a store window. Her gaze wasn't focused on the finery. Her mind continued to search for how to prove to Colin she wasn't lying about her loyalty to him and her abhorrence to Wilfred.

But could Colin have used Wilfred's words as an excuse to chase her away? Colin had said over and over her upbringing didn't matter. But it appeared he couldn't forget she was just a girl from the rookery. She'd never fit in with the Halsey's.

A crying baby swung her gaze from the window. A woman strolled by pushing a trolley with a squalling child.

Zeke's comment that she could be carrying the heir to Meath Hall burst into her mind. Her hands splayed across her belly. Have we already started a child? Her heart filled with the hope. Her mind dashed the idea. How could they have a marriage and a child if he didn't trust her?

But he said he loved me.

How can he love me and not trust me?

Her thoughts bounced back and forth. She wanted to believe if she returned and married Colin, he would love her and trust her. She glanced at the clock on the station tower. *Three-thirty!*

I'm late for my own wedding.

Livie spun the direction of the apartment and froze.

Walking down the street toward her was the very man she and Colin had tried so hard to avoid.

She pivoted to stare in a store window, hoping he hadn't noticed her.

He walked by, stopped, and retraced his steps. "Olivia, what a pleasant surprise."

Livie jumped even though she knew he was there. Running wasn't an option, he'd just chase her. She couldn't run in her long skirts.

Scream.

She opened her mouth, and Wilfred clamped one arm around her waist and the other over her mouth.

"I don't know if your new beau is stupid to let you run loose or if this is a trap. But I can guarantee, if you don't come with me without making a ruckus, I will make sure my dear cousin dies a long and painful death."

His gaze scanned up and down the street. By the scowl and intense scrutiny he gave the street, he expected a trap.

Fear for Colin had her mind scrambling to find something, anything to stall and hope Zeke and his friends were as good as Colin believed.

Wilfred jerked her down an alley before he removed his hand from her mouth.

"Wilfred. Ah thought you went back to Liverpool." She tried to keep her voice even and steady while inside she quivered with fear. What could she say to keep herself safe until help arrived? What would he believe? It had to be something that would make him re-evaluate his situation.

I could try to convince him I'm pregnant with the heir to Meath Hall. If he judged her to be lying she could end up dead and not have stopped the man from killing Colin either. This is so far-fetched he might believe her. If she could stall Wilfred for nine months it could give Colin time to return to England and have Wilfred locked up. She didn't expect Colin to want her after she spent the months with Wilfred, but she would have the satisfaction of seeing Wilfred in jail and Colin alive.

That was enough.

"Don't try to look innocent. I know all you women lie to get what you want." Wilfred grabbed both her arms. The glare and wicked set of his lips didn't harken well for her. Her knees started to give way.

His grip tighten as he yanked her upright, sending pain shooting up her arms.

She cried out.

"Hey! What's going on down there?" Two gentlemen stood at the entry of the alley.

Wilfred loosened his grip and cupped her elbow. "Everything is fine gentlemen." With a tight grip on her arm, Wilfred escorted her back past the two me, out of the alley, and half a block down the street to a hotel.

Once inside, he pulled her to the stairway.

No one would be able to find her if took her to his room. She'd end up beaten and tossed to the street like the other women in his life. The fear building in her caused her to squeak.

Wilfred didn't stop until he stood in front of a door. "Once you set foot in here, you'll not go back to Healy alive. If you don't want to end up dead, like him, you'll stay with me." He unlocked the door and pulled her in.

Her feet had become as heavy as cobblestones. Her heart ached knowing the agony Colin must be going through when he discovered her missing. Why did I leave the apartment? His accusations had stung and she wanted space. She had space now and the prospect she would never see Colin again.

She had to convince Wilfred she was here for him. It was the only way she could see to stay alive long enough for the Pinkertons to hopefully find her.

Livie shook off Wilfred's hold and held her back straight. Using her love for Colin to strengthen her resolve, she blurted out the first thing she could think of to perhaps stall any violence. "Ah'm with child from Colin."

She placed her hands on her belly and froze at the way Wilfred's lecherous gaze stole below her hands. Ripping her gaze from the man and concentrating on saving Colin, she continued, "This child is the heir to Meath Hall. Marry me, and in nine months you will have the heir and can oust Colin from your family estate."

Wilfred moved closer. His hand covered hers, causing her to shiver.

"How do I know you are with child? What kind of proof can you give me?" His hand slid down. He grabbed her through her skirts.

Livie jumped back, her face scorched with indignation. "You'll not touch me in so foul a manner again."

"You just said you would be my wife. I will have the law on my side and can touch you how and when I wish." Wilfred stepped closer.

"Ah've heard how you poot other women in the hospital. If you treat me as badly, you could kill the one chance you have of getting Meath Hall without going to prison. Too many people know about your attempts to kill Colin and me. If he dies, they'll coom looking for you. This way you can get your family's property back legally." Livie took another step away from the man as he scowled and thought through her comment.

He had to agree. It was the only way she could think of to save Colin.

Colin heard the door open and several pairs of footsteps coming down the hall. He strode across the parlor and was surprised to find the knob turn. He flung the door open as Zeke and two of the men he'd met that morning stopped.

"We've located Livie. She's with Canfield." Zeke put a hand on Colin's shoulder. "Two men reported a man being rough with a woman. My men investigated and discovered she's in his hotel room right now."

Colin's heart sank to his toes. What was she doing? "We have to get her. Canfield has put several woman in the hospital." He shoved by Zeke and started down the hall.

Maeve stepped in front of the door.

Damn! She knew he'd never use force on a woman.

"You can't leave this apartment with no plan and running off like a mad bull." Maeve put a hand on his arm. "Think with your head and not with your heart. That is your best chance to get Livie back alive."

Colin swallowed and hugged Maeve. "This is all my fault. I should have thought things through before I confronted Livie." He released his aunt and faced Zeke.

"We have to hurry. I don't trust Canfield to not kill her and come after me."

Colin stood in the lobby of the hotel watching Zeke use his status as a Pinkerton Agent to get information about Canfield. They had to get to the two before Canfield hurt Livie. Her leaving the safety of the apartment was his fault. He'd never forgive himself if she became one more victim of Canfield.

Zeke stopped in front of Colin but talked to the two agents behind him. "They're in room two-oh-six. Top of the stairs and to the left." His gaze landed on Colin. "We'll break the door down and capture Canfield. You get Livie out of there and back to the apartment. We'll get her account and yours when we have Canfield behind bars."

Colin nodded. As much as he'd like to thrash Canfield, getting Livie safe was his main concern.

They climbed the stairs and the three Pinkertons fanned out, one on either side of the door and

Zeke in front of the door. He drew his revolver and kicked the door in.

Colin didn't wait to be called in. He rushed through the door and stopped short.

Canfield's wild eyes bounced around in his eye sockets. He had an arm around Livie's neck and a knife pointed at her side. A side that was barely covered by a torn shift.

Colin let out a roar of rage and started to lunge at the man. Zeke caught him, holding him back.

"Don't do it. Hold that rage," Zeke ordered, clasping Colin's hands behind him like a criminal.

The criminal was the wild man pointing a knife at his woman.

A whimper caught Colin's attention. His gaze flashed to Livie's face. A large purple bruise had swollen the right side of her face. The fear in her eyes and tears trickling down her cheeks, clenched his gut and tore at his heart. He tried to pull free of his uncle's hold.

"I'll kill you for hurting her," Colin said, glaring at Canfield.

Canfield laughed. "You think a girl from the rookery wants a man like you. She needs someone to put her in her place." He kissed her temple. "Livie's been mine all along. You just were too blinded by her purity to see."

"No!" Colin roared and lunged forward.

Zeke pulled on Colin's arms still being held behind his back. "He's baiting you. Wants you to run at him so he has an excuse to kill her and you."

Canfield's wide eyes narrowed. He glared at

Zeke. "Who's this bloody big mouth?"

"The man to stop this nonsense," Zeke growled.

Colin's mind raced through all the conversations and intimate moments between him and Livie. He witnessed her fear and repulsion of the man holding a knife to her side. There was no way she loved Canfield.

Zeke tugged on Colin's arms, ripping him from his thoughts and against Zeke's chest. "I'm going to try and work us closer to them. Carlton will take a shot. You'll need to grab her and get the hell out of the way of the knife," Zeke whispered.

Before Colin even acknowledged, Zeke pushed him a step closer to Canfield and Livie.

Her crying eyes, bruised face, and stiff body proved she feared rather than cared for the man.

Another step closer.

Canfield shifted, putting Livie between them.

Colin kept his gaze focused on the six-inch blade at Livie's side.

Zeke took another step.

Canfield shifted again.

Zeke was giving his comrades an easier shot at Canfield.

"Go!" Zeke whispered and shoved Colin forward.

He lunged for Livie, dragging her to the ground and away from Canfield, curling his body around hers.

Three shots rang out.

A piercing pain struck his leg, but he held tight

to the shaking woman under him.

Chapter Thirty-three

Livie's heart ached. The agony on Colin's face when Wilfred taunted him had her wishing Wilfred would shove the knife in her heart. Now, laying under Colin, feeling his chest press into her as he breathed, his familiar weight, she hoped her running out on her own hadn't ruined her chance of becoming his wife.

He moaned.

Oh no! Had one of the bullets struck him?

Livie shoved out from under Colin, rolling him onto his back.

"Colin? Colin, did you get struck by a bullet?" She cradled his face in her hands. She loved this face. Loved everything about him. "Colin?"

His eyelids fluttered open. "Are you hurt?"

"No."

"Yes, you are. He hit you." Colin's fingers

gently touched the cheek Canfield had hit when she refused to undress.

She shuddered. After knocking her near senseless, he'd started ripping her clothes. She'd been an idiot to think she could strike up a deal with a mad man.

"Carlton, run get the police and a doctor."

Zeke's voice drew her attention to the three men standing with their backs to her and Colin. A body lay in a heap on the floor.

"Why did you leave the safety of the apartment?" Colin's question rang with every emotion churning in her body.

"I was upset that you still had doubts about my love." Now wasn't the time or place for them to reconcile, but she knew it would hang between them and perhaps fester even more, if she didn't.

"I shouldn't have had doubts. Once you knew I was in danger you have been honest about everything." Colin scooted to a sitting position.

She glanced down and her heart stopped. "You have a knife in your leg!" Livie waved her hands. "Zeke! Colin! Bloody hell!"

Zeke spun around and dropped to the floor beside Colin's leg.

"Looks like a clean stab. Hold still while I pull it out." Zeke grabbed the handle of the knife and pulled.

Colin winced and cursed under his breath.

Livie scrambled to her feet and gathered up the torn bits of her dress and handed them to Zeke. He raised his left eyebrow but didn't say a word as he bandaged the wound.

"Stay put until the doctor and police arrive." Zeke stood, rummaged around in the wardrobe in the room, and returned with one of Wilfred's jackets in his hands.

"You might want to put this on before everyone gets here."

Livie's cheeks heated. She slipped her arms into the sleeves that hung past her hands. But she was covered.

Colin patted the floor next to him.

She bit her bottom lip, knowing they needed to discuss her running away. Her gaze landed on the two men standing close conversing.

"They won't listen," Colin said, reaching up and capturing her hand.

He tugged gently, and she sat on the floor beside him.

"I'm sorry I doubted you and allowed you to shove me away." Colin grasped her chin, making her stare into his eyes.

Livie swallowed. She couldn't deny the trace of regret in his eyes. "Ah just wanted to get oot of the apartment and think. Your accusation stung. Ah've never given you any reason to think ah had any kind of interest in Wilfred other than helping Ellis out of Gaol." She grasped his hand. "When ah saw Wilfred coming toward me, ah didn't know wot to do. He saw me right off and ah couldn't run. Ah tried to make a scene, but he pulled me down an alley. Two men intervened and he dragged me oop to this room."

Her body trembled reliving Wilfred's wild eyes and menacing touch. "Ah told him I was with your child and if he took me back to Liverpool, he would have the heir to Meath Hall." She gripping is hand tighter. "I only said that to stall. Hoping he would be nicer to me and you and your uncle would find me, before he…"

Colin's gaze drifted to her belly. He slipped a hand through the jacket front and placed his hand on her belly. "Are you carrying my child?"

Tears burned the back of her eyes. She wanted to be carrying his child with every ounce of her being. "Ah don't know. It's too soon."

Colin pulled Livie onto his lap and held her head in his hands. He loved this woman. She'd gone through hell to sacrifice herself for his life. "It was quick of you to think of that, but he is a cruel man." He barely touched her bruised cheek. "I wish I could have killed him for the pain he's brought you and the other woman he's beaten."

"Ah'm glad you didn't. You say you want to kill him but after, you wod loath yourself."

She knew him so well. "I love you." Colin kissed her chastely on the lips. His finger tip glided over the bruise on her cheek. "Did he hurt you anywhere else?"

"You arrived before he had time." She sniffed and brushed at the tears on her cheeks.

"Livie, my heart claimed you from the first time I saw your copper hair and spirit. You're mine and mine alone. I don't care about your past. I want a future with you."

A smile graced her delicious lips. "Ah want to be yours, always."

He ignored the throbbing in his leg and drew her into a deep, soul-searing kiss. If any other Canfields came after their estate, he'd have Livie by his side helping him defend their life.

It was nearing midnight by the time they all gave their statements to the police, Canfield's body was hauled off, and Colin had been attended by a doctor. He smiled. Livie had refused to leave his side during it all. He understood why she'd slipped away. He'd been an idiot to think she would have continued to conspire with Canfield. He'd hurt her when he'd more or less accused her of still consorting or having feelings for the monster. His words had stung and confused her about his true feelings.

He smiled. While waiting for a doctor they'd talked it out, and he'd realized there wasn't another woman who could fill his life and heart like Livie did. Remembering that morning in the Liverpool alley when he'd first glimpsed her coat and copper hair, his heart had staked a claim on her at that moment.

Now, he stood in Maeve and Zeke's parlor, dressed in Zeke's good suit, standing with the Justice of the Peace, waiting for his bride to walk through the doors. They'd decided to go through with the wedding tonight. That way they could all board the train in the morning and head for Oregon with the tickets Zeke had already purchased.

Maeve walked sedately into the room and took

her place across from Colin. She winked and then turned her attention to the door.

Colin's breath whooshed out as his heart expanded three-fold. Standing in the doorway was the woman he was about to marry. Her skin glowed. Somehow, Maeve had managed to cover the purple bruise. Livie wore a body-hugging, deep emerald-green dress that made his body hum. He'd never seen Livie wear a dress that fit her so well. While it showed off her figure, the neckline was modest.

After a slow perusal from her head to her feet and back up to her face, he noted Zeke, holding Livie's arm and smiling like he was bringing Colin a great treasure. And he was.

They stopped in front of Colin and the Justice of the Peace.

Zeke placed Livie's hand in Colin's. "I don't ever want to hear you made this woman cry."

Colin nodded. He never wanted to see a tear in her eyes either. "You won't."

Zeke nodded and stepped over beside his wife.

Colin stared into Livie's beautiful green eyes. The love and happiness shining back at him told him the ordeals they'd went through were worth it. He'd spend the rest of his life making her happy and conquering the obstacles that came their way.

With the train leaving early in the morning, and no longer having the threat of Canfield, Colin had traded the tickets Zeke purchased for a private car. He and Livie boarded the private car an hour after their wedding. He had plans to make Livie's wedding night one she would not soon forget.

Inside the private car, Colin locked the door, pulled down the window shades, and commenced undressing his beautifully-wrapped wife.

"This dress is to be worn only for me," he said, starting on the buttons down her back.

"You like it? Ah've never had a dress that shows so mooch of me, but Maeve insisted it was the perfect wedding dress." Livie pulled her hair over her shoulder.

Her long white neck was too inviting. Colin kissed and nibbled as he took his time loosening the buttons. They had all night and the next day to enjoy one another in this private car. After that they'd be in a Pullman Car for seven days to Baker City.

"You're taking a long time getting me out of me dress," her voice purred.

He laughed. "I want to savor every minute." He sobered thinking of how close he'd come to losing her. He finished the rest of the buttons and spun her. Peering into her eyes, he slipped his hands under the dress and slid it down her arms and body, until it dropped to the floor around her feet.

Dropping kisses down her neck, shoulder, and across the tops of her breasts, he worked the hooks loose on her corset. Once that garment landed with a thump, he untied the front of her shift and sent it to the floor with her dress. Each garment he removed swelled his pride knowing this lovely woman was his.

Livie stood in front of him, her naked body a vision of loveliness.

"I never thought I would find a woman to spend my life with." He buried his face between her breasts and inhaled. His insecurity about being a man like Mr. Miller had kept him from having hope he could love someone enough to never lay a hand on them out of anger. But this woman had proven to him he wasn't a thing like that monster. Mr. Miller had never loved Ma. He understood that now. Love was wanting more for the other person and caring for their well-being over your own.

Livie clutched his head to her and kissed his hair. "Ah'll never leave. You're me heart and ah'd never be whole without you."

Colin raised his head and kissed her until he had no breath and ached to join with her. He placed her on the bed and quickly shucked off his clothes.

Tonight and most of the following day, he would show her how much he revered his new wife.

Epilogue

Colin stepped off the train in Baker City and turned to help Livie down. Zeke and Maeve stood on the train platform holding their sons and waving their arms.

Once Livie stood beside him, Colin turned and was knocked backward by a slender body slamming into him.

"You came! You came!" Shayla hugged him around the neck so fierce he could hardly swallow.

Colin pried his sister's arms from him and then hugged her back. "You've grown up." Before him stood a beautiful blonde young woman with sparkling blue eyes. Not the scrawny girl who followed him everywhere and hung on his every word.

He pulled Livie forward. "Shayla, I'd like you to meet my wife, Livie."

Shayla's eyes widened, her smile widened, and

she flung her young body at Livie. "Oh, I'm so happy you have someone and I have a sister."

Colin watched two of his favorite females hug. His heart couldn't get any happier.

"Laddie!" Ma's voice shifted his heart. She'd been his first love. They had a bond that was stronger than most mothers and sons. They'd endured Mr. Miller's beatings, he doctoring her, she taking beatings for him.

He opened his arms and gathered his mother against him. Peering over her shoulder, his gaze caught with Ethan's. The man who gave his whole family new life. The man who showed his mother how to love again.

Colin released Ma and shook hands with Ethan.

"Welcome home." Ethan's gaze shifted over Colin's shoulder.

He turned and found Shayla introducing Livie to Ma. Colin walked over, put his arm around Livie's shoulders and kissed her temple. "Ma, I found the love of my life on the trip here."

"Ah can see. Lassie, ye'll have yer hands full with ma laddie." Ma had a twinkle in her eye.

"Ah've found that out already," Livie said, wrapping an arm around Colin's waist.

He loved that she wasn't skittish about showing her affection in public.

Zeke, Maeve, and the boys joined the group and hugged Ethan and his family.

"I see you got my telegraph," Zeke said to Ethan.

"Yes. And the rest of the family will be here

tomorrow. We'll have a wedding reception for Colin and Livie, combined with Shayla's graduation."

Colin stared at Ethan. "Everyone?"

Ethan nodded. "Even Jeremy and his new bride will be here. Everyone wants to see you and Zeke's family."

This was the closeness he'd missed in England. He hugged Livie. "Tomorrow, you'll meet more family than you knew existed."

"Cam aloong, we've a meal waitin' for us at The Geyser," Ma said. linking her arm with his, and Ethan on her other side.

Colin slipped his arm through Livie's and Shayla linked with her, chattering all the way to the Grand hotel. Zeke and his family were close behind.

"Oh me!" Livie said as they stepped into the grandest building she'd ever seen. She stopped and stared at the stain glass on the ceiling of the open restaurant. "It's like a church," she whispered to Colin. She knew Colin had some money from all that he'd spent on her so far, but the whole Halsey bunch seemed to be well off.

"Halseys for nine?" the waiter asked.

"Yes, I believe you have a room in the back reserved for tonight and tomorrow night for us," Ethan said, putting a hand on Colin's mother's back and easing her forward.

Livie leaned close to Colin. "How many people will there be tomorrow?"

"I'm not sure. Some of the families could have grown that I hadn't heard of."

Hearing the pride in Colin's voice when he

spoke of his family added a glow to her heart. He believed in family and appeared to have a good one.

She thought of Mam living in poverty in the rookery and Ellis in Gaol. They both could have found a way out, like she did, but she still felt a need to make sure their lives improved.

She pulled Colin to the side when everyone entered the room. "When we're alone, can we talk about me family?" she asked.

"Of course. Your family is now my family." He kissed her temple and drew her into the room.

The following night Livie was dressed in one of the new dresses Maeve helped her pick out. Not only Maeve and Colin's mother and sister, but all the women, Darcy, Kelda, Rachel, and Clara, popped into the room she shared with Colin and helped her get dressed and fix her hair for the evening. She'd never been surrounded with so many strong-willed and opinionated women. It was invigorating and wearing at the same time. The person she liked the most was Jeremy's wife, Clara.

They found a few moments early in the afternoon, right after Clara and Jeremy arrived, to sit and visit. They came from completely different backgrounds but found a kinship in loving a man who had been brought into the Halsey fold.

"There you are," Colin swept her up in his arms and kissed her until her knees were weak. "You are the most gorgeous woman in this room."

"You are prejudice and a bit snockered." She giggled when he gave her an innocent look. "I saw you trying to keep up with your uncles over there." Livie put an arm around his neck. "Ah prefer a sober man who can remember all the things ah do to him." She nipped his ear and sauntered over to a table with Rachel and Maeve.

She sat down with a sigh and could have just watched everyone else the rest of the night. They all genuinely enjoyed the others company.

Shayla rushed over and sat beside her. "Colin says I can travel to England with you two and stay a month."

Livie smiled as her gaze traveled to Colin talking with Jeremy. Their gazes met. Colin winked and she blushed. Shayla wiggling beside her brought Livie's mind back to the present.

"That's wonderful!" It would be fun having a sister to do things with. But she would also need to learn how to be a baroness of Meath Hall.

The last of the family arrived. Livie stared without meaning to. "How does a man of color fit into the family?" she mumbled to herself.

Shayla laughed. "That's Jasper Smith, he works for Uncle Clay. So does Donny, the blind young man, beside him."

Livie knew Clay was blind from what Colin had said. She'd met Clay earlier and if he hadn't been introduced, the way he carried himself and navigated about the room, she wouldn't have known he was blind. She watched Donny move alongside Mr. Smith with the same long-legged stride and confidence as Clay. He stopped in front of Colin.

Her heart banged in her chest as Colin hugged

Mr. Smith and then the young man, slapping him on the back. The two fell into conversation as Mr. Smith wandered her direction.

He walked up to her, smiling like a man who'd found a pot of gold. "Missy, you must be one wonderful lady to have caught our Colin's eye. He looks pure happy." He pulled her into a hug and set her back down on the chair. "Yes, you done made this family proud."

Livie stared at the man's broad back as he sauntered over to Ethan, shook his hand and hugged Aileen, Colin's mam.

Donny followed Colin over to her. He extended his hand.

Livie grasped his calloused palm.

"Welcome to the family. We didn't think the world traveler would ever land a wife," Donny's comment netted him an elbow in the ribs from Colin.

"You're not the first person in the family to tell me this. Why did no one believe Colin wod marry?" She could tell all the comments had been genuine and not a joke.

"Because of his temper." Donny sidestepped, eluding another elbow from Colin and trotted away laughing.

"You have a temper?" She grabbed her husband by the front of his jacket. "Why haven't ah seen it?"

"Because, my beautiful wife, you have taken the fight right out of me. I only want to be a lover." He looked over both shoulders and said, "This is like a wedding night so we can slip away and I'll show you how much I love you."

Livie grinned, put her hand in Colin's and hurried out of the room behind him.

About the Author

All my work whether it's my romance or my mysteries have Western or Native American elements in them along with hints of humor and engaging characters. My husband and I raise alfalfa hay in rural eastern Oregon. Riding horses and battling rattlesnakes, I not only write the western lifestyle, I live it.

I love to hear from fans. You can find or contact me at:
patyjag@gmail.com
or my website – www.patyjager.net

Historical Western Romance
Gambling on an Angel
Improper Pinkerton
For a Sister's Love
Christmas Redemption

Halsey Brother Series
Marshal in Petticoats – Gil's story
Outlaw in Petticoats – Zeke's story
Miner in Petticoats – Ethan's story
Doctor in Petticoats – Clay's story
Logger in Petticoats – Hank's story

Halsey Homecoming Trilogy
Laying Claim – Jeremy's Story
Staking Claim – Colin's Story
Claiming a Heart – Donny's Story
A Husband for Christmas - Shayla's Story

Letters of Fate Trilogy
Davis
Brody
Isaac

Silver Dollar Saloon
Savannah
Lottie Mae
Freedom

Contemporary Western Romance
Perfectly Good Nanny
Bridled Heart

Historical Paranormal Romance
Spirit of the Mountain
Spirit of the Lake
Spirit of the Sky

Thank you for purchasing this Windtree Press publication. For other books of the heart, please visit our website at www. windtreepress.com.

For questions or more information contact us at info@ windtreepress.com.

Windtree Press
Hillsboro, OR